CW00840700

THE ATTIC ROOM

by

LINDA HUBER

Contents © Linda Huber 2015

All rights reserved

Cover design by The Cover Collection
http://www.thecovercollection.com/

All characters in this book are fictitious and any
resemblance to actual persons, living or dead, is entirely
coincidental.

Acknowledgements

Very special thanks go to Debi Alper, whose advice, support and encouragement helped me shape this book into the version we have here.

Thank you to my oldest school friend Anne Paterson, for living on the lovely Isle of Arran and in the Bedford area, and for her hospitality so many times over the years.

Many thanks to my nephew Calum Rodger and my sons Matthias and Pascal Huber for technical help and information, and to Pascal for his work on my website.

Special thanks too to Bea Davenport, for help with the book blurb, and to Debbie at The Cover Collection for the amazing cover image.

And to the many, many people who have helped and supported me in so many ways with this book and my others, both in real life and via social media – thank you SO much!

In memory of Kurt and Mum

Linda Huber grew up in Glasgow, Scotland, where she trained as a physiotherapist. She spent ten years working with neurological patients, firstly in Glasgow and then in Switzerland. During this time she learned that different people have different ways of dealing with stress in their lives, and this knowledge still helps her today, in her writing.

Linda now lives in Arbon, Switzerland, where she works as a language teacher in a medieval castle on the banks of beautiful Lake Constance. The Attic Room is her third novel. The Paradise Trees, 2013, and The Cold Cold Sea, 2014, are published by Legend Press.

Chapter One

Wednesday 12th - Friday 14th July

The house was empty without Claire.

Nina made coffee and took a mug out to the bench in front of the farmhouse. From here she could see right across the Firth of Clyde to the mainland, a mere fuzzy line in the distance today. The lunchtime ferry was inching out from behind the neighbouring Holy Isle, and the hills of Arran behind her separated a perfect summer sky from the sea. And the beauty of it all made a mockery of the fact that, two weeks ago today, she had switched off her mother's life support system and banished Claire into eternal peace. Far away from home.

Nina shivered. The world had changed, and it wasn't going to change back. For the zillionth time the lump in her throat expanded and dear God, how painful it was. Hot coffee slopped over shaking fingers, and Nina winced. She would never get used to this brave new world of hers. It was so bloody unfair – what had Claire ever done to deserve such a horrible death? Nina scrubbed her face with her sleeve. They'd been happy, her and Claire and Naomi. Three generations in one house didn't work for everyone but it had suited them, maybe because having the B&B meant that, in summer at least, the old farmhouse was full of people. Thank God Beth was around to help her cope. They'd been inseparable since primary school, and now the two of them ran the B&B. Nina pressed unsteady fingers on her hot forehead. It had been the three of them when Claire was alive.

And then some stupid kid with half a bottle of vodka inside him mowed Claire down with his motorbike. He'd died too, which made things no easier – she couldn't even rage at him now. The pain was never-ending.

The sound of the landline trilling into the farmhouse kitchen jolted her back to today. Another query about accommodation, no doubt, and Beth wasn't here to answer it. Thrusting out her chin, Nina forced herself to her feet and blew her nose on the way to the phone. She was coping – she *was* coping – and more importantly she was helping Naomi cope. Ten-year-olds needed stability as well as love and Naomi was damn well going to get both.

The voice on the phone was English and brisk. 'Ms Moore, good afternoon. My name's Samuel Harrison and I'm your father's lawyer. Mr Moore contacted us through the nursing staff yesterday afternoon, and requested that we call you. He wants to resume contact – I gather you've been out of touch for many years.'

For a moment Nina struggled to find the right words. 'I suppose you could call it that – my father died when I was three. You must have got hold of the wrong Nina Moore.'

There was a pause before Samuel Harrison spoke

again, his voice puzzled. 'O – kay.' Nina heard his fingers clicking over a keyboard. 'But you are Nina Claire Moore, born in Ealing, West London, now living on the Isle of Arran?'

'Yes,' said Nina, hearing the bewildered tone in her own voice too. What on earth was going on? 'My mother's family were originally from Arran, and we moved back here shortly after my father died.'

'I see. There must have been a misunderstanding somewhere. I'm working on this case for a colleague who's away at the moment, so I haven't met John Moore personally. He's in a hospice near Bedford. I'm sorry to tell you he's suffering from lung cancer, and my colleague's impression was that he was a father wanting to contact his daughter before it was too late. Could he be an uncle?'

Nina had to make an effort not to sound impatient. This was an absurd conversation to be having.

'I shouldn't think so. My father was Robert Moore, and as far as I know my mother had no contact with his family after moving back here. I wasn't aware I had any relations left on the Moore side.' She took a deep breath. 'And my mother died in an accident two weeks ago so I'm afraid there's no one I can ask.' She closed her eyes to keep the tears in. Thank God he couldn't see her.

There was silence for a couple of beats; the usual pause while people worked out what to say. Samuel Harrison did better than many. 'That's terrible. I'm sorry for your loss. Um, I'll go and see John Moore tomorrow, find out what's going on, and get back to you.'

Nina replaced the handset and stood staring at the

phone. What the hell was she supposed to make of that? Life was messy enough at the moment without something weird going on with her father… who she didn't even remember. Had Claire known this John Moore? If so, she'd never mentioned him. Which meant – what?

Bethany's car pulled up outside and Nina went to help bring in the shopping. Naomi hurtled out of the car and danced round Nina, her eyes huge and pleading.

'Mum! We met Ally and Jay in the shop and they're going pony-trekking starting Friday for a long weekend and there's a place free, can I go too? Ally's mum said she'd book it for me if you said yes. Please?'

Nina took a deep breath. A long weekend pony-trekking sounded like the best possible way to help Naomi ease into the new normal and have fun holidays, especially as there was no summer visit to her father for the girl to look forward to this year. Alan and his new family had moved to South Africa and Naomi was going for Christmas.

Nina stroked the girl's blonde hair, so like her own, and kissed Naomi's nose. 'Sounds brilliant! You'd better call Ally's mum, then.'

Naomi whooped and disappeared upstairs with the phone. Nina and Bethany grinned at each other.

As they unpacked the shopping Nina told her friend about Samuel Harrison's call.

'How very odd,' said Beth, staring. 'Sounds like he's got hold of the wrong daughter for the right father, or something like that. Moore isn't an uncommon name.'

'He had my full name and date of birth – place of birth, even,' said Nina. 'What I really don't get is why Mum never mentioned this John Moore. Unless... hell.' Claire hadn't mentioned John Moore, but maybe she'd tried to.

Bethany touched her shoulder. 'What's up?'

Nina closed her eyes for a moment; the memory was so terrible. 'After the accident, you know, the first day in hospital before she had the brain haemorrhage, she wanted to tell me something. She was saying things like 'I'm sorry' and 'I should have told you' but it was all so garbled and then she lost consciousness and -'

And she had never heard Claire's voice again.

It was late the following afternoon before Samuel Harrison called back, sounding guarded. Nina took the phone into the deserted living room and sat down.

'Ms Moore, I've got more news for you and I'm afraid it's not all good. I went to the hospice this morning, but John Moore wasn't well enough to see me and in fact he died a little later. He's left a will, made with my colleague a few years ago, with instructions for it to be opened in your presence. You must be related, but I haven't found anything so far that explains the connection. Are you quite sure your father didn't have a brother?'

Nina's head was reeling. She cleared her throat. 'I'm – almost sure he didn't.'

She'd never known her father, of course, but – actually, why the hell wasn't she absolutely sure?

The lawyer was speaking again. 'I'll get onto the General Register Office; they'll have all the information we need. Would it be possible for you to come down to Bedford for a day or two? We could read the will and work out what would be best for you.'

Nina thought quickly. With Naomi on a pony all weekend, this would be the ideal time to sort out whatever needed sorting in Bedford. She could fly down tomorrow, see Samuel Harrison, and be back by the beginning of the week. It would do her good to get away from the island for a day or two, and as Beth and her husband Tim lived in the barn conversion next door they would be around for Naomi – exactly what was needed right now.

Two o'clock on Friday afternoon saw Nina stepping into the arrivals building at Luton Airport. She'd spent the flight thinking about the almost faceless blur in her mind that was her father, not even sure if the blur was a memory or something she'd seen on a photo. Come to think of it, photos of him hadn't exactly been strewn all over the house while she was growing up, and she couldn't remember ever seeing photos of any other Moores. Nina knew she'd lived in Bedford with both parents when she was a toddler, but her memories of those days were hazy to non-existent. Was there an Uncle John in her little life all those years ago? She simply couldn't remember.

Two very different emotions were fighting for place inside her as she looked round the arrivals hall for the lawyer – uppermost was a definite 'oh no not all this as well' feeling, but – what on earth was going on here? *Was* John Moore her uncle? Even a distant cousin would be a find – there could be a whole family waiting in Bedford, and with Naomi being her only blood relation Nina wasn't going to worry about how distant other family members were. But then – wouldn't any family in Bedford have kept in touch with Robert Moore's widow and child? So maybe it *was* all a mistake. Nina set her shoulders; worst case, she'd have a wasted journey, but at least it was giving her something fresh to occupy her mind. The grief swirled up again and she pushed it down. This was neither the time nor the place to throw a wobbly.

As soon as she set eyes on Samuel Harrison Nina smiled to herself, remembering what Beth had said that morning. 'Be careful, Nina. You don't know what kinds of sharky old lawyers there are around the place.'

This was almost certainly no shark, and definitely not an old one. He must have been about the same age as she was, with fine features set in milk chocolate skin, and jet-black cornrow plaits just tipping his collar. There was an appealing air of enthusiasm about him as he stood holding a card with 'Nina Moore' printed in large blue letters. Apart from the sober grey suit he didn't look in the least like a lawyer. Nina pulled her case across the arrivals hall.

He strode towards her as soon as he noticed her, hand outstretched. 'Nina? Hi, I'm Sam. Was your flight okay?'

Nina shook hands – his handshake was warm and firm – and allowed him to take her case.

'Fine, thanks,' she said, following him to a dark blue Zafira. 'I'm glad you could meet me.'

He nodded. 'We'll drive to my office in Allerton and open the will, and then go on to the hospice in Bedford. It's not far.'

Nina settled into the passenger seat. Sam Harrison

seemed an easy person to be with; attractive too, now she thought about it. Nina sighed. It was ages since she'd done more than go out for the odd dinner date. Being a single mother and B&B-owner meant that relationships had taken a back seat while business and her daughter were right up in the front row.

'Do you know any more about John Moore?' she asked, as Sam drove into Allerton, a bustling little place close to both the A6 and the M1. It was a lot bigger than Brodick, the largest town on Arran, and Nina sniffed dolefully. Her island nose wasn't used to exhaust fumes and the smell of a busy town.

'I've got his hospice admission sheet,' said Sam. 'His GP's down as next of kin, so his death was registered by the hospice. I haven't heard from the General Register Office yet. The admission sheet's a bit odd, but you can have a look for yourself and see what you think. This is our office now.'

He pulled up in front of a red sandstone building. There was a combination of dentists' and lawyers' practices inside, noticed Nina, going through the old-fashioned revolving doors. Sam's name was at the bottom of a list of five on a plaque on the office door.

He saw her looking. 'Junior partner, that's me. My grandfather established the firm, so I'm carrying on the family tradition.' He opened the door and stood back for her to enter.

In spite of the age of the building the offices were bright and airy. Nina followed Sam along a corridor and into a small room with stark white walls and black and chrome furniture. A Chagall print above the desk provided a vibrant splash of blue and green, and Nina gazed at it admiringly.

Sam fetched coffee then sat down at right angles to her, a slim folder in front of him. Nina straightened in her chair. This must be the will. And maybe the answer to the mystery of who John Moore was.

It was very short. Sam read it aloud and then explained the details, and Nina sat gaping at him, her heart pounding. John Moore, a man she knew nothing about, had left her over two million pounds – two *million* pounds – plus a house. With no mention at all of how they were related. How in the name of all that was sensible could this be? Hot confusion made sweat break out on her forehead and she leaned back in her chair, struggling not to hyperventilate.

Sam put the will to one side and pulled a sheet of thin white paper from the folder. 'It's a straightforward will, though it's unusual that it makes no mention of your relationship to John Moore,' he said. 'Quite legal, though. But Nina, have a look at this – it's John Moore's hospice admission form. His name was John Robert Moore.'

Speechless, Nina stared at the sheet of paper on the table top. John Robert Moore. And her father had been Robert Moore. Her hands began to shake. Dear God… who was this man?

'But – if his second name was Robert, he can't have been my father's brother…' Her voice trailed off. If he wasn't her uncle…

Sam put the will back into its envelope. 'It doesn't seem likely, I agree.'

'I – I don't get it. If he was some sort of distant cousin

15

he wouldn't have left everything to someone he'd never met, would he? He'd have left it to the cat and dog home or his best mate or – something.'

Nina realised the implications as soon as the words were out of her mouth. Somehow or other, John Moore must have been her uncle. And it must mean too that he had no other family to leave his fortune to, so she and Naomi were still alone in the world. For a moment the disappointment was crushing; she hadn't realised how much she'd been hoping to find more relatives here, distant ones, maybe, but family was family. Two tears escaped and Nina wiped them away before Sam noticed, forcing herself to concentrate on what he was saying.

'Don't worry, we'll find out who he was. I suggest we go by the hospice now – I said we'd collect John's belongings – and then on to the house. We might find some papers there to explain the mystery. I guess you're staying overnight? Do you want to stay in the house itself?'

The thought of sleeping alone in a dead man's house was unnerving. Nina hesitated, wishing she knew more about the Moore side of the family – she should have asked Claire before it was too late. But neither of them had known 'too late' would come so soon.

'I'll have a look and then decide,' she said, turning back to the admission form. John Moore's date of birth was the 15th of October. Her father had been born in October too, but in the stress of the moment she couldn't remember the date. How shameful, her own father – and unnerving to realise how little she knew about him.

Nina thought about this during the short drive

to Bedford. Why had Claire spoken so little about her husband? Was there some kind of family secret about Robert Moore? Of course Claire been in other relationships over the years; she had moved on. But even so, that was no excuse for her own ignorance now. She'd never been interested enough to probe into her father's family, and the thought didn't make her feel proud today.

On the other hand, if this John Moore had left her all his money, it was difficult to see why *he* hadn't been in touch with *them* before. And surely if Claire'd had a bust-up with a rich relation in the past she would at least have mentioned it at some point? Think as she might, Nina could find no explanation.

Chapter Two

Friday 14th July

The smell in the hospice took Nina straight back to the day of Claire's death, and she bit down hard on the inside of her cheek to banish the dizziness swirling round her head. After the accident both Claire and the motorcyclist were helicoptered to Glasgow, leaving Nina to make the agonisingly slow ferry-crossing and then drive to the hospital, well over an hour away. That day she'd felt as if she was standing outside her own body, watching the terrible events unfold. Claire's poor battered face... and her pitiful attempts to talk that first hour, and then the slide into coma from which she had never awakened. The memory still took Nina's breath away.

Pushing the thoughts aside, she followed Sam into the hospice reception area. The building was an unattractive seventies concrete cube on the outside but quite homey and cheerful inside, with blue-uniformed nurses rustling along the corridor, and floral prints on the walls. John Moore had suffered and died here, and she – apparently his only relative – had never met him and didn't know who he was. Poor John Moore. But it was preferable to dying the way Claire had. Nobody knows their future, thought Nina soberly. Carpe Diem; how true that was.

A middle-aged nurse handed over John Moore's suitcase and a black plastic bag of soiled clothing and Nina, feeling more and more like an imposter, signed for them.

'I gather you didn't know John,' the nurse said. 'But we put him in the chapel in case you wanted to see him anyway.'

Nina blinked at the woman, consciously preventing her mouth from falling open. The thought would never have crossed her mind. Apart from Claire's she had never seen a dead body, but that had been enough for her to know there was nothing frightening about a corpse. Like the cliché said, the body was a shell, and when life had gone there was nothing of the person left inside. That hadn't stopped Nina shedding horrified, disbelieving tears over dead Claire on her hospital bed, but she wouldn't do that for John Moore.

'I won't recognise him, but I guess to make sure I should see him,' she said, noticing the look of respect Sam gave her.

The nurse led her to a dim little chapel, where a vase of red roses on the altar perfumed otherwise musty air and provided the only real colour. A solitary coffin was set on a wrought iron stand, and Nina followed the nurse across the room. In spite of the brave words apprehension wormed its way through her gut as the older woman slid back a wooden panel to reveal the face of John Moore and his right hand, resting below his neck.

Nina winced, leaning on the coffin to steady herself.

He wasn't an old man, but his face was deeply lined as well as being yellow and emaciated, and his greying hair was sparse. The cancer had marked him. What a horrible way to go. But not as horrible as...

'I've no idea,' she said, her voice echoing round the bare little room. 'Was he – a nice person?'

The nurse closed the coffin, nodding. 'He was very brave,' she said, putting a hand on Nina's shoulder as they left the chapel. 'He had a lot of pain, but we helped him with that and fortunately he didn't linger long. He'd only been here ten days when he died.'

Sam was waiting outside, and Nina went into the ladies' to recover. She hadn't expected the sight of John Moore to shake her, but it had. Dear God, this was all so impersonal. She pressed wet hands to her face, feeling her cheeks hot under the coolness of her palms. She was this person's nearest relation, but she still felt – empty.

Sam took one look at her and guided her towards the car, his right hand under her elbow. 'Come on. The sooner we find out what relation John Moore was to you, the better you'll feel.'

Nina nodded. It was true. Everything would seem more organised when she could file her newly-found deceased relative into a box in her head labelled '42nd cousin John'. There was no reason for her to feel guilty about this man; it wasn't her fault she hadn't known of his existence until Wednesday.

John Moore's house wasn't far from the town centre. Nina was silent as the car passed through the usual kind of urban sprawl; streets lined by chain stores and supermarkets, anonymous in their normality. She was beginning to regret her decision to come here; the thought of Naomi, who was probably still on a pony, sent heavy waves of homesickness all the way through her. But then, Naomi was so thrilled about her trekking weekend she would barely notice her mother's absence, and they could phone soon and have a long chat. Even so, real life on the island felt very far away right now and it wasn't a good feeling.

Sam drove down a wide road where the shops were smaller, their fronts making a colourful patchwork on both sides, then crossed a bridge and turned into a narrower street beside the river. They were in a residential area now, tall houses on the left facing a wide strip of grass stretching down to the river on the right. Nina gazed out at well-kept flower beds, shady trees, and people on benches enjoying the sunshine. It was nothing like Arran, but it was nice here.

'This is it,' said Sam, negotiating a narrow iron gateway and pulling up in front of a large, square house.

Nina craned her neck to get a better view, amazement robbing her of speech. Had John Moore really lived alone in such a huge place? It was detached, a well-proportioned building made of red brick, with generous – and dirty – windows, and a lot of them, too; there were three storeys here. Dormer windows on the top floor indicated that the attic space had been renovated at some point. A wilderness of green ivy ran up the walls, almost obliterating the downstairs half of the house and stretching up to the roof in places. The front garden was a weed-infested patch of gravel, and high wooden fences separated the plot from the properties on either side. It was obviously an expensive, solid house, but the outside at least was in need of a huge makeover.

'Is it flats?' she asked as Sam pulled out the front door key.

'No, it's all one house. Remember John Moore was wealthy. I gather he was big in property but he sold his business when he was diagnosed with cancer,' he said, unlocking the door.

Nina pulled out her mobile to see the time. Hell, it was nearly five o'clock. Unlikely now they'd uncover the secret of John Moore's identity today; Sam would want to go home soon.

'Why don't I leave you to search for documents while I have a quick look round to see if I should stay here,' she suggested, stepping over a pile of newspapers jostling for place behind the front door.

Inside, the house looked exactly like what it was – the home of a single man who was no longer young and who hadn't cared enough to make it a pleasant place to live. Nina's heart sank. The hallway was dim in spite of the glass door separating it from the entrance porch, and the maroon carpet extending up the stairs and stretching towards the back of the house did nothing to brighten the place up. A grandfather clock was tick-tocking in the darkness further down the hallway, and Nina felt her shoulders creeping up.

She opened the nearest door and wandered into a generously-proportioned room, furnished with old-fashioned and possibly valuable pieces. A sombre air of genteel shabbiness hung over the place. Nina sank down on a cracked leather sofa – bloody hell, what was she doing here? She should be in the farmhouse, waiting for her girl to come home, not sitting in semi-darkness – these were the windows with ivy growing over them – in a house that had come straight out of the nineteen forties. On the other side of the hallway she could see Sam searching through a desk in the study where the lighting was even murkier. The dusty smell of old books wafted towards her.

Dismayed, Nina trailed further down the hallway. There was a loo here, so the bathroom proper must be upstairs, and it was all so dingy. They probably filmed the last Frankenstein movie in here, she thought, pushing the kitchen door open and giggling nervously when it creaked. Sound effects and everything, and the very smell seemed to come from the first half of the previous century too. A hotel was beginning to sound like a very good idea.

The kitchen wasn't bad, though, about the same vintage as their own on Arran, with a big gas cooker and a microwave. Whatever his taste in furniture had been, John Moore had liked his kitchen functional.

The last door was beside the kitchen, and Nina put her head in, expecting to see a pantry, but found herself looking into a slip of a room with a single bed, a wooden chair, and a small table. The old 'kitchen maid's room'? The window faced the back garden, and she saw another patch of gravel. John Moore hadn't been a gardener, then.

She could hear Sam's feet thudding on wooden floors upstairs now. What a massive old place this was, and how unbelievable that it was hers.

'Four big bedrooms, all chock-full of furniture,' he said, running down to join her in the hallway. 'The attic room's almost empty and very dusty; I would leave it alone in the meantime. Nina, I have to go. What do you want to do?'

Nina glanced back at the small bedroom and came to a decision. 'If I can find sheets etcetera for this bed I'll stay here. Sam, thanks a million. Was there anything helpful in the study?'

''Fraid not. I found some documents and a couple of photos in the desk; I left them on top for you to look through.' He leaned against the kitchen doorway, brown eyes fixed on hers. 'I might still hear from the GRO today, but I'll come back in the morning anyway if that's all right. Give you a hand to search the rest of the place.'

'Well – if you're sure,' said Nina, relieved. With a bit of luck it wouldn't take long to get things sorted out. A speedy return to the island was the aim of the game here.

He rummaged in his briefcase and handed her a business card. 'Don't worry, we'll get this cleared up. Here are the keys for this place. I'll come back about ten tomorrow. Oh, and there's a hotel with a good restaurant about two hundred yards further along this road, in case you need it.'

Nina waved as he backed out of the driveway, then locked the front door against the world. Apart from the clock, the house was deathly silent. Her courage sagged briefly before she pulled herself together. This was her house now and there was nothing scary about that. She had plenty to do, not least of which was going to Sam's hotel to see if they could provide dinner. Nina pulled her case towards her new bedroom, chin in the air. Maybe by the time Sam came back in the morning, she'd have solved the entire mystery.

Chapter Three

Claire's Story – Bedford

The flat door banged shut behind Robert, and Claire leapt up, balling her fists in frustration as Nina's small voice wailed from the bedroom. Typical – she'd been sitting down for exactly five minutes after spending an exhausting day with a teething toddler, and now Robert was off God knows where with George Wright, leaving her babysitting like a good little wife. Well, she wasn't. She was trying her best to be a good mother, but the good wife bit might be over.

'Hush, baby. It's all right. Go back to sleep,' she whispered, smoothing the sparse blonde hair from Nina's forehead and kissing the damp little brow. She hummed softly, *The Skye Boat Song* followed by *The Northern Lights of Old Aberdeen*, smiling in relief as Nina's eyes closed again.

Back in the living room of their tiny Fulham flat, Claire lifted the phone to call her mother. These early-evening chats with Lily in Edinburgh had become her lifeline. Robert was so cold these days, so hurtful when he spoke to her – it was unbelievably restful to talk to Lily, who loved her. Claire punched out the number, blinking back tears. Yes, her mother loved her, but that didn't stop Lily constantly advocating 'making a go of your marriage', like she and Dad had.

But Rob's latest escapade was something that even Lily couldn't just smooth over.

'He's bought a house, Mum!' Claire blurted it out before Lily had finished saying hello. 'I didn't know a thing about it until he announced it over dinner as if he was telling me he'd bought a new pullover!'

'Oh my goodness. What kind of house?'

'An old one, apparently. It's in Bedford, by the river, and we're moving next month. Two reception rooms, four bedrooms plus an attic. And I can only sound like a catalogue because I haven't even bloody seen it!'

For once, Lily didn't immediately launch into a variation of 'marry in haste, repent at leisure', and Claire was grateful for this much at least. She knew the whirlwind courtship hadn't been time for her to get to know Robert properly, but he'd been the man of her dreams back then, all chat and charm. Not to mention good-looking. He was a walking cliché – tall, dark and handsome. Three years and a baby later, her feelings had changed and so had his; he hardly spoke to her now. Face it, Claire, she thought, blinking miserably. He's not the man you thought you married.

'Oh darling. But maybe it'll be a chance to get yourselves back on track? A fresh start in a new place? When do you move?'

Claire cast her eyes heavenwards. Lily was back on her 'work at your marriage' pedestal, but maybe she was right. Giving up on the relationship when she had a two-

27

year-old daughter wasn't something to be done lightly.

Claire was astonished when she did see the house. Where had Robert found the money to put down a deposit on a place this size? He barely gave her enough to cover the housekeeping and Nina's clothes. She wandered round the upstairs rooms, planning in spite of herself. This largest one would be a great master bedroom, and Nina could have the one opposite, a lovely big room with a bay window. She sighed. If only she could turn the clock back to the first weeks of her marriage, those heady days of being in love. Rob was twelve years older and came across as worldly-wise and sophisticated. He'd made her feel special, and although even then he'd been a little... reticent, it had only added to the attraction. Claire squared her shoulders. In spite of their recent problems, Robert was planning a shared future in this house. She would do likewise.

'Mummy's,' said Nina, holding up a handful of Jelly Tots. Claire bent and allowed her daughter to feed her the hot, sticky mess. Nina beamed, and Claire kissed her, licking the sugar from her lips afterwards. She stood up to see Robert in the doorway, hands on hips and a sneer on his face. As usual he looked immaculate, the crisp white shirt contrasting with the blackness of his hair.

'For God's sake, look at you. Stuffing your face as usual. No wonder your figure's gone to pot. Where's your self-respect – you can't blame having the baby after all this time.'

Claire didn't reply, because hell, he was right. Before

her pregnancy she'd been a small size ten and now she struggled to get into a fourteen. She allowed herself too many little treats these days because they made her feel better, but Robert cared about her appearance. He'd loved her old skinny-as-a-rake figure, and while he'd said nothing when she was pregnant, this past year or so he'd been – rude. Distant. Putting her down, humiliating her in front of other people. It was horrible.

Robert stamped downstairs to speak to the plumber, and Claire took Nina's hand and went up to the attic room. Wow, she thought, staring round. A huge floor space, lovely sloping ceiling, cute little windows – this would be a fantastic room for Nina in a few years. The little girl was running up and down, her face one big beam, and Claire laughed too, pretending to chase her. Nina shrieked, and Claire scooped her up and hugged her, looking round with sudden determination. The way forward was clear in her mind now.

With a lick of paint and some nice modern furniture, this house would be an amazing home for the three of them. It was time to do something about her marriage. She had a child. A happy family life was worth fighting for.

Chapter Four

Friday 14th - Saturday 15th July

A search round the first floor of the house revealed a good-sized bathroom with an electric shower, an airing cupboard with all the bed things she would need, and a couple more wooden chairs. Nina settled into the downstairs bedroom quite comfortably. The upstairs rooms, though larger, didn't appeal to her. Apart from John Moore's own room – and no way could she sleep there – they were poorly lit and smelled musty. Nina spread her things about the little 'maid's room', then grimaced. Quarter past six, oh, golly – Naomi would be back at the farmhouse by now, chattering away to Beth about the day's ride, or maybe having a bath to get rid of the aches and pains after four hours in the saddle... if only she were there to see the pleasure and excitement on her child's face. Unhappiness washed over Nina. It was years since she'd been away by herself like this. She wasn't used to her own company, that was the problem, and this wasn't a good time to phone home, either. They'd be busy with the guests' evening meal in the farmhouse.

Stop being a wimp, woman, she thought, grabbing

her handbag. Go for dinner, you're hungry. Things'll look different when you have a good meal inside you.

Half an hour later she was sitting at a single table by the fireplace in an elegant Georgian dining room, a very nice salmon steak in front of her and thinking that having a solo dinner in a posh hotel was something else she wasn't used to. The other diners were all couples or family groups, but the waitress made her feel at home and Nina arranged to have breakfast there too. For a few moments she regretted her decision to stay in John Moore's uncomfortable house, but then – what would she do stuck in a hotel all evening? What a weird situation this was. This time last week she'd been on the laptop, helping Bethany get them started again after the break caused by Claire's death. Little had she known then that in a week's time she'd have inherited a fortune from a man she'd never heard of and be dining all alone in a Bedford hotel.

It was still light when she walked back to John Moore's house, and the contrast of the pleasant river bank to the dinginess inside hit Nina like something physical as soon as she opened the front door. She shook off the feeling of depression. There was a job to be started here. To work, woman. You can do this.

At the desk she sat staring at the pile of papers Sam had found, apprehension rising in spite of the brave thoughts. God, it was creepy here... and if John Moore was her uncle it was entirely possible that she would come face to face with a photo of Robert Moore, or Claire – or, heaven forbid, her own younger self. Quickly, Nina pushed the pile away. Something about this place was giving her the jitters big-style, and faces from the past would be easier to cope with after a good – she hoped – night's sleep. She pulled out her phone.

A long conversation with Beth reassured her that she wasn't alone in the world, and one with Naomi made her laugh. The little girl was bubbling over about her pony ride, in tones of childlike happiness that had been missing since her grandmother's death. It was great to hear her so bright again, though Nina knew that no-one grieved in a straight line. She herself could be almost content one minute, and then the senselessness of Claire's death would hit her yet again. Thank God she was never further than a phone call away if Naomi needed her. Permanent accessibility had its advantages.

It was well before seven when Nina awoke the next morning. The curtains in her bedroom didn't quite meet in the middle, and sunlight slanting through trees in next door's garden was creating flickering shadows on the wall beside her bed. She watched them for a few seconds, then stretched luxuriously and swung her feet to the floor. Parquet, no less, though a rug for her toes would have been nice. But never mind, it was a beautiful morning and even John Moore's dreary décor looked better when the sun was shining.

Returning to the house after breakfast, she ran up to the airing cupboard for a couple of towels for the downstairs loo. Heavens, by the looks of things John Moore hadn't splashed out on towels since the nineteen eighties; these were all either threadbare or stiff as boards. What on earth had the man spent his money on? Nina grabbed two of the least ancient ones and was turning for the stairs again when the attic doorway caught her eye. Eight or nine steps above, it was set in the middle of a little landing, a solid, wooden door painted dingy white, a raised T-shaped panel on the lower part.

Nina stood motionless, staring at the door. That T-shape... what was it reminding her of? Something was jumping up and down just beyond memory, and she couldn't pinpoint it. Nina shivered, and ran on downstairs. It couldn't be anything important, an old door...

Sam's documents in the study were all bank-related, apart from receipts for medication that John Moore had bought online. He'd worried about his thinning hair, apparently, and was prone to heartburn. A lump came into Nina's throat as she leafed through them, sorting the photos into a separate pile. How pitiful it all felt. Poor sick John Moore, with no-one to care.

Now for the photos. She took them to the window where the light was better, dismayed that most were of places, not people. Two she put aside to look at again. One showed a woman and a small boy standing in a doorway, too far away to be recognisable, but maybe a magnifying glass would help with that. The other was a terraced house with a tiny patch of grass in front, the same small boy and a cat sitting on the garden wall.

Nina shrugged – these wouldn't help solve the mystery. But surely there must be more photos – Sam had been searching the desk, so these were probably floating around the drawers, as photos had a habit of doing. There could be albums somewhere too, and

John Moore might have kept more recent images in his computer. According to the receipts there must be one somewhere.

She stared round the study. There was no computer in sight, but between the windows was a rather nice secretaire and when she opened the cupboard part underneath, lo and behold there was a laptop. Great — if she could get on the internet here it would make life much easier. Sending emails with her phone was plain fiddly.

Happier, Nina went to see if the kitchen would reward her find with a hot drink. A rummage through the food cupboard produced a packet of coffee well within its sell-by date, and the two cartons of long-life milk on the bottom shelf were okay too. She rinsed the old-fashioned filter machine and set it brewing.

The smell made the kitchen seem more homelike, and Nina checked the remaining cupboards while she was waiting. There was a large selection of plates and glasses, but no perishables anywhere and the fridge was switched off. John Moore must have known he would never come back here. Did someone help him clear the kitchen, or had he done it himself? Dear God, what a depressing thought that was. She found a roll of bin bags in a drawer and dropped most of the remaining food into one. There was a small supermarket along the road; she would buy a few necessities later, to tide her over the weekend. With any luck she'd be able to go back to Arran on Monday or Tuesday.

Or — no. There would be a funeral, and under the circumstances she would have to stay for that. Come to think of it, she might even have to organise it. Something else to talk to Sam about. Nina's heart sank. The island with its lush green hills and healthy sea breezes seemed very far away today.

Soberly, she tied the bin bag and took it to the outhouse in the back courtyard where the dustbin was. It was only when she was back inside that the thought struck her – she'd gone straight out to the bin without thinking about it; she'd known where it was. She hadn't noticed it yesterday – or had she? Of course it was the logical place for a dustbin to be, but hell, how spooky that was.

The doorbell bing-bonged, and Nina hurried to let Sam in. Thank God, another human being. He was wearing jeans and a dark grey T-shirt today, and Nina was startled to see appreciation shining in his eyes as he grinned at her. Help – the last thing she needed here was an appreciative man, nice as he was. And the very fact that she'd thought of him as 'nice' said everything, didn't it? She smiled briefly and led the way into the study.

'I found John's laptop, but that's about all,' she said, resuming her search in the secretaire.

'Great. This model is pretty new, a mate of mine has one,' said Sam, booting the machine up on the desk. 'Shit, we need a password to get in here.'

Nina scowled at the screen, where the white field was blinking mockingly. There was no way to guess what John Moore's password was.

'We're going to need one of those geeky IT people,' she said.

Sam closed the laptop. 'I'll get onto that on Monday.

You can still have guest access to the Internet, might be useful. What do you want to do now?'

Nina glanced round the room. The tall bookshelves housed only ancient paperbacks and travel books. The secretaire was a dead loss, and Sam had been through the desk already.

'What we need to find is where John Moore kept his birth certificate and so on. Let's go through the rest of the house. There might be something useful in his bedroom.'

In John Moore's room the bed was made up, the duvet cover and sheet newly-washed and un-slept-in. Sam opened drawers in the tallboy, and Nina saw piles of folded underwear and jumpers.

She plumped down on the bed, frowning and thinking aloud. 'This is seriously weird. John Moore was terminally ill. He lived alone, and went into a hospice to die. So why is his bed freshly made up? The kitchen was cleared of anything that might go off, but there were half-empty boxes of rice etcetera. There's nothing personal lying around, and all his correspondence has either gone, or been put away where we haven't found it yet. And absolutely everything was unplugged.'

'You're right,' said Sam. 'You know what I think?'

Nina sat pondering, then nodded. 'He's had someone in to clean the place; someone who didn't know he was never coming back. He was rich, he might have had a regular cleaner. But Sam, that doesn't explain the lack of bank cards, passport, that kind of thing.'

'Maybe there's a safe somewhere,' said Sam, going back out into the passage. 'And what about his post? Was it redirected to the hospice? Or somewhere else?'

'I could ask at the post office,' said Nina. 'And hang on – let's look in the case they gave me at the hospice. There might be something among his stuff there.'

The case revealed a small pile of correspondence consisting of a handful of circulars, a car magazine, and two bills, one of which was from a cleaning company.

'Bingo,' said Nina. 'I'll call them and see what they can tell us. This says they were here on the eighth.'

Poor John Moore. He'd gone into the hospice and arranged for a cleaner to depersonalise his house. And now she thought about it – where were all his friends? As far as she knew there was no one clamouring for a funeral.

She keyed in the number on the cleaner's bill while Sam went to fetch more coffee. Fortunately, the company worked Saturdays, and when Sam came back with a fragrantly steaming mug in each hand she waved a page of notes at him.

'If you ever need cleaners, these are your guys. I spoke to Joanne who was very cooperative but she can't really help us. The company have been cleaning the house once a week for five years now, but they hardly ever saw John Moore. Joanne said she'd only spoken to him a handful of times since the start. He phoned them a couple of weeks ago and said he was going away, and told them to do the place and then close it up until further notice, and -' She paused and pulled a face at Sam. 'There were two large bags of shredded paper to be disposed of. Of course they're long gone now, and she has no idea what they were.'

Sam handed over her coffee and perched on the edge

of the desk.

'Okay. So he got rid of all the stuff he didn't want anyone to see after his death. But he'd hardly have shredded his birth certificate, would he? Of course he might have a safe deposit box at the bank, but that'll have to wait till Monday too.'

Nina sat sipping. It was beginning to sink in that this was her house now. She would have to decide what to do with it. Sell it? Keep it and rent it out, or live in it?

I don't want to live here, she thought. It was an absolute gut feeling. This wasn't a happy house, with the dim ground floor rooms, those closed-up bedrooms upstairs, and the long, dark attic room on the top floor.

... and the long, dark attic room on the...

'Shit!' she whispered, horrified, and buried her face in her hands. She hadn't been up to the top floor yet. How had she known about the room there?

'Nina? What's wrong?' Sam was bending over her, his hand on her back.

Nina could hear the panic in her own voice. 'There's one big room on the top floor of this house, with a wooden floor and a sloping roof and rafters. It's dim and spidery and scary, and Sam, I haven't been up there yet, how do I know that?'

He rubbed her arm and Nina fought to regain control. If nothing else, the sudden memory showed that she and John Moore were in some way connected. She must have been in this house as a very young child. It was the only explanation –and that was how she'd known about the dustbin too. She took a shaky breath. Now that the first shock had gone, she could see that it was logical – John

Moore was a relation, so naturally she would have been here to visit. Maybe she'd even played up in the attic. Rainy day games or whatever.

'Let's go and look,' she said.

Nina's heart was beating uncomfortably fast as she ran upstairs, Sam close behind her. She pushed the attic door open and clicked the light switch, staring round. Another short flight of eight stairs led up to the room proper, and it was exactly as she'd described it – one long space under the roof. Boxes were piled up on one side of the dusty wooden floor, and a pile of old mattresses lay near the windows facing the river. A single lightbulb hanging from the middle rafter was throwing shadows into the corners, and the windows were small and dirty, keeping more light out than they allowed in. Nina went over to the window overlooking the river and ran a finger along the window ledge. The dust was thick.

And something up here was spooking her out well and truly; she could feel the hairs rising on her arms.

Sam sneezed. 'I think we can assume for the moment that we won't find anything useful here.'

'There might be photos back there,' said Nina, staring at the crates and boxes stacked against the wall. But even if there was, what help would they be? What she needed was a family tree showing how she and John Moore were related. In spite of the warm weather the room felt clammy, and Nina shivered. The atmosphere up here was almost choking her. Or was it the dust?

Sam was already running downstairs, and Nina hurried after him. Dear God, this huge old place. The logical thing would be to sell it, but whether or not she'd find a buyer for a house in this state was anyone's guess. All she could hope was that Sam could deal with the business side of things for her, because no way did she want to be stuck here all summer doing stuff with John Moore's house and belongings. And they still hadn't found anything to connect her with her benefactor.

'My bet's on a safe,' said Sam, going back into John Moore's bedroom. 'Let's check all the walls, and the rest of the furniture on this floor. But Nina, whatever the relationship is, you are definitely John Moore's heir, and one way or another we'll find out how the two of you are connected next week.'

Nina's heart sank. Home soon was sounding less and less likely. 'What I can't understand is why my mother didn't tell me about him.'

'Maybe it's a very distant relationship. Or maybe she didn't like him – and she couldn't have known about the inheritance. There are any number of reasons.'

Nina sighed. It was true, anything was possible. Half an hour's work revealed nothing new, however, and Sam left, saying he was playing squash that afternoon.

At the front door he turned and touched her shoulder. 'I'd like to take you out for dinner tonight, how about it? There's a great pizza place in Bedford, if you're into Italian food.

For a split second Nina hesitated. Why was he asking? No way did she want any kind of romantic involvement; her emotions were all tied up with grieving for Claire and helping Naomi deal with her grief too. On the other hand, she had to eat, and she could make her feelings clear if the need arose. And Sam was fun; they had a good rapport.

'I love Italian food,' she said at last. 'And dinner would be great, if you're sure you haven't had enough of me for one day. But one thing, Sam – it's on me. You've been so much help, I'd like to repay you a little.'

He saluted and accepted, leaving Nina hopeful that he had no ulterior motive for asking her out. Or maybe 'hopeful' wasn't quite the right word... she wanted another relationship someday, didn't she? She wanted to find a 'significant other'? Someday yes, she thought, heading back to the kitchen. But 'someday' was neither today nor tomorrow.

Chapter Five

Saturday 15th July

Alone again, Nina wandered through the ground floor rooms, picturing her relative here. It was so odd – John Moore could have got in touch any time, but he'd waited until it was too late for them to meet. Or did he think he'd have a week or two longer? Nina shivered. How horrible, and shit, she had forgotten to ask Sam about the funeral. Oh, well, it would be a nice cheerful topic if they ran out of things to say tonight, she thought, then shook herself. Now she was getting morbid. This wasn't how she'd have chosen to come into a fortune, but it had happened and whatever his reasons were, John Moore had obviously wanted her to have it. With his millions about to become her own she could indulge in an afternoon's retail therapy with a perfectly clear conscience. Her wardrobe could do with a few additions.

Head high, she locked the front door behind her and headed for the town centre. On the way she passed the Post Office, and on an impulse went in to inquire about John Moore's post. The assistant went to check.

'Yes, the hospice didn't accept Mr Moore's post after

his death, we've been holding everything here,' she said. 'I'm sorry, I can't give it out to you today.'

'Can I arrange to have it delivered to his home address on Monday?' said Nina, thinking quickly. By the looks of things she'd be here till the middle of the week at least, and she could make fresh arrangements after that.

Lunch at a salad bar and a two-hour shopping spree cheered her up considerably. Her situation right this minute, though undeniably unusual, was actually all good news. She had inherited enough to make financial problems things of the past. She would put some of the money into the B&B – they could build the extension they'd been talking about for ages and double their business next year. And how amazing it was to go shopping and not worry too much about prices... oh yes, she could get used to this...

On the way back she called in at the supermarket and bought two bags of provisions, including a bottle of wine. A few little treats would make all the difference to living in John Moore's house. Her house.

She arrived 'home' and walked into the dimness of the hallway, determinedly thinking cheerful thoughts. She would phone Naomi in a bit, and get the day's news. Right this minute her daughter would be bouncing around on her pony, having a ball. Happy thought for the day. Now, the grey silk top she'd bought to wear tonight was gorgeous but shop-creased, but she'd spotted John Moore's iron in the tall kitchen cupboard that morning. Hopefully it worked, or she'd be heading straight back into town...

Whistling to fill the silence, Nina opened the cupboard

and reached for the elderly steam iron on a shelf near the back, noticing for the first time the tin beside it, a small flat tin that had once contained shortbread. She gave it a little shake and knew immediately that one search might be over, anyway – that sounded like papers in there... Fingers shaking, she prised the lid off.

Inside was a thick wad of banknotes and a smaller bundle of papers, and bingo, John Moore's birth certificate was there, as well as a couple of bank cards and an old cheque book, and his passport. Nina unfolded the birth certificate and peered at the old-fashioned – was it copperplate? – writing. None of the names meant anything to her, except John Moore's. His father had been John Moore too. Wishing with all her heart she knew more about the Moore family, Nina opened the passport at the photo page and felt the kitchen reel around her.

She had almost no memory of her father. They'd been on trips to the seaside, she knew, and the zoo, when she was a toddler, but – she remembered nothing of these. He wasn't quite faceless because Claire had an album with photos of Nina's baby years and of course her father was on some of these. Some, but not many, she thought suddenly, clenching her fists to stop her fingers shaking. Claire had included very few photos of Robert Moore, and when you thought about that it was difficult to understand why.

And now this face on John Moore's passport photo, rejuvenated by however many years, could easily have been her father on one of those old baby photos. The same chin, the same flat nose, the heavy eyebrows, the receding hairline. Shit, oh shit. Of course passport photos were always terrible, and there could well have been a strong family resemblance between Robert and John Moore, but...

Nina stared at the date of the passport. It had expired last year, so this photo was over ten years old. A horrible churning sensation started in her gut. Was it even remotely possible that John Robert Moore *had* been her father? That Claire had lied all those years?

For a second Nina felt as if she'd been slapped across the face, and she raised cold hands to her mouth, feeling her fingers tremble against her lips. No. That couldn't be... such a huge lie, all those years... Impossible.

Dazed, she poured a generous glass of wine and took it upstairs to the bath. She needed warmth; she was shivering. Lying in fragrant, soapy water, she tried to think calmly. A horrible, logical progression to the entire scenario was seeping into her head.

She knew very little about her father because Claire had told her very little. As a young girl she'd asked about Robert Moore's family and was told they were all dead. End of conversation. Nina's stomach churned uncomfortably as she realised that Claire had made the Moore family taboo long before little Nina was old enough to know what was happening. That was why she'd never asked much about her father; that was why she wasn't sure about her own grandparents' names. As a topic, the Moore family had been very strictly off-limits. And in all the years she'd never challenged the boundaries Claire had set.

And now – what if her father wasn't – hadn't been – dead? What if John Moore... but no, no, Claire wouldn't have invented Robert Moore's death, because that would have been cruel, and her mother hadn't been a cruel person. John Moore must have been Robert's brother, or cousin… Even cousins could look very alike. Like Tim and his cousin Angus, who was best man at Beth and Tim's wedding. Everyone joked that Bethany should check very carefully to make sure she was marrying the right man… The thought wasn't comforting for long.

If Claire had lied, she must have had a very compelling reason…

Nina stood in the bathroom drying her hair with one of John Moore's towels and thinking about her mother. She and Claire had been close; they lived together and worked together – and fought as mothers and daughters do, but the bond had been a strong one. Nina bit her lip. Their life on the island had been far away, both physically and chronologically, from their old life in England. Claire might not have shared a long-ago secret. But dear God, what possible reason was there to lie about a rich relation? And what relation?

Nina reached for her make-up bag. There was no way she could puzzle all this out for herself; she would have to wait until Sam got the information from whichever authorities on Monday.

Sam's restaurant was by the river, in a tall conservatory full of greenery. Water bubbled up from a little fountain in the middle of the room and trickled down a series of small pools into a shallow stone basin. Nina gazed round, feeling the tension leave her shoulders. The walls were sponge-painted orange at floor level and faded gradually to yellow up at the ceiling. It wasn't quite like being in Tuscany, but it must be the next best thing – exactly what she needed after John Moore's house. She smiled at Sam over the menu.

'This is a lovely place! What do you recommend?'

He opened his menu. 'Okay, my favourite starter is the one with Parma ham and melon, and the one beneath it with olives and shaved parmesan is great too. You get garlic bread with the olive one. For the main course I often have one of the tortellini dishes. The mixed fungi one is fantastic, and so is the 'Tortellini alla Roma'.'

Nina chose the olive and garlic starter and Tortellini alla Roma and sat back, sipping her wine. She hadn't told Sam about finding the passport yet, but it didn't seem polite to launch into business straightaway. She glanced up to see him gazing across at her.

'Spit it out,' he said.

Nina put her glass down. 'I was wondering if it would be rude to talk business and say I've found John Moore's birth certificate and his passport, and unfortunately they don't take us any further, except for the interesting detail that he could have been my father's twin.'

'Ah,' he said, frowning. 'Of course it's not rude. I wouldn't worry till you know the facts, Nina. Brothers can look very alike.' He sat fiddling with a piece of bread, and she waited.

He looked up again. 'You know, I can identify with your problem. I don't remember either of my birth parents. My mother was only seventeen when I was born, and she died a year later after a drugs overdose. I don't think she knew who my father was, so for all I know he could be alive. I was adopted by an amazing couple from Allerton, and they're the ones I call Mum and Dad.'

'They must be very proud of you,' said Nina, leaning back as the waiter appeared with the starters, glad of the short interruption. The evening had taken a slightly disturbing turn – Sam had trusted her with an intimate part of his past. Of course, he knew a lot about her, things she wouldn't normally tell strangers. He'd balanced that out now and it somehow removed them from the situation of lawyer-and-client-out-to-dinner – so maybe he did want to be more than her lawyer. Help. She would have to be careful; there was no space in her head for a lovesick lawyer, even if he was 'nice'.

She gave him a quick smile and lifted her fork. 'Tell me more about the arrangements.' Business was definitely the safest option.

She listened attentively as he told her what John Moore had organised. 'As you know I'm executor of the will. That means it's up to me to settle the estate and make sure it's given over to the heirs. That's you. I also have to organise a cremation, but John Moore didn't want a funeral service and he didn't leave any special instructions about the ashes, so you can have a think if you have any preferences about that. And on Monday morning we should hear back from the General Register Office; then we'll know who's who.'

Nina heaved a sigh, relief making her feel quite light-hearted. Not so complicated after all, brilliant. The horrible uncertainty would soon be over.

'It's great to know I'm in such efficient hands. You have an interesting job, don't you?'

He wrinkled his nose. 'Not really. You're the most interesting thing that's happened in the last three years. All I do most of the time is draw up contracts, and I'm the most junior partner with no real hope of becoming more senior in the foreseeable future. I've been mulling over a change of direction for a while now.'

'What would you do?'

He shrugged. 'Look for something business-related, I guess. Maybe do a course. It's all a bit up in the air at the moment. Tell me about you. What do you on your west coast island?'

Nina talked for a few moments about the B&B, telling him how they'd started with one room and then added five more as time went on.

'We get loads of business from Easter till about October, but very little the rest of the year. So balancing the books can be tricky, but it's worth it. Arran's a fantastic place to live,' she finished.

Sam reached across and squeezed her hand, not letting go. 'Sounds like John Moore's legacy will make a difference to you. Any plans yet?'

Nina removed her hand from his grasp. Time for some plain speaking. 'What I need to do first is get my life back on an even footing after Mum's death, and help Naomi do that too. I need time and space to recover, Sam. All this with John Moore really is too much, and I have to put Naomi first.'

And she should be with her girl right now, she thought miserably. Mind you, the phone call to Arran before Sam arrived tonight had reassured Nina that Naomi was having the time of her life. The pony-trekking weekend was to continue until Wednesday. John Moore's millions were going to come in handy.

'Of course, I understand,' said Sam, looking at her helplessly. 'I'm sorry. I'd like to think we can be – friends.'

He was more than nice, thought Nina. If they'd met at another time in a different place... But they hadn't. She raised her glass. 'Me too. To the future!'

They clinked, but Nina could see he felt rejected. His eyes swivelled round the room before he eventually came back to business. 'I'll draw up a death announcement for the newspapers on Monday, maybe some of John Moore's friends will get in touch. That could be helpful.'

Yes, thought Nina, but wasn't it a little strange that no one had got in touch already? Of course it was summer, people were away, and maybe they'd had better things to do than visit dying men in hospices... it would need a good friend to do that. Not many people had visited Claire in hospital, it was just too damned painful to sit watching her vegetate while a machine breathed for her. Nina understood perfectly; she'd hardly been able to stand it herself.

It was almost eleven when Sam pulled up in front of the house.

'Nina, I'm sorry but I'm away all day tomorrow. It's the squash club's annual outing, and as I'm secretary this year I arranged it and I have to go.'

The expression on his face was downcast, and Nina smiled wryly. His apology could only mean that otherwise he would be back on her doorstep, which was not what she wanted. God bless the squash club. She made her voice bright and cheerful.

'Sounds great! Where are you going?'

'Stratford. Guided tour plus 'A Merchant of Venice'. I'll text you a picture, shall I? Then first thing Monday morning I'll get on to your business, and I'll call to tell you what's happening as soon as I know. What'll you do tomorrow?'

'I guess I'll start clearing. Clothes, books and stuff. I'm not going to keep the house.'

The decision had made itself, so it must be the right one.

Sam didn't sound surprised. 'The estate shouldn't take long to settle. You can have it on the market by the autumn.'

Nina closed the door behind him and trailed through to the kitchen. Hopefully, by the autumn this house would be a distant memory and John Moore's millions would be safely in the bank on Arran.

CHAPTER SIX

Monday, 17th July

The blackmail letter arrived sometime between eight-thirty and nine-fifteen on Monday morning.

By half past eight Nina was scurrying towards the local supermarket, huddled under one of John Moore's better umbrellas and trying to avoid the worst of the puddles. The easterly wind blowing a gale against her added to the misery; controlling the big umbrella was challenging to say the least. If she hadn't needed some basic necessities like bread and bin bags, she would never have attempted it and how she was going to manage the return journey, with full shopping bags, she had no idea.

The river was full and flowing more swiftly than she'd seen it so far, its waters brown and muddy to match her mood. Her sojourn here had been bearable in sunny summer weather with Sam around to talk to, but after thirty-six hours in her own company Nina felt tired and jaded.

Being an heiress isn't all it's cracked up to be, she thought, scraping damp strands of hair away from her eyes. She had all that money, yet here she was, staying in a pretty sordid house, and now she had to go out in a monsoon – or it would be if it wasn't so bloody cold – and buy her own bread. Talk about Monday morning. She was doing something wrong here. And thank heavens, here was the supermarket.

The rain had slackened off to a drizzle when she emerged clutching her bags of provisions, and Nina pulled up her hood and left the umbrella to its fate in the stand by the door. There were at least another three in the coat rack at 'home'.

The letter was on the mat when she opened the door, and Nina stared at the single envelope. John Moore's held-back stuff was supposed to be coming this morning; surely there should be more post than this. She lifted the thin envelope and went on through to the kitchen.

Oh – this hadn't come by post. Nina stared at John Moore's name printed in Times New Roman on a sticky label on the envelope. There was no address, no stamp. From a neighbour, maybe – or one of John's elusive friends? But why the label? She sat down at the table to open it, and pulled out a single A4 sheet, folded in four. The print here was Times New Roman too, large-sized and italicised.

Horror chilled its way through Nina as she read.

Did you think you'd paid me off? Did you think I'd go away? Wrong both times, paedo. You don't have enough money to pay for what you did. Do you think I don't remember screaming my poor little head off while you and your paedo mates got off on it? Pervert, paedo, and now you can pay. It'll cost you double this time. £4,000. And I'll be back for more. Like you were, pervert.

Nina dropped the letter on the table and leapt to her feet, hands over her mouth. Dear God, what a disgusting letter. John Moore – a paedophile? Could that be? Shit, shit, what on earth should she do now?

Phone the police, the rational part of her brain said immediately. Blackmail's an offence, no matter who did what, and the police could find out if there was any truth to the allegations.

Feeling sick to her stomach, Nina hurried through to the study for the phone directory she'd noticed there, and looked up the number of the police station. The person she spoke to was calm and reassuring, told her someone would be round in fifteen minutes, and warned her not to touch the letter again. Nina broke the connection and called Sam's number. He should know about this too. Loneliness crept through her as she waited for him to connect. If only Beth were here and not hundreds of miles away. And oh, if this had all happened a few short weeks ago she'd have had Claire to call on both for help and for information about John Moore. The images the letter was conjuring up were appalling. Nina squinted at it on the table.

...screaming my poor little head off...

Dear God but she had done that too, up on the top floor of this house... she had screamed too...

Nina dropped her phone on the table and stumbled to the downstairs toilet where she vomited hot, burning liquid into the bowl. When the spasm was over she splashed water on her face and stared at her reflection, sheet-white in the rust-marked mirror. Get a grip, woman, the police'll be here any minute. They'll know what to do. And Sam, hell, what must he be thinking, she'd called his number, dropped her mobile, and ran.

He was shouting her name down the phone when she picked it up.

'I'm on my way,' he said when she told him. 'I'll be with you in ten, okay?'

'Yes,' she said dully. 'I'm fine, don't worry.'

A muffled thud in the hallway made her jump, but it was only the postman. Nina's fingers shook as she sat in the kitchen, sifting through the bundle of letters and ads from the past couple of weeks. But thank God, apart from the gas and electricity bills there was nothing here that needed attention.

The doorbell rang and she trailed through to answer it. Two police officers were standing there, a grey-haired older man with a comfortable face and a blonde woman who looked very severe but was probably only twenty-five or so. They introduced themselves as Detective Inspector David Mallony and Detective Constable Sabine Jameson. Nina led them into the kitchen where they stood beside the table, reading the letter where it lay, their faces grim. DI Mallony pulled on gloves and eased both envelope and letter into plastic folders.

'Nasty,' he said. 'Must have given you quite a shock. And this John Moore is - ?'

'He's dead,' said Nina, feeling better now she could hand the letter over to experts. 'He died last week and I've inherited this house, you see. I didn't know him and I'm not sure what relation he was to me. His – my lawyer's finding out about that today.'

It sounded strange as she said it, but DI Mallony

merely nodded.

A sudden idea came to Nina and she sat straighter. Maybe science could help her. 'Is there a test I could get done to find out about the relationship, even though he's dead? A DNA test or something?'

David Mallony sat down, his expression giving nothing away. 'There is, but if it's a distant relationship it can take a while to get the results. It's not like a paternity test which is back in a day or two.'

'Could you arrange for me to take a paternity test?' said Nina. A negative result would be exactly what she wanted, much better than an old marriage certificate or family tree.

'I think you'd better tell me why you want it,' said David Mallony, staring at her over the table. 'Is there any doubt about who your father is?'

Nina took a deep breath. All she could do was tell the truth. She was in the middle of explaining when the doorbell rang and Sabine Jameson went to let Sam in. He touched Nina's shoulder and sat down beside her.

David Mallony listened without speaking, his face grave. 'I see. Well, we can certainly arrange a paternity test though I imagine you'll have to pay for it yourself.'

'Nina – I've heard back from the GRO. They traced your birth certificate. John Robert Moore was your father,' said Sam, putting a hand on her shoulder again.

Nina winced. How stupid, her own birth certificate – it was the logical starting place; she should have thought of that herself. It must be at home, in the folder where Claire kept all the important documents, but for the life of her Nina couldn't remember ever seeing it. And why on earth that should be was difficult to understand.

She glared at Sam. 'Hell. But that can't be right. There must be some mistake. I still want the test.' She raised her eyebrows at David Mallony.

'Of course.' His voice was quite neutral.

Nina nodded. Thank God he'd agreed. Surely the test would show that she wasn't John Moore's daughter. And when she was safely back on Arran she would research Robert Moore's side of the family. It might be something Naomi would enjoy helping with, too.

Sam leaned towards her. 'You're doing the right thing; a test'll give you certainty. Oh, and the cremation's organised for 10 a.m. Wednesday,' he said, and David Mallony took a note of the details. Nina was silent. A cremation with no service, no mourners, no funeral flowers. How tragic. A sordid end to any kind of life. But oh, God, what had John Moore done? Was there any truth at all in that blackmail letter?

David Mallony asked several more questions about John Moore, the house, and if she had noticed anyone hanging around since she arrived. Nina answered as well as she could, wondering all the time if she should tell them about the moment when she'd felt she remembered crying up in the attic room. But it was so vague – what child didn't cry at some point? Yet the phrase 'screaming my poor little head off' had stirred something deep inside her, some long-forgotten terror.

Say nothing for the moment, she thought. She could tell the police later if she remembered anything more concrete. Anyway, there was nothing to say that the accusation in the letter was true, and even if it was, John

Moore was beyond prosecution now.

The two detectives had a look round the house, spending quite a long time in the study, then left, taking John Moore's laptop with them and telling Nina to go to the police station for a cheek swab later that morning.

Nina closed the door and turned back to the kitchen, where Sam was making coffee.

'Are you all right, Nina? What an ordeal.'

'I want to go home,' she said, sinking onto a hard wooden chair and rubbing her face with both hands. She would phone Beth as soon as Sam had gone, and – but dear God, she couldn't tell her friend over the phone that she thought she remembered screaming in the attic owned by a man who might turn out to be her father and who had now been accused of being a paedophile... She would break down and howl before she'd said six words. A sob escaped before she could suppress it.

Sam put a mug of coffee in front of her. 'Nina, talk to me. I can see there's something more.'

She turned her face away. This was way too personal to tell someone she'd only known a few days, even if he was her lawyer and 'nice'. And fancied her. Especially if he fancied her.

'It's nothing,' she tried to say, but the words came out in a cracked whisper.

...*screaming my poor little head off*... Fuck, fuck, that was a memory, she could remember screaming, there had been a lot of screaming...

What had happened to her?

Sam tried to grasp her hands and she yanked them away, conscious that she was shaking all over now.

'Nina, you can tell me, or you can tell the doctor. Whatever this is you can't deal with it alone. Which do you want?' He was holding his mobile, thumb poised to tap.

Nina stared at him, bleary-eyed. She didn't want to confide in him, but perhaps she should. She needed an impartial opinion, and telling Sam would be better than having him summon yet another stranger here.

'I – when I read the letter I remembered screaming too, upstairs in the attic room,' she whispered, not looking at him, unable to stop her teeth chattering.

For a moment there was silence, then Sam reached out and squeezed her hand very briefly. Nina fought for control over her breathing. It was a relief to have told someone, though Beth would have been a better someone.

'But Nina – if that's an accurate memory then - '

'Then the allegations in that letter could well be true,' said Nina bleakly. She took a deep, shaky breath, then another. 'Sam, I know. It's so horrible – I just don't remember enough. Hell, I was only three years old when we left this house, nobody would - '

She broke off, yet more horror flooding through her as she realised what she had said. This house... it had been this house, her gut instinct was shrieking that now.

Another thought crashed into her head. This could be the reason for Claire's flight from Bedford and the Moore family. Maybe they hadn't left because Robert Moore died – Claire could have been running from an abusive John Moore. But how could she find out, all these years later? Nina swallowed, her throat dry and painful.

And of course, of course, hell – this would be why Claire took over the application for both their passports so firmly. Nina closed her eyes, remembering. She hadn't thought anything of it at the time; she signed the appropriate pages and left the bundle with Claire to 'send off with all the paperwork'. Shit. She'd been twenty-two, Naomi was a toddler, and Claire had 'done the donkey work', as she called it. Did she do it to prevent Nina noticing her father's name on her birth certificate? Nothing seemed more likely now.

Dear God, where was this going to end?

'I think you should go to a hotel,' said Sam. 'Don't forget, whoever wrote that letter is out there somewhere.'

Nina stared out of the kitchen window. Rain was dripping from the ivy growing up the garden wall. 'There's no reason to think he'd harm me. All I want is to finish up here as soon as I can and then go home, Sam. Back to Arran.'

'I'll do everything I can to get you on the first possible plane north. Let's wait and see what the police say when they get into John Moore's computer. They might find an explanation there.'

Sam left soon after and Nina set her shoulders. She was going to get on with things here. First stop was the police station for her cheek swab, and then she would continue what she'd started yesterday, bagging John Moore's stuff.

But how scary it was that John Moore, whether or not he was her father and whether or not he was a criminal – had known about her all the time. The thought made her feel invaded, as if he'd been snooping about in her life.

By evening she'd made good headway clearing John Moore's possessions and organised with a charity shop in town to take some bits and pieces. It felt good, having a menial task to do, and it gave her time to think. Either John Moore was her father – and she was still hoping he wasn't – or he was a more distant relation. He may have abused the letter-writer in the past, but it was also possible that the writer was nothing more than a mean chancer after the money. After all, a sick, single man might pay up simply to stop someone making a false allegation.

Nina shook her head. It sounded logical enough when you thought it through like that, but somehow her gut instinct was jumping up and down again, telling her that a piece of the puzzle was still missing. The best thing would be to stay here a few more days and get things sorted out before she headed north again. Slowly, she walked through the house, trying to remember being here as a child. But nothing came to mind. You couldn't force memories, she knew that; they had to come by themselves.

At five o'clock the doorbell rang. Sam stood there, clutching a laptop, his face a mixture of exasperation and apology.

'Nina, I'm sorry. I wanted to keep you company this evening but I'm in court first thing and something new has come up – so I've got masses of reading to do on the case before morning. I've brought you this; I thought it might be useful now the police have taken John Moore's laptop.'

Nina was touched. 'Thanks, Sam, that's kind of you. And don't worry. I have a gourmet microwave meal for one waiting in the fridge. I've decided to stay on for a day or two anyway, till we know more.'

His face lit up. 'Excellent. I'll make us pizza tomorrow night, shall I? I do a real mean pizza.'

Nina accepted, wondering if she was doing the right thing. But you could have too much of your own company, and with all these vague feelings and uncomfortable memories welling up it was better not to be alone too much.

CHAPTER SEVEN

Claire's story – Bedford

Nina's third birthday was a big family event. Lily and Bill came down from Edinburgh for a few days, so all four grandparents were there, plus Robert's Aunt Emily and the Wright cousins. Claire congratulated herself on getting the whole family together for the first time since her wedding. That was what families did, wasn't it – they gathered under one roof and celebrated the grandkids' birthdays. And as Robert went out of his way to demonstrate to the older generation what a brilliant father he was, the birthday party had gone off rather well.

'I see you're making a go of it,' said Lily, approval in her voice.

They were washing up after the party. A dishwasher was high on Claire's wish list, especially as the Wrights spent more time in her home than they did in their own. But Robert held the purse strings and as yet he hadn't considered it. Claire shivered, in spite of the hot dishwater. Robert should open a joint account; it really bugged her that she had to ask for every single thing.

She was doing her best – she had lost weight and was genuinely trying to take an interest in Rob's hobbies and his work. Mind you, his only hobby was going out with George Wright and heaven knows what the two of them got up to. Robert barked at her every time she opened her mouth, too. It felt as if she was the only one trying to save the marriage. Of course there could be another reason for his crabbiness – maybe his property business was going through a bad patch. That didn't excuse the churlish behaviour, but it might be a reason for it. People did let off steam on their nearest and dearest.

'I'm doing my best, but it's not easy, Mum,' she said at last. 'Rob spends more time with George than he does with me. Sometimes I wonder why he married me.'

'That's men for you,' said Lily, hanging up her dish towel. 'Maybe if you made the place a bit more… modern? Welcoming?'

Frustration fizzed up inside Claire. 'I'd like nothing better but he won't cough up for new stuff. All the furniture apart from what's here in the kitchen came from his Mum and Dad's old place. I had nothing to say about buying the house and now I have nothing to say about the furnishings. I feel like a servant most of the time.'

'Oh, don't be so melodramatic,' said Lily. 'It's good quality stuff. Maybe you can replace it little by little.'

Claire shrugged. Her mother had always been good at whistling in the dark.

As soon as his in-laws returned home Robert reverted to

his old insulting manner, and Claire found herself avoiding him and beginning to hate him, too. Her suggestion that they talk things through with a marriage guidance counsellor met with ridicule, and he started calling her 'fat cow', even in front of other people. The constant jibes about her weight hurt – she was a size twelve now and anyway, had he only married her for her matchstick figure? It was beginning to look like it. She couldn't even remember the last time they'd had sex.

But the most disturbing thing of all was he'd started to push her around a bit. Oh, nothing you could call violent, but he'd chivvied her out of the way a couple of times, and recently he'd taken to brushing past her a shade too closely, forcing her to move aside. Claire knew it was the kind of thing that people said would only get worse. She couldn't go on like this; she'd done her best but the marriage was dead. She should leave. The thing was – what would she use for money? She had no training, no prospects, and a three-year-old daughter. Could she swallow her pride enough to ask her parents for help? That wasn't a decision to be taken lightly.

Things came to a head one Saturday afternoon a few weeks later. Claire had an emergency dental appointment – she'd lost a filling and it was giving her gyp – which meant leaving Nina at home. The Wrights were there too; George and Robert were up in the attic as usual, along with several bottles of beer, and loud laughter wafted down at regular intervals. George had taken up photography; his camera was permanently round his neck and he'd set up a dark room at home. Whatever photos he took caused a lot of hilarity whenever he and

Robert got together but he never showed them to the women. Claire had to fight to keep a pleasant expression on her face when George was around, but if she didn't the jibes were worse.

Fortunately Jane had come too that afternoon and was doing a jigsaw with Paul and Nina, glass in hand as usual. Claire hesitated in the living room doorway; hell, that was Jane's second G&T, she'd be pie-eyed by tea time if she went on like that. It might be better to take Nina with her. But watching her mother have a tooth filled would put Nina off dentists for life...

'Hey, leave some for me,' she said lightly, shifting the gin bottle back to the sideboard. Jane smiled, and Claire decided to risk it. Nina adored Paul, anyway, look how she was hanging on the six-year-old's every word. Removing her now would only cause a scene, and Claire didn't have time for that.

She arrived home late afternoon to find Jane asleep on the sofa and no sign of the children. Shaking the other woman, Claire saw it wasn't as much sleep as a drunken stupor that was afflicting Jane. The men were out, if the absence of jackets in the hallway was anything to go by. Hell, she should never have left Nina – and what was Robert thinking, leaving his daughter with a drunk woman?

'Nina! Paul!' she called, running upstairs.

Nina's bedroom door banged opened and the little girl stumbled out and ran towards Clare, arms outstretched. There were tear-stains on the child's face, and Claire scooped her up and held her tightly, horrified to feel the little body tremble in her arms. What on earth was going on here?

'Sweetheart? What's the matter?'

'Paul's crying. Daddy said he was bad,' said Nina, squeezing Claire's arm in a painful grip and pushing her other thumb into her mouth. Claire stroked damp curls into place and kissed the hot little head.

'Why? Did Paul hurt you?'

She knew that Paul's exuberance was sometimes difficult for Nina to keep up with. Nina shook her head and removed her thumb long enough to reply. 'No. Daddy was cross. He was in the attic... he hurted Paul and then he - ' She sobbed into Claire's neck.

Claire carried Nina into the bedroom. So Robert had been in a temper with the children – nothing new, but as far as Claire was aware he'd never struck them before. But then maybe she didn't know everything.

Paul was sitting on the floor, his face blotchy and a wild expression on his eyes. There was an enormous red lump on his forehead and his small frame was shaking with every breath. Aghast, Claire crouched beside him, Nina in her arms.

'What happened, Paul?' she asked, stretching a hand out to him. 'Did you bang your head?'

He slid away from her. 'He – Uncle Robert said... ' The words seemed to stick in his throat and he stared at Claire, his eyes wide, then giggled nervously.

'Where is he, darling? What did he say?'

Claire reached out again but Paul pressed himself against the bed.

'He – he said I – we – were bad. He said we're always bad and he – he – he hit – us. I ran away and I banged my head on the attic door and Uncle Robert shouted and Nina – Nina was scared.'

Claire's arms closed round her own child. Right. She had come to the end of her tether. No matter how loud and disruptive the children had been, there was no excuse for violence. And there was every reason to leave a man who would strike his own daughter.

Nina had fallen asleep in her arms, and Claire laid her on the bed, noticing grimly how exhausted the child was. As soon as Nina awoke she would examine every inch of her skin and check for bruises. And then...

And then they would leave. Anger was fuelling her determination now and her hands were shaking almost as much as Paul's. That was it. She was finished here and finished with Robert too.

Tomorrow, she and Nina would 'go for a walk' and they would take a train up north. She wasn't helpless; she would find a job in Edinburgh, and Mum and Dad would help her. Outrage filled her mind as she considered this might not be the first time the children had suffered under Robert's hand. Paul obviously wasn't lying; the child was distraught.

'Come on, Paul lovey,' she said, tucking the duvet round Nina. 'Let's put some magic cream your head and then we'll phone for a taxi to take you and Mummy home, will we? You can be all safe and warm again there.'

The child was looking at her with a closed expression on his face, but he allowed Claire to take his hand. She sighed. Paul didn't have a regular home life, but his mother loved him when she was sober, and he had stability at school. And she certainly couldn't take him to Edinburgh. But she could take Nina – and she would.

A lump came into Claire's throat as she led Paul downstairs. How much in love she – they – had been, what high hopes she'd had at the beginning of her marriage. She'd known Robert for – what? – just over four years. Four years which had made her life a million times better, because now she had Nina. And Nina was more important than anyone – or anything – else.

Her mouth tight, Claire rinsed a washcloth under the tap in the downstairs toilet and wiped Jane's face with it. She had done this many times before, but today would be the last time. This time tomorrow, both Jane and Bedford would be out of her life forever.

CHAPTER EIGHT

Tuesday 18th July

The doorbell rang when Nina was swallowing her last bite of toast on Tuesday morning and surfing the news sites on Sam's laptop. She glanced up to see a police car parked outside and hurried to the door. Hopefully they'd found out something that would set her mind at rest about John Moore. Hearing that the anonymous letter was from a vicious conman trying to trick a sick man out of his money would be the best possible start to the day. You heard about things like that all the time and John Moore would have been an easy target, in his condition.

DI Mallony was standing on the doorstep, staring at the ivy-covered walls.

'No real news yet, but I thought I'd stop by anyway and tell you how things are progressing,' he said, following her into the kitchen and accepting a mug of coffee.

'All I want to know is who I am in relation to John Moore. And it would be great to hear that the blackmail letter is a pack of lies,' said Nina frankly.

'I can imagine, but all I can tell you is that John Moore has no criminal record and he isn't on the sex offenders register. And apart from your own, there are no fingerprints on the anonymous letter. If you come across another, call us straightaway. That letter wasn't the first.'

'Okay,' said Nina, remembering the bags of shredded papers the cleaner had told her about. She wasn't likely to find the letter's predecessors. He hadn't been kidding when he said 'no real news', she thought glumly. But no news was good news, wasn't it?

She cupped her hands round the comforting warmth of her mug. 'So what else is there to do?'

'John Moore's laptop's being investigated; we should have more information about that later today,' said David Mallony, draining his mug. 'I'll be in touch. Oh, and I've marked your paternity test 'urgent'.'

Nina closed her eyes in relief. Thank God for technology. Old records might fail her, but the test would remove all uncertainty. And surely Claire hadn't lied all these years...

'I'll be here all day,' she said, accompanying him to the door. Things were moving along, not exactly a mile a minute, true, but they were moving. And in an odd way, the very fact that the police weren't treating it as super-urgent was reassuring too.

And at least John Moore didn't have a police record as long as Brighton pier. Nina grimaced. She could still hope he was a nice innocent reclusive forty-second cousin. It was frustrating being stuck in limbo like this, but on the other hand it was giving her the chance to get the house cleared. Look on the bright side, Nina. She would get those bundles for the charity shop finished now.

The doorbell rang again while she was looking for the string, which had disappeared completely since the previous day. Nina jogged up the hallway to the front door. This was turning into quite an 'at home' day, and she couldn't think who this caller could be. Sam was expecting to be in court till lunchtime at least.

A worried-looking middle-aged woman was standing on the doorstep. Frowning, she peered short-sightedly into Nina's face and then beyond her into the darkness.

'Hello, dear, is everything all right? I live next door, we only got back last night but when I saw the police car this morning I had to come and see...'

Aha, thought Nina. This would either be a nosy busybody or a genuinely concerned neighbour, and either might be able to provide her with some useful information.

'Come in and have a coffee,' she suggested, holding the door open.

The woman, whose name was Pat Cox, didn't need a second invitation. Nina made fresh coffee, reflecting she'd be hyper for the rest of the day at this rate. Pat listened to her account of the past week with a horrified expression, though Nina didn't mention the anonymous letter. She didn't want the sordid little story to be all over Bedford by lunchtime.

Pat rubbed her face. 'Oh my goodness. I'd no idea. I knew he wasn't well but we didn't think for a minute... He always kept himself to himself, Mr Moore, a nice quiet gentleman. And this past fortnight we've been away on holiday, Florence and Rome and then a week at Rimini, such a busy resort, dear, you should see the crowds on that beach. Oh dear. Nigel'll be right sorry to hear this.'

A concerned neighbour, decided Nina. Good.

'Do you know anything about John's friends?' she asked.

Pat looked thoughtful. 'Like I said he kept himself to himself, your uncle. I can't say we knew him but he was a good neighbour. He was away a lot of the time – the house was often dark in the evenings. Being next door of course we noticed that.'

Nina was silent. She had introduced herself as Nina Moore, saying that John Moore had left her the house. Pat had put two and two together and come up with what was probably the most likely solution to an outsider. There didn't seem to be anything Nina could say without telling Pat way more than she wanted to. But it couldn't do any harm to press for as much as the other woman knew about John Moore.

'My mother had no contact with John for as long as I can remember,' she said, topping up Pat's mug. 'Do you know if he had any other family, or good friends, even, in the area – people who came round to visit, maybe?'

Pat shook her head. 'A young man visited quite a lot a while back. I always assumed he was a nephew or something. We noticed him because he always parked in front of our place. We haven't seen him for a while, though. And sometimes there would be older men, too, friends, I suppose. But nothing much, like I said... Oh dear. When's the funeral?'

'He didn't want one. I'm here to clear the house as much as I can this week and then it'll be going on the market.'

Pat stood up. 'Well, I won't keep you. What this place needs is a team of decorators, and then a big family living

73

in it. It would make a lovely family home and being so close to London you'll sell it no bother.'

'I hope you're right,' said Nina. 'Thanks for coming by, Pat. It's good to know that John had nice neighbours.'

How hypocritical, she thought, closing the door behind the woman. But the picture of John Moore was becoming stranger with every person she spoke to. Few visitors to the house, a cleaning lady he'd exchanged a mere handful of words with in five years, neighbours who barely knew him. The man seemed to have been a positive recluse, and really, it was hard to imagine Claire marrying someone like that. Claire had been a real people person, she'd loved having friends and family around her. But then again, if opposites did attract... Nina shrugged. There was no way to know what had happened back then. She would just have to wait for the test results. And hallelujah, here was the string.

She was bringing bundles of bedware down to the study, which had turned into a kind of half-way house for goods on their way to the charity shop, when her mobile rang. Goodness, it was Beth, what an odd time... Hell, was Naomi - ?

Nina's heart thundered into top gear and she spoke before Beth had the chance to say hello. 'Is Naomi all right?'

Beth's voice was calm. 'She's fine, lovey, but she fell off her pony this morning and sprained her wrist, so it's no more riding for her this week. She wants to come and join you, Nina. What will I tell her?'

Nina gripped the phone. Her baby was hurt and she was stuck at the other end of the country. Shit, why the hell had she ever come here? 'Oh God. Has she seen a doctor? Let me speak to her?'

'Yes, I took her to Lamlash for an X-Ray and she honestly is fine, Nina. Tim's taken her to help him buy more canoeing stuff, but she's upset about losing the rest of the trekking course and she wants to be with her mum. Any sign of your business finishing?'

Homesickness rattled through Nina – she wanted nothing more than to be with Naomi. If she was on Arran they could go long walks along the beach and she could help Naomi get over the hurt wrist and the disappointment. As it was...

Nina thought swiftly. She could hardly expect Beth to take care of a bored, frustrated ten-year-old and run the B&B at the same time. 'Of course she can come here. Do you want me to find out about flights?'

'No, I'll do that. We'll get her on one today, I promise. Speak soon.'

Nina broke the connection and stood still. Naomi was coming here to this dingy, depressing house, to be right in the middle of a police investigation for blackmail and possible paedophilia, and Nina couldn't even tell her daughter what relation John Moore was to them. And yet –

I am really pleased, thought Nina, standing there grinning at the piles of sheets on the floor. Naomi was coming; that would brighten things up and give them both something fresh to think about. Should they stay here or go to the hotel? Which would Naomi prefer?

Stay here, she realised after just two seconds' thought. Naomi would want to explore the house and help get everything packed up. Okay. They couldn't both sleep in the downstairs bedroom, so...

She was arranging a pair of single beds in one of the upstairs rooms when Sam arrived with tuna sandwiches and two large chunks of Black Forest Gateau. Over their meal Nina told him about the morning's events and he listened, sandwich in hand.

'Wow, you've been busy. And as the police have pinched my job finding out about John's family I've taken the rest of the day off. I can take you to meet Naomi if you want. I'm afraid we might be looking at a trip to Heathrow.'

He was right. Nina left Sam in a coffee bar to give herself some time alone with Naomi, and hurried through the arrivals area in Terminal 2. Thank heavens it was midweek. At least the airport was less busy than at the weekend. Which meant it was mobbed without being completely chaotic, she thought, skirting a group of irate people who appeared to have lost their relative. Bouncing up and down on the balls of her feet, Nina checked the board – the plane was down. Not long now till she could hug her girl and oh, how brilliant was that?

'Mum!' Naomi flew towards her and flung herself into Nina's arms. 'Oh Mum, Mrs Anderson wouldn't let me finish the ride though I told her my arm was okay and the doctor said it was only a sprain too.'

Nina hugged back gently, fighting back the desire to laugh at Naomi's aggrieved expression. She took hold of the bandaged wrist and examined it.

'Oh sweetheart. Doesn't it hurt?'

'Not much. They gave me pills at the hospital. It's not fair. I was getting on so well.'

She put one arm round Nina's waist as they walked towards the exit, cuddling up, and Nina squeezed back gently. This was a time for one hundred per cent sympathy.

'It's such bad luck, but I promise when your wrist's better we'll get you on another trek. You've got all summer on Arran this year so we're bound to manage something.'

Naomi nodded, her expression still glum. Nina kissed the honey-coloured hair and hugged Naomi closer, feeling the tension in the child's body. This wasn't all to do with a sprained wrist and the loss of a couple of days trekking. Naomi had the death of her grandmother to contend with as well, not to mention having contact with her father reduced to Skype conversations. And a mother who'd deserted her...

The little girl sniffed disconsolately. 'Are we going back to Bedford now?'

'Yes. The lawyer's driving us back. Sam Harrison. He's helping us this afternoon because the police have taken over some of his work to find out how we're related to John Moore.'

'The *police*? Why?'

The news at least had the effect of distracting Naomi from her misery. Nina hugged the girl again. She had already concluded that there was no point trying to hide what was going on from Naomi, so the explanation would give her daughter still more food for thought, even though Nina was going to keep schtum about the paedophilia part for the moment.

'Because a letter arrived for John Moore yesterday, trying to blackmail him – that means threaten him to make him do something, and that's illegal. So I called the police. Look, here's the coffee shop where we're meeting Sam.'

Naomi was quiet on the drive back to Bedford. They were a mile or two south of Luton when her mobile rang, and she had an animated conversation with her father in Cape Town. Nina listened, holding Naomi's hand. They were both in the back seat, which made poor Sam look like a chauffeur.

Eventually Naomi clicked off her mobile and blinked up at Nina. 'Dad says he sprained his wrist when he was about my age too, when he fell downstairs. He said it was better in a week or two. Oh, Mummy, I wish it had never happened. The others'll be out there riding right now. And we were going to gallop on the beach at Kildonan tomorrow, and take the ponies into the sea. It's not fair.'

Naomi subsided, nestling up close again, and Nina's heart sank. Naomi had way too much to cope with at the moment, that was what wasn't fair. She wasn't usually a clingy, cuddly child. It was time to be supermum for a while, make sure that their dead relation's non-presence in their lives didn't worry Naomi any more than she was worried already.

'Ladies. What do you want to do about food?'

Nina glanced out of the window. They were approaching the exit for Bedford. She and Sam had discussed possible dinner plans on the way to Heathrow, but Nina wanted to see how Naomi was before making any decisions. Originally of course she'd been supposed to go to Sam's flat for pizza. Nina sighed. She could tell Naomi wasn't in the mood for fun evenings out.

'I think we'll go straight back to the house, Sam,' she said. 'Naomi's tired – and of course I want to show her everything, too.' This last was added on quickly as Naomi stirred indignantly. Silly me, thought Nina, grinning in spite of herself. Ten-year-olds didn't get tired, they were almost grown-up already, not babies...

Sam's shoulders drooped and for a brief moment Nina felt guilty. But Naomi needed a cosy evening with Mum and lots of cuddles. And she was the luckiest woman in the world to be able to give her daughter just that.

Chapter Nine

Wednesday 19th July

Naomi was still asleep in her bed by the window when Nina awoke the next morning, and for a few glorious moments she lay still, gazing across at her daughter. How miraculous it was that this perfect being had grown inside her. That her tiny, beautiful baby had developed into such an amazing creature. Mother love must be the greatest emotion possible, she thought, particularly when the children were young and vulnerable. But maybe mothers never lost the feeling no matter what age their children were; maybe she would look at Naomi and feel exactly the same when they were seventy and fifty.

They'd gone to bed early in the largest front bedroom, which in spite of Nina's apprehension had scrubbed up rather well. There was nothing she could do about the drab paintwork, but a couple of green and blue blankets from the airing cupboard made brilliant throws for the beds, and the pair of blue glass vases she found in the living room cupboard made a second splash of colour on the chest of drawers. Anyway, Naomi was so spaced out by the thought that they'd inherited this enormous house from a 'sort of cousin' that she didn't notice the drabness of the décor. What they should do with the house, and her wrist, were her sole topics of conversation, even when they'd gone to bed and were whispering together like two schoolgirls.

Today would be different, Nina knew. Naomi was no fool. The question about why they didn't know the exact relationship between them and John Moore wouldn't be long in coming, and the blackmail letter would get a grilling too. Well, the only thing to do was tell the truth, thought Nina. Tell the truth and shame the devil, like Grandma Lily used to say.

She thought about her grandmother's words while she was getting dressed. Both Lily and Claire were always so insistent about never telling lies. It was difficult to see why Claire had lied by omission, never mentioning their rich relative in the south of England. She couldn't have forgotten about him – or had she wanted to forget? And oh God, if John Moore turned out to be her father... that would be such a huge lie... the biggest lie in the world. Nina pushed the thought away.

She lifted the newspaper from behind the front door and stood leafing through it. The death announcement should be in today, yes, here it was. 'Peacefully, at St Michael's Hospice on Wednesday, 12th July... John Robert Moore... Relatives and friends are respectfully requested to contact the family in Bedford about funeral arrangements.'

Unconventional, but it was what they needed in the circumstances. It would be interesting to see what kind of response they had. Mind you, unless people were very quick off the mark with their questions all she'd be able to tell them was that the cremation had already taken place. It was to be that morning, and Nina wasn't going to attend. She would think up some other remembering-family ritual for her and Naomi to do together, something special for Claire, Grandma Lily and Grandpa Bill that didn't quite leave out John Moore. She wasn't going to make this into something more important than it was; it would be insincere to pretend that John Moore had meant something to her. But – oh God, if he was her father...

'What's for breakfast?' Naomi was standing in the doorway, dressed in jeans and a rather grubby pullover.

Nina smiled. Supermum was allowed to use bribery, wasn't she? 'Just toast, but we'll go into town later and have lunch – you can choose a place. The sales are on, we might find you something nice to wear.'

The landline rang while Nina was spooning coffee into the machine, and Naomi ran to answer it.

'Mum! It's that lawyer!' she yelled, and Nina raised her eyes heavenwards. Tact wasn't Naomi's strong point.

Sam was chuckling when she lifted the phone. 'I've been called many things, but 'that lawyer' isn't one of them. Is she okay?'

'She's fine, but she's spitting nails about her missed trek. Is there any news?'

'No. I called to say I'll phone the crematorium this morning and organise about the ashes. Do you want them scattered in the garden of remembrance there?'

'Yes. Thanks.' Nina felt guilty. Should she be doing more with John Moore's ashes? If he did turn out to be her father, and if the accusations made in the anonymous letter were false, she might regret leaving everything to Sam. But then, if John Moore had cared what happened to his ashes he would have left instructions.

'I'll come by late afternoon to let you know what they say.'

Surprised, Nina agreed, and sat nursing another cup of coffee while Naomi finished her third piece of toast then ran upstairs to reorganise her things in John Moore's chest of drawers. Nina mulled over her coffee. It was hard to see why Sam wasn't just planning to phone and tell her what he'd arranged for the ashes. She couldn't shake off the feeling he wanted more contact than she did. Oh yes, she liked him, and she knew that if life had been less messy and distressing she might well have felt differently about his dinner invitations. But a death in the family – or two deaths, as John Moore was family too – plus a grieving daughter, plus a big mess here – it was all too much. She needed Naomi and she needed to find peace before she could think about anything else – and she needed Sam to respect that.

The phone in the study shrilled out again and she jumped up to answer it, limping on her left leg, which had gone to sleep on the hard kitchen chair. Why was everyone calling on the landline today? Oh, her mobile was switched off. She hadn't wanted anything to disturb her and Naomi the night before. Nina switched it back on and lifted the house phone.

'Hello?'

A stranger's voice answered, and Nina's knees began to shake as she listened to the high-pitched, distorted voice. She held on to the desk with her free hand, feeling her breath catch in her throat.

'Nina, Nina. It's you now, you have the money, but it's not your money, is it, Nina? You did nothing to earn it. I did all the earning and all the suffering, and I want payment for that and I'll get it, too. Mind that if you know what's good for you. I'll be in touch.'

The line went dead. Nina dropped the handset and fell to her knees on the study floor, clutching her middle. Shit, shit, she had spoken to the scumbag blackmailer. Her stomach heaved and she clutched it, oh God she was going to be sick. He had known her name...

Still shaking, she forced herself to her feet and stood leaning on the desk, panting. Please let Naomi stay upstairs, please, her daughter mustn't see her like this; she'd be scared witless. But that terrible voice... had it been the blackmailer? Or some other pervert after the money... David, she had to call David Mallony, right now this minute. Fighting to keep control of her gut, Nina scrabbled on the desk for the number of the police station.

David came to the phone himself. 'I'll be with you in fifteen minutes,' he said, and the very neutrality in his voice sent a further shiver down Nina's spine. 'I was coming round this morning anyway. There've been some developments.'

Nina was left holding a dead phone. She stood there, her breath coming in short pants. The developments weren't going to be good news, she had heard that loud and clear. They must have found out something about John Moore, something that was too horrible to tell her over the phone. And hell, Naomi was right here in the middle of it all. Oh, what should she do, what should she do? Loneliness crept into her head as she realised that apart from Sam, there was nobody she could call on for help.

'Mum! What's wrong?'

Naomi was beside her, putting her arms round her, cuddling her. Nina held on tightly, feeling Naomi's heart beating next to her own and breathing in the scent of her child. Blessed calmness crept through her. This, right here, was the single important thing in her life. For Naomi, she could – and would – do anything.

Strengthened, Nina made sure her voice was reassuring. 'It's all right, darling. Remember I told you John Moore had been sent a blackmail letter? Well, the – I think that was the blackmailer on the phone. It gave me a fright but I've called the police and they're coming round. Naomi, darling, I want you to be very good and stay upstairs while they're here.'

She saw refusal in Naomi's face and went on firmly. 'I promise I'll tell you afterwards what's going on, but some of the things DI Mallony might want to talk about aren't for you to hear yet.'

The doorbell rang before Naomi could answer, and Nina kept the girl hugged to her side while she answered it. David Mallony was there with Sabine Jameson.

'This is my daughter Naomi. She's going upstairs while we talk.'

Naomi tugged at Nina's sleeve. 'Can I go right up to the attic room? I could see what's in those old boxes?'

Nina opened her mouth to agree, but David was

85

already speaking.

'Right – um – hello Naomi. Ah, Nina, I should have told you – don't touch the boxes, will you?' he said, looking from Nina to Naomi in a way that made Nina feel giddy. She listened incredulously as he went on.

'We might need to, um, fingerprint them later. In fact it might be an idea if DC Sabine here goes upstairs with you, Naomi.'

Nina gaped at him. Why on earth would the police want to fingerprint the boxes in the attic? They didn't look as if anyone had been near them for decades. The sick feeling returned to her stomach. What was going on?

The young detective followed Naomi upstairs, and David Mallony turned to Nina, his face grim.

'You can guess it's not good news,' he said, as they went into the kitchen and sat down.

'We found large numbers of pornographic images on the hard drive of John Moore's computer, most of them involving young boys. Children. Paedophilia. I'm sorry.'

Nina inhaled sharply and clapped both hands to her mouth. So the horrible suspicion had become even more horrible reality. For long seconds she couldn't speak. She was living in this man's house, using his towels, drinking his coffee. And she'd stood beside him in his coffin and felt pity, shit, she'd admired him for being brave... and all the time he'd been the worst kind of low-life possible.

'Christ. What can I tell Naomi?' she whispered.

David Mallony leaned towards her. 'You'll have to think about that. We don't know yet if he simply kept the images for his own gratification, or whether he was involved in distributing them – or making them.'

Nina's head reeled. This was getting worse and worse. What if -

'Oh God – does that mean the blackmailer was telling the truth?'

But the answer to that must be 'yes'... dear God... Her relation had been the absolute worst kind of pervert, for nothing could be worse than abusing children. And oh, fuck... had it only been other children? Or had she been abused too? Had she 'screamed her poor little head off'?

Her gut spasmed as she stared in horror at David Mallony, seeing the sympathy in his eyes. The only thing that would make her feel a tiny bit better was if John Moore was no relation to her at all. And that seemed so very unlikely now.

'Have you found out his relationship to me?' Her voice came out a mere whisper, and continued silently in her head. Please let him be a ten millionth cousin a billion times removed, please...

His voice was heavy. 'Bad news again, I'm afraid. There's a marriage registered between him and Claire Lily Donaldson. One child, Nina Claire Moore. And there was no divorce.'

Nina thudded her fist on the table. What the shit had Claire been thinking? This would be why she left Bedford with Nina, and she must have had her reasons for keeping the paedophilia a secret, but it had still been wrong. It was all very well holding something like that back from a child, but Nina should have been told as soon as she'd grown up.

David Mallony nodded approvingly. 'That's right. Be angry. Don't get into the victim role. All this is nothing to do with you, and you'll cope best if you think like that. The DNA test will confirm the relationship. In the meantime we're going to have to search this house, and we'll bug your landline in case the blackmailer calls again. And if he does I think you should move out of here.'

'Oh God – I don't know what to do for the best.' Nina rubbed her face with both hands. 'Is there any reason we can't go home straightaway?'

But if they did that, she would only have to return at some point to finish the business with the house. How very much better it would be to get it all organised first and then never darken John Moore's door again.

'It's up to you,' said David.

Nina bit her lip. She might as well get the job finished. It wouldn't take long, a planning session with Sam and then she could sign anything necessary, clear the house and then be off... and they would manage it quicker living here than in a hotel.

'Okay. I'll stay in town another day or two but if anything more happens we'll go to a hotel. That was why you sent the policewoman upstairs with Naomi, wasn't it – in case there are boxes of nasty photos up there.'

'Yes. But don't worry. If there's anything to be found we'll get it out of here,' he said. 'Now, tell me what this caller said, as exactly as you can remember.'

When the two officers left Nina checked the time. Shit, it was twelve already. What a stomach-turning way to spend a morning. She turned to Naomi, who was standing in the hallway, her face one big question mark.

'Right, Miss,' said Nina briskly. 'Information. First of all, the police have found out that John Moore was involved in some sort of – of illegal business. That's why he was being blackmailed. So he was wrong and the blackmailer was wrong too. Secondly, and I don't understand this myself yet, but there's a possibility that John Moore was my father. The test results will tell us that and they should be back in a day or two so let's wait for them before we get carried away about that, okay?' Half-truths maybe, but this way she'd have a bit more badly-needed thinking time.

Naomi's eyes were fixed on Nina's. Nina reached out and hugged the girl quickly. Thank God her daughter was old enough to understand this much, at least. Pretending that everything was all right would have been next to impossible.

'Thirdly, the police are coming to have a look round here, to see if there's any evidence that might help them investigate the illegal business. They're going to tap the landline too, in case the blackmailer calls again, so don't you answer that phone, ever, no matter what. And fourthly you are one mucky pup, skedaddle upstairs and change that disgusting pullover before we go into town.'

Naomi giggled, then caught Nina's arm. 'Mum – it's going to be okay, isn't it?'

Nina hugged her again. 'As Inspector Mallony said, it's really nothing to do with us, so yes, it'll be okay in the end. It's a bit messy at the moment, though, but you don't have to worry about that. Okay?'

Naomi shot off upstairs, and Nina pulled out her mobile. Under the circumstances it might be best if she disturbed Sam's lunch hour to tell him what was going on. He listened without interrupting, and his voice was angry when he spoke.

'What a bastard, threatening you like that. Are you okay?'

'I'm fine now. It was horrible at the time. And apparently John Moore is my father, Sam. I feel sick about that.'

'I know. Some of the queries I put through came back too. You have a couple of cousins as well, but no one that could upset the will so nothing changes there. If you wanted to get in touch with them we could find them for you. Nina, I was wondering if you and Naomi would like to go for a picnic by the river – there's some kind of water event on today. I think Naomi might enjoy it, and it would get you out of the place when the police are searching it. What time are they coming?'

'About four. That sounds perfect; she's a real water-rat. Thanks, Sam.'

His voice was warm in her ear. 'Great. I'll bring the grub.'

Nina put the phone down and stood staring at it. Cousins? So they did have family in England...

CHAPTER TEN

Claire's story – Edinburgh

'Squirrel, squirrel!' cried Nina, running across the grass in Princes Street Gardens, losing both her red Christmas mittens in the process. Claire and Lily laughed.

'She's having a ball here, isn't she?' said Lily, as Claire returned from retrieving Nina's mitts.

Claire could only agree. Her gaze swung from the dark heights of Edinburgh Castle towering above them, to the shoppers up on Princes Street, a colourful mass of well-wrapped-up bargain hunters doing the January sales. And Nina wasn't the only one who was enjoying Edinburgh life. It wasn't until she came home to stay with her parents that Claire realised how much time she'd spent in Bedford walking around on tip-toe, afraid to make her presence felt in case Robert lashed out with another hurtful remark.

Marry in haste, repent at leisure was dead right, she thought, watching Lily point out the people at the top of the Scott Monument to distract Nina from chasing squirrels. It had taken the geographical separation from Robert before she'd allowed herself to think too much about it. Living with Mum and Dad was so restful in comparison. And in the few weeks since their arrival Nina had become chattier, laughing more too, which made Claire angry. Even a baby like Nina was sensitive to the atmosphere in a house, and after what Paul said that awful afternoon in Bedford there was no way of knowing how long Robert had been bullying the children – without her noticing a thing. She hadn't been much of a mother to her child, but she was going to change that now.

'I want to stay in Edinburgh, Mum,' she said quietly, and Lily squeezed her arm.

'Of course you can stay. I'm sorry things haven't worked out for you and Robert, but you tried, and your Dad and I'll help all we can. It's a good thing I'm not working – you can find a job and I'll be there to take care of Nina.'

Claire squeezed back. Her parents had always done the old-fashioned thing. Mum was housewife and Dad was breadwinner. It was the right arrangement for them.

She straightened her shoulders. The 'holiday' was over. She would go to the job centre tomorrow; she couldn't expect her parents to support her and Nina indefinitely. Another problem was that the Morningside semi where she had grown up only had two bedrooms, so as well as a job she would have to find a flat. Life in Edinburgh would be a lot less luxurious than life in Bedford, but then money couldn't buy the important things anyway.

And oh, Lord, she'd have to get things organised with Robert, child support and so on. All he knew was what she'd told him when she called from King's Cross before boarding the train for Edinburgh – that she didn't like his behaviour and wanted a 'trial separation over Christmas'.

Not that she'd had any idea of returning, but it was as well to give him time to get used to the idea. He phoned every few days, trying to persuade her back to Bedford, but all she heard in his voice now was insincerity. He would be missing someone to keep the place clean, of course. How on earth could she have been so taken in by his good looks and charm? Unbelievable, how naive she'd been. But that was over.

She called Robert that night and informed him curtly that she wanted a divorce. It was easy to be brave when your abusive soon-to-be-ex-husband was several hundred miles away, and Claire congratulated herself on her decisive tone.

Robert, however, was equally firm. 'I'm not discussing this on the phone,' he said, and she could hear the anger in his voice. 'I'll come up to Edinburgh at the weekend. But I warn you, Claire, I'm not giving Nina up. She's my daughter too and I want her back here, with or without you.'

Claire gripped the phone, her fingers shaking. She would tell Robert what she thought of him, right now, in case her new-found bravery deserted her when he was standing in front of her.

'Oh yes? You love her so much you bullied her and Paul and frightened them both half to death, not to mention hurting them,' she said, distance allowing the sneer in her voice . 'That's abuse, you know. It's despicable. Paul told me all about what you did that last afternoon, oh, yes. Not much love there, was there? If I went to the police with a story like that they would stop you seeing Nina first thing and you know it.'

There was silence at the end of the phone. His breath had caught when she'd spoken, so she'd taken the wind out of his sails anyway. Apparently he did know that hitting small children was unacceptable.

'We'll talk at the weekend,' he said at last, and hung up before she could reply.

Claire thought carefully about how best to arrange her meeting with Robert. No way was she inviting him to her parents' home; she would take him somewhere in town. It might actually be an idea to ask Lily to come along for moral support – Robert would be more restrained if his mother-in-law was there too. But then, it was hardly fair to drag Lily into her mess of a marriage.

In the end she decided to meet him alone, in a coffee bar on Hanover Street near Waverley Station. That would be better than parading up and down outside with Robert making snide remarks and possibly even threats. She and her friends used to go to 'Saluti a Tutti' on Saturday nights when they were teenagers, and the proprietor, a fatherly Milanese, would chase them out at midnight with a great deal of Scottish-Italian humour. Today, she was glad to see him still manning the espresso machine. If Robert tried anything on, she'd only have to shout and Guido would come running.

It wasn't an easy conversation. Robert arrived at the coffee bar while she was standing chatting to Guido, who melted away tactfully. Claire gathered her courage and frowned at Robert, who greeted her with his most charming smile, called her his 'wee lassie' for the first time since before she'd been pregnant and would have hugged her, too, if she hadn't sidestepped. He ordered her favourite cappuccinos for them both and he was calm, witty, articulate – in fact he turned his considerable powers of persuasion on full strength, and Claire realised anew why she'd fallen for him in the first place. This time, however, she knew it was an act, and when he paused to sip his coffee she told him quite bluntly that her mind was made up.

'We've grown apart, Rob,' she said, determinedly holding his gaze. 'There's no way we can start again, and I don't want to, either. Nina and I are staying here in Edinburgh and that's that. And you know you'd never get custody. If I reported what you'd done, Paul would be well able to tell the police or social services what happened, and so would Nina. She talks away nineteen to the dozen now. And we know why she didn't talk as much in Bedford, don't we?'

How mean she was, blackmailing him like that. If every father who had ever struck his children lost custody, there would be an awful lot of fatherless kids in the country. A sad but true fact, even in these enlightened days. And of course it was equally true for mothers, though she had never lifted a hand to her child. But a lot of people did, and Robert was probably going to tell her all about them right now.

He was staring at her, and she noticed with interest that his face had gone white with a red splodge of colour on both cheeks. She had touched a nerve there. Good.

'All right, Claire,' he said at last, his voice tight. 'If that's the way you want to play it, then so be it.'

He pulled out his chequebook and started to write. 'I'll give you this. It's a one-off, and it's a lot more than you'd get if you reported me and went through the official channels, believe me. In return you can get right out of my life. I don't want to see you or hear from you again, and the same goes for Nina. Got that?'

He slid the cheque across the table and she lifted it. Fifty thousand pounds. Bloody hell, how unbelievable. Fifty thousand pounds. He was selling her his daughter. Did he have that kind of money – and if he did, where the hell had it come from? She swallowed, then managed to speak calmly.

'Very well. I'll tell her you had an accident and died, will I, when she asks? And never fear, Mum and Dad don't know the gory details. I'll put this in the bank on Monday, Rob, and if it bounces I'll go straight to the police.'

It was an empty threat, of course. For what would the police say when she told them that her husband had hit her daughter – not marking her, mind you, for Claire had checked the same evening and there wasn't a hint of a bruise on Nina – and then offered her fifty thousand pounds to get out of his life? She had no proof that Robert had struck the children, just the word of a six-year-old who was upset anyway because his mother was lying downstairs pissed out of her mind.

Claire could see Robert was trying hard to control his temper, and she stood up, smiling into his face. For once she had the upper hand and it was a powerful, intoxicating feeling. A pay-back in a small way for the hurt he had caused her.

'Goodbye, Rob. Forever.' Conscious of Guido grinning

behind the counter, Claire swept outside, leaving her cappuccino half-finished.

It was the kind of exit that belonged in a trashy film, she thought, laughing out loud as soon as she rounded the corner. Well, that was the end of her connection to the Moore family. Emily was the only one she'd really liked, but Robert had never sought much contact to his aunt.

And poor little Paul... It was a pity she couldn't help him, but she had to look out for Nina first. Anyway, when Paul told his mother about Rob's behaviour she would do something about it. Even Jane must rate her child higher than a bottle of gin.

It wasn't until she was in bed that night, Nina asleep in the too-small cot beside her, that Claire began to wonder if she'd done the right thing. They hadn't even discussed the divorce. And what reason did Robert have to pay all that money in exchange for her silence – for that was what he'd done. She still didn't know where on earth his money came from.

A new thought slid into her head. He must be involved in some kind of criminal activity. That was the only explanation; he was doing something illegal, something that would put him in prison if it was found out. And if the police or child welfare people got involved, whatever it was would be discovered. So possibly she was doing wrong too, accepting the money. Had he done something really wicked? Something that would shock her so much that she would go to the police, if she knew what it was? But no. Not charming Robert Moore. It would be embezzlement or fraud or something sordid like that.

Claire lay gazing across the dimness to Nina, whose plump, rosy cheeks looked at least three times as healthy as they had in Bedford, and came to a decision. Nina deserved a good life. Fifty thousand pounds would make the difference between managing comfortably, and scrimping. She would take the money and forget all about Robert Moore. So what if he made his money embezzling other crooks – she knew nothing for sure. If she reported him she would lose the fifty thousand that was going to buy them all a future.

So she would just hold her tongue. It was much the best way for Nina.

CHAPTER ELEVEN

Wednesday 19th - Thursday 20th July

The police arrived as they were leaving to go to the 'Riverside' event in the country park further down the river. David Mallony stood in the hallway as five other officers clumped past and went straight through to the study.

'Nina, here's the warrant to search this house. I'm not sure how long we'll need, but we'll leave everything tidy for you.'

'That's fine,' said Nina, aware that Naomi's eyes were growing rounder by the second at the sight of the police calmly taking possession of the place. 'Naomi and I each have a caseful of clothes in the front bedroom upstairs, and you'll see I've bagged most of John Moore's clothes and bedding. Help yourselves to whatever you need. Shall I give you a key to lock up when you're done?'

She glanced round. Sam had taken Naomi outside to the car.

'You will include the boxes in the attic?' she said. 'I'd hate to come across pornographic photos but I do want to look through them in case there's anything family-related up there. Oh, and the cleaning service told me they removed a load of shredded paper before I arrived. Heaven knows what was there and please, if you do find anything disgusting, take it right away from here. The thought that I'm related to that man is – stomach-turning.'

'Don't worry. We'll check everything,' said David Mallony. He gave her a brief salute and turned into the study.

'What did he say? And why did *he* -' Naomi was hunched in the passenger seat of Sam's car, an aggrieved expression on her face. ' - not let me stay to hear for myself what the police said? I'm not a baby!' She glared at Sam.

Still shaken, Nina got in the back and for a moment had to concentrate on remaining calm. She would never understand how Claire had managed to keep such an awful secret all these years. Nina shuddered. John Moore must have been blackmailing Claire in some way. It was the only explanation; her mother would hardly have chosen to act like that. What a swine the man had been. Claire had probably – no, she had definitely acted against the law in saying nothing. Imagine if she was still alive – she could have ended up facing charges. Child pornography was a bit different to stealing petty cash or cooking the books.

And – dear God in heaven – had any child suffered abuse because Claire hadn't reported John Moore? That was something they would know by the end of the investigation and the answer was going to be 'yes'. And Claire must have known that. Bile rose in Nina's throat and she swallowed, feeling it burn all the way to her stomach. How terrible... Claire's silence had condemned who knows how many kids to vile abuse. And her mother had *lived* with this knowledge...

Naomi turned from the front seat and pouted at her. 'Mum! I wanted to - '

'They're looking for evidence of the illegal business, Naomi.' Nina gave herself a mental shake. She couldn't think about the ramifications of Claire's silence now, with Naomi upset and waiting for an answer. The truth and nothing but the truth, but not quite the whole truth, that was what she needed here. 'And of course anything that would lead them to the blackmailer. We don't know who that could be. And Sam was right to take you to the car. Things like this aren't suitable for children to hear about.'

Naomi scowled at Sam, then turned back to Nina. 'I bet I can understand. What kind of illegal business is it?'

Nina struggled for words. Not the whole truth indeed. 'I don't know exactly, Naomi, and I don't really want to know either. I'm afraid John Moore wasn't a very nice person.'

Naomi was silent, and Nina slumped in her seat. How much did Naomi know about paedophilia? 'Stranger danger' had been a theme in their lives, of course, but Nina had never seriously considered they would come into contact with a paedophile. No one did. But the day when she would have to explain more about John Moore's 'illegal activities' was coming, nothing was more sure than that. She should start getting her ideas together about how best to phrase things so that a ten-year-old would understand without losing her faith in the entire human race. Not an easy task.

The Riverside Water Party, set up by a trio of small lakes in the country park, was lively and crowded, with competitions for children and displays of aquatic sports and other activities. Naomi was fascinated by the water rescue dogs, several of which were enormous Newfoundlanders, and for a long time refused to be tempted away from their stand by the lakeside. Nina and Sam left her to it and settled down under a tree a short distance away where they could keep an eye on her.

'I hope I didn't stand too hard on the poor kid's toes back there,' said Sam, passing Nina a smoked salmon sandwich. 'She was none too chuffed when I insisted on leaving you alone to talk to the police.'

'I'm glad you did,' said Nina fervently. 'I have no idea how best to explain all this to her. Don't worry, Sam, she'll come round. She hasn't got over her Grandma's death yet, and losing part of her trekking holiday isn't helping.'

To her dismay, however, Nina saw that her daughter was still very miffed with poor Sam. Naomi came back for something to eat with a sullen expression on her face.

'Mum, can I go and buy an ice cream? I don't like fish,' she said, turning her nose up at Sam's cool box. 'Or chocolate yoghurt.'

Nina pulled out her purse, refraining from pointing out that both appeared regularly on the table at home and Naomi had yet to voice an objection. If only peace of mind was as easily purchased as ice cream. She would part with any amount of John Moore's fortune if she could buy something to help Naomi through what had turned into the worst summer of both their lives.

She watched unhappily as the girl trailed over to the ice cream van and back, demonstratively giving Sam a wide berth. As soon as she'd handed over the change she was off again back to the dogs.

'Don't worry,' said Sam, as they packed up the picnic. 'I know it's not personal.'

He was right, thought Nina. But she could have done without yet another complication. Sam was the closest thing she had to a friend down here, and now Naomi had taken a scunner to him, as Grandma Lily would have said.

The party continued with music and dancing, and it was after ten when Sam pulled up outside John Moore's house, Naomi half-drowsing in the back. Nina undid her seat belt. Had the police found anything? Heavens, she had butterflies in her tummy about it – they might have come across something that would change the whole situation. Oh, if only…

She turned to Sam. 'Want to come in and see what the police have been up to?'

'You bet,' he said, pulling the key from the ignition.

Naomi bounded up in the back seat. 'The police! Are they still here?'

The police were gone and the house was tidy, though Nina saw signs everywhere that things had been disturbed, moved, rummaged through. The smell of old books in the study was almost choking, and Nina wrinkled her nose. They must have flicked through John Moore's entire collection. It was unnerving, even though this wasn't her home. Her house, but not her home. And what had all those policemen found in her house?

'Mum! They've left some boxes from the attic in the living room!' said Naomi, who was wide awake again, running from room to room.

Nina went to look. There was a note from David Mallony on the uppermost of three cardboard boxes on the coffee table.

'All the 'good' photos are here. We're taking two further boxes to the station for investigation. Those still in the attic contain clothes and china.'

Nina breathed in deeply. It sounded as if the 'further boxes' contained pornography. Thank Christ she hadn't left Naomi to explore the attic by herself the other day.

Sam patted her shoulder. 'I'll make coffee, shall I?' he said. 'You'll want to have a look at these.'

Nina opened the smallest box. It was almost full; there were dozens of small, black and white photos, the kind that would be pre-1960.

'Bo – ring!' said Naomi theatrically.

''Fraid so,' said Nina, glad that the girl wasn't itching to look through the photos. 'I can sort them out, and show you any that are interesting later, okay? Look, it's late. Why don't you scoot off and have a nice bath before you go to bed? You can use my new body lotion.'

To her relief Naomi took the bait and disappeared upstairs. Nina stared round the room, looking for somewhere to lay the photos out to sort through them. The table under the window with its two drop leaves seemed the best bet. She moved the ugly crystal bowl from the table top, and soon created a good-sized surface to work on.

'I don't think those black and white ones'll show anything very interesting,' she said, putting the small box to one side and accepting a mug of coffee from Sam. 'My father would be a child in these. What I'd really like to find are photos of my parents together, maybe some of me as well. And anything else with people, too.'

Sam opened the second box. 'Hm. None of these seem to have a date on them,' he said, stirring the photos with his index finger. 'They're all colour, though, so they'll be more recent. Why don't I sort them into those with and without people, and you can arrange the people ones?'

Twenty minutes work was enough to convince Nina she had a mammoth task on her hands. Surely most families didn't have half as many snaps as this; one of her relations must have been an enthusiastic amateur photographer. She found several photos of John Moore, but none of her mother or herself, though there were several dozen with strangers. Some included the woman and the little boy who were on the photos Sam had found in the desk, but there was no way to tell who anyone was. Not one of the photos had names or dates on them, and there must be dozens still in the box. Who on earth had taken them all?

'This is hopeless,' said Nina at last. 'Or at least it's a long job and I'm tired. Let's call it a day. How about a glass of wine to finish up with? If you open it I'll check on Naomi.'

Naomi was reading in bed, her eyelids drooping, and Nina's heart melted. Poor kiddy, she must be thoroughly upset by everything that had happened, and none of it was her fault. Time for some TLC.

'Night, lovey,' she said softly, sitting down on the edge of the bed. 'And don't worry, things'll get back to normal soon. Have a think about what you want to do tomorrow. You can choose.'

Naomi's lip trembled. 'I wish I could be at home with my Gran.'

Nina hugged her. 'Sweetheart, your Gran will always be a part of you, and of me too,' she whispered. 'We'll always miss her, and you wouldn't want not to, would you? But you know she'd want us both to be happy and live our lives well. So let's do that. For her.'

Naomi smiled sleepily and snuggled into her pillow. Nina tucked the duvet round the little girl and kissed the sun-browned face. What a good feeling it was that she could comfort her child with the sheer force of her words. She should make the most of this phase while it lasted; in a couple of years Naomi wouldn't be hanging so trustingly on everything her mother said. And how wonderful to have a daughter and to know that they loved each other.

Downstairs, Sam had opened a bottle of Merlot. 'Well? Are the troops settled down?'

He handed over a ruby-filled glass, and Nina sipped. With Naomi beside her and Sam to help, she was going to get through this.

'Almost asleep. Thank you, Sam. I had a great time, and Naomi did too, though you might find that more difficult to believe.'

'Don't worry. I can see she's a great girl.'

They sat there talking about children and parents and photos and houses, and Nina was startled when she looked at the clock and saw that it was after midnight. Sam left, squeezing her hand and promising to be in touch the next day. Nina watched him go, feeling the awkward silence of the old house envelope her when the sound of his car had gone. Oh, how tired she was. Creeping into the bedroom, she saw that Naomi was sleeping on her front, one hand under her cheek and the other trailing on the floor. Nina tucked her in again and slid into her own bed. It had been an interesting evening in more ways than one.

Buttered toast in one hand and coffee steaming aromatically by her side, Nina pored over the photos she and Sam had organised last night. Naomi was still asleep, so she could take the chance to do some more sorting. She poked about in the box of colour snaps they'd started on last night. Bloody hell, there were dozens of them. And really, what good would it do, searching through boxes of John Moore's ancient pics? She wasn't even sure what was she looking for. The photos might tell her something about her father's life, but she already knew he'd been the biggest scumbag in creation. He himself had deemed the snaps fascinating enough to keep in the attic, so she was unlikely to find them any more interesting.

Discouraged, Nina opened the third box. More of the same. Oh! There was something else, too, under the photos.

She extracted a folded piece of paper and smoothed it out on the table. Well. Now this was interesting. Names, addresses and phone numbers, about twenty in all.

There were two Moores here, they might be the distant cousins Sam had mentioned. Had the police seen this? Nina reached for her phone.

'Yes, we photographed it yesterday,' said David Mallony. 'We'll be investigating these people, but it was in that box of normal photos so I shouldn't think it's anything more than an old address list.'

'Okay,' said Nina. 'Um – is there any word about the paternity test?'

She knew she was being naïve, hoping it could still come back negative, but you never knew. People won at the lottery every week, didn't they?

She could hear the sympathy in David Mallony's voice.

'You'll be the first to know when it comes. But Nina, don't get your hopes up.'

Nina turned back to the photos. It was difficult not to hope. Nobody wanted a monster for their father.

With no great enthusiasm she lifted a handful of photos and started to divide them into 'with' and 'without' people piles. There were such a lot of landscapes here, country pictures with farm buildings, why on earth would anyone photograph bare fields with the odd stumpy tree, and – shit!

It was her, her and Mum and John Moore, sitting on a bench, in fact it looked like one of the benches on the other side of the road here, by the river. Hell, yes, that was Claire, her hair dark and curly and a strangely subdued little smile on her face. It wasn't an expression Nina could remember seeing before. Claire was holding little Nina, a blonde child with solemn features and a doll clutched in her arms. She couldn't have been more than about two, here.

Hot tears burned in Nina's eyes. She didn't need the test result now. This photo was telling her loud and clear that those old records she hadn't wanted to believe were telling the truth all along; John Moore was her father. She could even remember that doll – Susie, its name was, she'd taken it to Edinburgh and then to Arran, played with it for years.

She scrabbled wildly in the box and soon had a row of family photos in front of her. Her and Mum, her and the boy she'd already seen in a couple of pictures, her and... her father...

Nina stared at the three photos where she and John Moore were pictured. A solemn child, a smiling, strutting man. Did the child in those photos really look afraid and unhappy, or was she projecting that because she knew about the paedophilia? Nausea welled up, almost choking her; she had to breathe through her mouth for a few moments. She still didn't know if he'd been an active paedophile or had 'merely' collected vile pictures. And – if he had abused other children, he could have abused her too. It was the blackest thought of all. There was no evidence of it and she had no memories, but... she'd been crying on the top floor... On the other hand, according to David, the images on John Moore's computer were of young boys, and paedophiles were attracted to either girls or boys but not both – weren't they? She didn't know enough about it, that was the problem. But it wasn't impossible that she'd been abused. Dear God, it wasn't impossible.

Forcing herself to remain calm, Nina went to fetch

more coffee. It's better to find out the truth, she told herself. If she knew the worst then she could deal with it and get on with her life. But how could she possibly find out what had happened all those years ago? The hazy memory of her crying in the attic room wasn't enough.

She went back and stood in front of the 'family' photos. If she hadn't known about the paedophilia the thought wouldn't have entered her head. There were a couple of wedding snaps she hadn't seen before, Claire and John Moore, and oh, Grandma Lily and Grandpa Bill. A lump grew in Nina's throat as she saw how slim Claire was in those days before motherhood, and how happy she looked, like a little girl playing at weddings – and... what was making her uneasy about these photos? Other people were there too, a young woman with a toddler and another man, as well as several older people in various combinations. Two of them might be her other grandparents. Nina stared at the photos, then shrugged and laid them down. Hopefully she could get in touch with those distant cousins Sam had turned up; they might be able to help. Or would they turn out to be as horrible as John Moore?

Her phone rang and she grabbed it. Sam's voice brought normality back into what had already become a bad day. She told him about the photos and the list of names.

'Well, I certainly think it's worth trying to find them,' he said. 'The ones called Moore must be relatives. And Nina, remember – your mother was looking out for you.'

Nina blinked unhappily. It was true, but the fact remained that Claire's silence had allowed John Moore to abuse heaven knows how many kids after the two of them left. It was very, very difficult to get her head round that, and it didn't sound like Claire, either. Something monumental must have happened to make her behave like that. Nina put the thought to the side for the moment and arranged with Sam to have lunch together the following day.

Ending the call, she switched her phone right off. She would waken Naomi and take her down to London for the day. They would do some sights, go shopping, maybe go to a show if anything was available. Life had been depressing for long enough; a day out with her daughter was exactly what they both needed.

And what a pity it was that the whole bloody mess would still be here when they got back.

CHAPTER TWELVE

Friday 21st July

Nina took one look at the cheap envelope lying face down on the mat and ran to the kitchen for a knife. Shit, oh shit, this was going to be another horrible letter. Crouching behind the front door and praying Naomi wouldn't choose today to get up early, she flipped the envelope over.

Oh. Her own name and this address were clearly handwritten, and unlike Monday's letter, this one had come by post. Maybe it wasn't anonymous. She wiped away the sweat that had broken out on her brow.

Still squatting by the door mat, she considered whether or not to open the letter. There was no one she could think of who would be writing to her here. It wasn't Beth's or Tim's handwriting, and apart from Alan in South Africa, no one else who might conceivably write to her knew she was here. Nina rose to her feet and trotted into the kitchen for her phone. A quick call to the police might be best.

Sabine Jameson was dubious. 'Hm. It doesn't sound like an anonymous letter. Hold the envelope by one corner, and open it with a knife. Then use the knife to open out the letter,' she said. 'Call me back when you've read it.'

Nina sat down at the photos table to open the letter, keeping an ear open for Naomi. No way did she want her child any more involved in anonymous letters and paedophilia than she was already. Fortunately, Naomi was sleeping the sleep of the exhausted tourist. They'd had a great day out yesterday, with lunch in a crêperie, a visit to Greenwich and then a boat trip back to the centre. To round off the day they went to an outdoor 'oldies' cinema and watched 'E.T.' for the zillionth time, with the added attraction that they were out there under real stars themselves.

As always, the end of the film brought tears to Nina's eyes. A lost little creature going home. It brought back to her how very much she wanted to be back home, even though without Claire, home was a different place. They would have to deal with the change in the old farmhouse, remember the past with love and move on with joy, as Claire would have wished. A lot of reorganising lay ahead on the Isle of Arran, and John Moore's hard cash would undoubtedly make things easier.

Nina blinked unhappily. 'We'll go back early next week.' She spoke aloud, using the paper knife from the desk to assist the kitchen knife. Sam would be able to carry on here without her physical presence.

It wasn't easy to get the single sheet of paper from the envelope without touching it, but at last she managed to ease it out. The same handwriting was on the letter, and Nina spread the sheet with the knives, her heart sinking as she read.

113

Dear Nina Moore,

Please forgive me for writing to you like this, but I know you recently inherited a large fortune. Please consider that there are people less fortunate than you. My husband was in an accident in May, and he no longer earns a living wage. £500 would mean nothing to you and everything to us. After all, it's not your money, is it, you did nothing to earn it. Please, Nina, be generous and help a family in need.

Yours sincerely...

The signature was illegible, though the address wasn't, Nina noticed wryly. Did this person imagine she was going to stick £500 in an envelope and send it off just like that? No way. And who the hell could it be from? No one knew about John Moore dying and leaving her a fortune... but no... that wasn't quite true. The staff at the hospice and the crematorium would know he was rich, and anyone could have seen the death announcement in the paper. It might even be from someone who'd visited the hospice, or delivered something... Nina sniffed, then looked at the letter again.

In a way it was true, what the letter writer said. She could easily spare £500 now. But there would be more begging letters; she couldn't give money to everyone who asked for it and she didn't want to, either. Nina folded the letter, thinking.

Maybe she should make one big donation, to a children's charity, for instance. That way she would be doing good and also showing Naomi that helping people was the natural thing to do. They could choose a charity together – Naomi would enjoy doing some research on the internet. Or they could look into one of those sponsorship arrangements, maybe support a child in India. Yes, good idea. But now she'd better phone Sabine Jameson and tell her it was just a begging letter. The first, but probably not the last.

She was making the connection when her fingers slowed and a frown came over her face. There was something vaguely familiar about the language on that letter...

'After all, it's not your money, is it, you did nothing to earn it.'

Wasn't that very similar to what the anonymous caller said on the phone?

Sabine Jameson listened to her fears. 'I'll tell the boss when he gets in, but there isn't much to go on there. We'll have a look at it later. Oh – Nina – your test result's back. Ready for it?'

Nina gripped her phone. 'Positive, isn't it?'

'I'm sorry. I know you were hoping for a negative result.'

Nina broke the connection and stood fighting disappointment. The last vestige of hope was gone; John Moore was her father. Well, there was nothing she could do about that. She wasn't responsible for his crimes. What she needed to do now was find out enough about the past to give herself peace of mind, and the best way

115

to do that was to sort through these wretched photos.

'Mum! I've had cornflakes, can I email Jay?'

Nina jumped, then went to hug Naomi. 'Heavens, you got up quietly! Yes, of course. You can have an hour online, shoot bubbles or something after your email, and by that time I'll be finished with the photos and we'll think of something fun to do when Sam arrives.'

Naomi raced upstairs to clean her teeth, and Nina went back to work. By half past eleven she had another row of 'people' on the table. As well as the family with the little boy she found four photos of the same little boy with some older people. On two of them he was sitting on a middle-aged women's knee, looking much happier than on the other photos. The woman was smiling too; maybe she was his grandmother. Which could well make her Nina's grandmother too, or an aunt. Was this woman one of the people on the list? Abandoning the photos, Nina pulled out the address list and scanned it again. She should see if she could find any current phone numbers for these Moores.

'Anything interesting?'

Nina jumped for the second time that morning. Sam had come into the room without her hearing. This must be her day for being crept up on; she should watch her back. She grinned at Sam. 'Hello! How did you get in?'

'I arrived at the front door as Naomi was coming downstairs and she saw me through the glass,' he said, joining her at the table. 'And guess what, she's speaking to me today. She said, 'Mum's miles deep in those boring old photos again' and went into the study. What have you found?'

Nina showed him the letter and pointed out the similarity to the threatening phone call. He grimaced, tapping his fingers on the table.

'Oh Nina, I don't like it. Even if this is a coincidence, it means that every begging letter you'll be wondering about a possible connection.'

'I know. I want to get away from here asap, Sam. All this hassle isn't worth it; I need to get on with my life. And the paternity test result was positive, by the way.'

He grimaced again. 'I'm sorry. I have all the paperwork ready for you to sign so there's nothing to stop you going home. We can continue with the business stuff by e-mail and phone. And unfortunately I'm away myself for a few days at the beginning of the week; I have to see a client in Devon. It was arranged three weeks ago and I can't get out of it.'

Nina stood straighter. 'That settles it. We'll leave on Monday.'

Happier now that the decision had been made, she showed Sam the 'people' photos.

'Wow. You're incredibly like your mother, aren't you?' he said, picking up a photo showing a young-looking Claire with her new husband.

Nina went to look over his shoulder. A very young-looking Claire... The thought that had hovered over her brain the other day came sharply and horribly into focus.

'Shit,' she said. 'Mum looks about thirteen here. Do you think – oh Christ.'

The thought was appalling. A paedophile would enjoy having a wife who looked so much younger than she was. Dear God no.

Sam put the photos down. 'Nina, don't go there,' he said in a low voice. 'They're both dead, it's over. We only have to sort out what's relevant to you.'

He opened his briefcase and pulled out a magnifying glass.

'I borrowed this from our secretary. A vital piece of secretarial equipment when you have to work with old documents. She has two so you can hang on to it for a few days.'

He was right, Nina knew. John Moore's actions were nothing to do with her. She pored over the photos with the glass, but although it made the facial expressions clearer, it didn't help identify the people. Definitely, it was time to leave the winding up of her father's estate to the lawyers, and go home and enjoy the rest of the summer on beautiful Arran.

'Nina, look.' Sam had lifted the list of names. He pointed to one about halfway down. 'Emily Moore. And the address is in Biddenham, that's a village a couple of miles outside Bedford. Maybe she still lives there.'

Nina stared at the list. Emily Moore, 15 Long Meadow Lane, Biddenham.

'Wow. I hadn't realised that. Let's try the phone number.'

The number was unobtainable, though, and Emily Moore didn't figure in the phone book either.

'We could drive by and have a look,' suggested Nina. 'Even if Emily's not there anymore, one of the neighbours might know something.'

Sam pulled out his car key. 'Good idea. Let's go.'

'This is boring. You said we would do something fun,' said Naomi, as Sam drove along the main road towards Biddenham.

Nina thought swiftly. Compared to the day before, an outing to find someone they didn't know must be boring to a ten-year-old, but she wasn't prepared to let Naomi stay all alone in John Moore's house when there were unknown weirdos at large writing revolting letters and making funny phone calls. Nina twisted round in her seat and made a face at her daughter.

'I know, sweetie, but look at it this way. You can count your blood relations on the fingers of one hand. I can count my blood relations with my left thumb. Emily Moore might be another one. It would be sort of worth it if we could find her, wouldn't it?'

Naomi sniffed. 'You said John Moore wasn't a very nice person so Emily might not be either. You could find her yourself and if she was nice I could go and see her too. All this driving about looking for her is so incredibly mega-dull.'

'I know,' said Nina helplessly. 'I'll make it up to you, I promise.'

'That doesn't help now.' Naomi turned away theatrically and retreated into her ipod, staring out of the side window.

Nina glanced at Sam and hid a smile at the apprehensive expression on his face. He obviously wasn't used to sharing car-space with sparring mothers and daughters. Not that she often sparred with Naomi... Mind you, puberty wasn't a million miles away and they would know all about theatricals then. Sam raised his eyebrows at her when they stopped at traffic lights and she winked the eye Naomi couldn't see.

Long Meadow Lane was a quiet, leafy little place, with tall trees and bushes bordering the lane on both sides. Nina sat looking from right to left as they crept along in search of number fifteen. The houses were large and almost hidden behind the greenery; it seemed rather an affluent little area. Nina sighed. Her own branch of the Moore family lived in less well-to-do accommodation. Claire left the riches behind when she left John Moore all those years ago...

If only they knew what had gone on in her mother's mind back then. What a heavy burden Claire had carried all those years, if she'd known about the paedophilia. *Had* she known? Why hadn't Claire divorced John Moore and agitated for child support, alimony, whatever, instead of lying about his death? That lie meant John Moore had never supported his own family. It didn't seem right.

Nina shivered. It was so true, there were things that no amount of money could buy. As soon as this thought came into her head she realised something else. Claire had made so very sure the break was absolute, never demanding the support that was hers by right – so the odds were she *had* known about the paedophilia. Bloody hell. What a terrible hold John Moore must have had over Claire to buy her silence all those years. Not knowing what had gone on between the pair of them was turning into the worst aspect about the entire business, and it was hard to see how they'd ever find out. So as well as finding a father she didn't want, she'd lost the mother she thought she'd known...

Number fifteen was near the top of the lane, and Sam pulled up at the gateway. A long, rhododendron-lined driveway led down to the house, a low bungalow with an obvious garage conversion at the side. It was freshly painted in crisp white and had a swing set on the front lawn.

Leaving Sam and Naomi in the car, Nina went to ring the bell. The front room window had no net curtain, and she looked in on a large collection of cacti and an orange cat sleeping in the middle of them. No one was home, however, and she turned back to the lane.

'I'll try the neighbours,' she said, leaning in the passenger seat window.

Naomi gave another theatrical sigh, and Nina handed over her mobile. 'Naomi. We'll have a look round here first and then go for lunch. Why don't you use the time to find us a nice restaurant or pub in the village?'

Naomi brightened considerably and sat up straight to do her research.

A young woman answered the door at the next house, a toddler on her hip and about three-year-old twins crowding round her feet to see what was going on. She shook her head when Nina asked about Emily Moore.

'Sorry, can't help. I'm the nanny here. There's a young family at number fifteen, I do know that much. You should ask old Mrs Peters at number twenty. She's a terrible gossip; if anyone around here knows, she will.'

Nina laughed and thanked her. Number twenty was diagonally opposite, and she waved to Sam and Naomi as she crossed the lane. Fortunately Mrs Peters was at home, though mid-sixties would have been a better label than 'old'. The 'terrible gossip' part of the nanny's description fitted well enough, though.

'Emily Moore? Yes, that was quite a while ago mind you; she was here for years and I don't think she was ever married, either, lived alone, she did, she was a nice lady but rather withdrawn if you know what I mean, not the sort to pop round for a cup of coffee and a chat, though she did come to the Woman's Institute when they built the community hall. Are you a relative?'

'I think I might be. I'm researching my family at the moment and I found her name. Do you know where she is now?'

'I don't even know if she's still alive. She went to live in an old people's place near Luton, oh, about ten years ago now. If she is alive she'll be about eighty, but she was always very fit, I must say. She went into the home, or maybe it was sheltered housing, you know, the kind of place where you can be quite independent but there's someone to call if you ever need help, anyway she went there because she broke her hip and though it healed all right it was never as strong as it had been, and she had become very short-sighted too and she thought it was risky living alone as she did, which is quite sensible, though it must have been a blow to leave her house after all that time.'

'Yes. Thank you very much, that's very helpful,' said Nina breathlessly. She made her escape and jogged back to the car, wondering if there was a Mr Peters or if Mrs Peters was so loquacious because there was nobody to talk to most of the time.

'Right. So Emily Moore must be a generation older

than John Moore,' said Sam when Nina reported back. 'And if she wasn't married then she's a genuine Moore and not a connection by marriage. That's important too.'

'I'm starving,' said Naomi. 'I found a pub with a garden restaurant up at the top of the lane. There's a children's menu but I'd like scampi if they have it.'

They had lunch in the garden of Naomi's pub, then Nina and Sam sat with the laptop trying to find out about accommodation for the elderly near Luton while Naomi sat picking at the rubber band bracelet she was wearing, the bored expression back on her face.

'Do you think if we start phoning round they would even tell us if she was a patient or resident or whatever?' said Nina, staring at the depressingly long list of care homes they'd compiled. 'They might have confidentiality rules or something.'

'Very possibly. I think you should engage me as your lawyer. You are trying to trace family after learning that your father was alive till recently – perfectly true – and I'm helping you. People often give more info to a lawyer than they would to any old Joe Plumber.'

'Okay. At least John Moore's estate can afford to pay your bill,' said Nina, and he pulled out his mobile.

Naomi sat with her chin propped on both hands while Sam called the first home.

'Can't we go back to the house now? At least I can watch telly there,' she said in a low voice, her lower lip trembling.

Nina nodded. 'I'm sorry, Naomi. You're being very

good. Extra Brownie points, you can think what you want to spend them on.'

'Yay!' Naomi beamed. 'Brownie points' was an old family tradition, awarded for particularly good behaviour and used for more expensive treats.

They adjourned to the house in Bedford, where Naomi commandeered the living room with the TV. Nina and Sam went on with their search in the study, Nina accessing contact details while Sam made the calls. All the homes were cooperative enough to reply that no, there had never been an Emily Moore from Biddenham in their facility.

After the eighth negative call Nina went to make coffee. She was organising mugs on a tray when Sam strode in.

'Nina, I've found her! At The Elms, on the outskirts of Shefford. Emily Mary Moore, she's seventy-nine, been there for ten years, from Biddenham. I told them you'd be in touch about going to visit her. They said she's a nice old lady, quite fit and very bright.'

Nina inhaled sharply, clasping both hands under her chin. She'd found a relative who was a 'nice old lady'. Tears came into her eyes.

'That's – amazing,' she said slowly. 'Thanks, Sam. I'll see if I can visit her this weekend. But – a seventy-nine year old lady – can I really start a conversation about John Moore's paedophilic tendencies and his death and by the way my mother was killed by a manic motorcyclist last month?'

He sipped his coffee. 'Maybe in the first place you should simply introduce yourself as John Moore's lost

124

daughter. I imagine she'll know who you are and you can take things from there. She could turn out to be a very distant cousin who doesn't know much about your father.'

'You're right. But she might know if the other names on the list are relations too. And I could show her the photos. Sam – she might be my great-aunt. Oh, I hope she'll agree to a visit.'

Tears were still pricking in her eyes, and Nina tossed her head impatiently. Getting emotional about it wouldn't help anyone. But oh, she hadn't known how good it would feel to find someone who was actually related to her.

And what would Naomi think about a visit to Emily Moore, she wondered, putting the phone down later after arranging with one of the staff to be at The Elms at half past two the following afternoon. Emily was out on a trip with some of the other residents that afternoon but had left instructions when she heard about Sam's call, so wow – they were going to meet a relative tomorrow.

Naomi's face fell a mile and a half at the mention of an afternoon in a sheltered housing complex, and Nina was racking her brains to think of something that would make the idea attractive to a ten-year-old when Sam beat her to it.

'Tell you what, Naomi – and Nina. We'll go and have lunch with my parents in Allerton tomorrow. Then Naomi can stay there while we visit Emily. Mum and Dad always have a crowd of grand-kids round at the weekend, Naomi, and one of them's about the same age as you. I know my dad's hoping that Amy'll help him paint the garden fence and I'm sure he'd be very pleased to have another pair of hands too.'

'O – kay,' said Naomi, and to Nina's surprise she smiled at Sam.

'Won't your parents mind?' said Nina, when Naomi had gone back to the television.

'My mum's Italian. It's family, bambinos all the way. And like I said, my sisters usually deposit their kids at Mum's on Saturdays and go into town. I'll phone her from the office – which reminds me I should get back there and do some proper work.'

Nina waved as he drove off. Sam was turning into a bit of a rock here and she wasn't sure what she thought about it. Part of her wanted to banish her connection to Bedford and John Moore to the dim and distant past, but with Emily Moore nearby that was unlikely to happen now. And there were other cousins, too... And now nice-guy Sam was becoming someone she might – might – want in her life. In some capacity. Nina sighed, and went to join Naomi shooting bubbles on the internet. Her mind wasn't going to be clear about this till she'd won some certainty about what had happened, and some distance, too.

Chapter Thirteen

Claire's story – The Isle of Arran

Claire stood at the farmhouse door looking across the Firth of Clyde. The mainland was invisible today; it looked as if the sea went on and on, almost forever until it merged into the cloudy sky. For the first time since they'd moved here, the view failed to inspire a sense of achievement. The family dream of opening a B&B on the Isle of Arran where Lily had grown up was a dream no longer. Robert's criminal cash had made the venture possible, but how little that meant today.

Her father was dead. It was the worst thing that had ever happened to Claire, much worse than the breakdown of her marriage or the suspicion that Robert might have been violent towards their child. That was all well in the past; Nina was at school now and was thriving. This would never go away.

Claire stared up at white clouds chasing briskly across the sky. It was almost beyond comprehension. Her father had been one of those tall, wiry people who could eat anything and never put on an ounce, he was fit – he played tennis and went hill-walking almost every weekend; he was a happy, easy-going kind of person, not even a whiff of a problem with his blood pressure – yet now he was gone. An infection, they said after the post-mortem, and it had attacked his heart.

Claire knew she had to hold things together for Nina. At six, her daughter was well able to understand what was going on and of course she was grieving too; she'd loved her Grandpa. And Claire knew helping Nina was the best way to help herself. Having little rituals – lighting Grandpa's candle when it got dark, looking at a star for Grandpa, taking care of Grandpa's garden – it all helped create a sense of continuity.

The awkward part was that losing her grandfather so unexpectedly prompted Nina to ask a whole lot of questions about her supposedly dead father, and Claire was hard put to find answers. How she wished she'd never started this; she should have told Nina from the beginning that Daddy had been bad to them and that was why they never saw him now. It was dreadful, lying to her child like this. Worse still, Nina soon noticed that her mother didn't enjoy these 'Daddy' conversations and stopped asking about him, which only increased Claire's guilt. Fortunately Lily, who had never approved of the lie and was now the only other person in Scotland who knew that Robert was alive, refused to speak about him to Nina, saying 'I don't remember, ask your mum,' when Nina tried to talk about the Bedford years.

Claire turned back into the kitchen, crossing the room to touch the photo stuck on the fridge with a magnet. Mum, Dad and Nina on the top of Goatfell, the highest peak on the island; she'd taken it the day Nina walked up for the first time. Pride was shining from her father's face as he stood there with 'his girls'. Claire turned away before Nina noticed what she was doing. Fathers were an awkward subject. Of course Robert himself had wanted the break to be complete, which said everything about the kind of father he was, but still... Nina had never had the opportunity to love her

father. It wasn't fair. Look at Bethany down the road, with a Dad and two Grandpas and several strapping uncles all living close by on the island. Claire rubbed her eyes.

'Mummy? Are you okay?'

Nina was standing behind her, a sweet, concerned expression on her face. A lump rose in Claire's throat and she kissed the wrinkled little brow. 'I'm fine, lovey. I was remembering your Grandpa. It's good to remember, you know, even if it makes you sad. Come on, let's make some scones for teatime.'

Nina allowed herself to be distracted, but Claire's thoughts were in turmoil as she measured out flour and butter. Remembering Robert and his wealth brought home their own financial situation. Her parents' Edinburgh semi hadn't sold well; it was in need of what the estate agent had called 'some modernisation', and the market was sluggish. They'd wanted a good ten thousand more than they eventually accepted. Claire didn't want to put all Robert's cash into the farmhouse in case she needed it later for Nina, so the renovation was on hold in the meantime, which meant the B&B venture wasn't bringing in as much cash as it could.

But it was Robert more than the money that was the real worry. Claire hated the stupid, false situation she was in. Nina thought her father was dead, and that was just –

wrong, and now the child was old enough to understand more it might be time to put things right. It had been three years now, Robert could have changed. Maybe she should find out what he was doing these days. It was something to consider, anyway.

Claire put the tray of scones into the oven and was setting the timer when a new, terrible thought struck her so hard she actually staggered. Dear Lord – what if she died as suddenly as her father? What would happen to Nina then? Lily with her arthritis would be pushed to cope with a six-year-old... It wouldn't take much investigation for anyone concerned to find out that Nina's father was alive and well – the poor child could end up living in that awful old house with the father she believed was dead.

The thought almost took Claire's breath away. Definitely, they would have to change things. If Nina got to know Robert a little, she would be prepared if anything did happen to her mother.

'You're being daft, lass. You're not going to die anytime soon.' Claire could almost hear her father's voice, and oh, how she wanted to believe that, how very much she wanted to think she'd be there for her girl until Nina was a grown woman and could take care of herself. Fear swirled round Claire's head; she could land under a car next time she went down the Bay for the shopping. No one knew what the future held.

That evening Claire wrote a letter to Robert, asking if he would consider seeing Nina if they went down to London for a weekend.

In the morning she tore it up.

Chapter Fourteen

Saturday 22nd July

Nina could have guessed Sam's mother was Italian even if she hadn't been told. Cascata Harrison was small and plump with dark hair piled on top of her head, and shiny brown eyes that lit up when she saw Naomi. Surrounded by grandchildren, she looked like a typical Italian Mamma and Nonna, and she obviously revelled in her role. For a moment Nina felt as if she'd landed in one of those Hollywood perfect-happy-family rainy-Sunday-afternoon kind of films. No sooner had she thought this than the youngest child, a toddler of about eighteen months, brought reality right back to centre stage by being sick on the kitchen floor.

'Welcome to the madhouse,' Sam said to Nina as a younger woman rushed to help the child.

Sam's mother rolled her eyes, shut the door on the clean-up operation and squeezed both Nina's hands before turning to Naomi.

'So this is Naomi. What gorgeous hair. You'll break a few hearts before you're too much older,' she said in faultless English, kissing Naomi on both cheeks.

'You don't sound Italian,' said Naomi, and Glen

Harrison clapped the little girl's shoulder.

'Well spotted. She hasn't actually lived there since she was five,' he said.

'But I go back every year for a holiday,' said his wife, taking Nina's jacket. 'Call me Cassie, Nina, everyone does. Sam told us you have a lot of business – we can take care of Naomi as much as you need us to. All you have to do is ask.'

It was impossible not to like Sam's parents, thought Nina, watching them fuss over their son and joke with each other. This was what she'd never been part of, a big normal family having fun with each other. And yet they weren't quite a normal family, with dark-skinned Sam and his white adoptive parents. But the love was there; she could see it shining out of Sam's face when he spoke to his mother. And the pride in Glen Harrison's eyes when he listened to Sam talking about last week's court case was unmistakable. You didn't need to share blood to be a family.

Sam's two sisters, their husbands, and five children ranging in age from one to nine were all in the garden, running around, helping to lay the table and arguing good-naturedly.

Cassie took Nina's arm. 'Come and help me with the salads. We'll leave Sam to sort out the drinks with his Dad.'

Nina looked outside where Naomi was playing with Sam's oldest niece, throwing balls for Cassie's dog, a Westie named Kira. A dog had been top of Naomi's wish-list for ages, and Nina smiled ruefully as she followed Cassie into the kitchen. 'Let's get a dog' would be topic of the week now.

'Sam said you're having problems getting your father's estate settled. I'm sorry for your loss,' said Cassie, removing plastic containers from the fridge and transferring their contents into a series of bowls.

Nina leaned on the worktop, sighing inwardly. Cassie's motherly presence and her words brought back exactly what she'd lost, and it wasn't John Moore. Sam had been discreet, so Cassie presumably didn't know about Claire's death. Nina straightened up and gave Cassie a smile. Sympathetic as Sam's mum was, this just wasn't the time. The realisation that she had no one in Bedford to confide in struck anew.

'I didn't know him. My mother left him when I was very small and we had no contact after that, so the loss feels a bit unreal, somehow.'

Cassie patted her shoulder. 'I didn't know. Sam didn't go into details. Then I'm doubly glad you've found another relative to visit – family's important. And you mustn't worry about Naomi, she'll be fine here.'

Lunch was an exuberant, noisy meal in the garden, with the children sitting round a smaller table beside the big one. Nina was grateful that none of the adults made any attempt to question her about her family; they had evidently been forewarned and it did make things easier. Sam's sisters and their husbands were good company; their good-natured banter was the kind of exchange Nina often had with Beth and Tim. A fresh wave of homesickness swept through her. It would be so great to be back on Arran next week, working in the farmhouse, digesting whatever Emily Moore would tell her about the family, and planning what she would do with John Moore's fortune.

At two o'clock Sam stood up. 'We'd better get going, Nina. Emily might be a stickler for punctuality and we don't want to make a bad first impression, do we?'

Nina reached for her handbag. 'We do not. Naomi, I'll see you later. Have fun and be good.'

It was her standard 'goodbye' phrase, and Naomi barely glanced up long enough to wave as Nina and Sam left the house.

Nina was silent on the way to The Elms, thinking about the questions she wanted to ask Emily Moore. The relationship between John and Emily. John's parents. If there was any other family nearby. And hopefully Emily would recognize some of the people on the photos she'd brought.

And of course the more awkward topics. Did Emily know about the paedophilia? But of course she didn't – hell, she didn't even know if Emily Moore was aware that John was dead.

The Elms was an attractive grey stone building, three storeys high with a well-kept garden where groups of people were sitting under tall, shady trees. Behind the main building was a little row of ten cottages, each split into two apartments, and Emily lived in one of these. It was everyone's vision of the perfect old people's home – residents out in the garden, their children and grandchildren around them on a Saturday afternoon. Happy families yet again. Nina bit her lip. And here they were, coming to visit with death and paedophilia in their pockets. I hope we don't frighten poor Emily into the middle of next week, thought Nina, as Sam pulled up in the last of the 'visitor' parking spaces.

Emily Moore's cottage was number 3a, and Nina wiped damp palms on her trousers as she walked along the pathway. The door opened before they reached it. Emily was small and grey-haired, and the eyes smiling up at Nina and Sam were dark blue and intelligent behind thick brown-rimmed glasses.

'Hello, dear. So you're the Nina Moore who thinks we're related – and I think you're right, too. Come in and sit down, the pair of you,' she said, indicating a two-seater sofa and a reclining chair grouped round a little coffee table.

Nina presented Emily with the pot plant she'd bought on the way over, feeling quite weak with relief. This *was* a 'nice old lady', and one who was clearly very sharp too.

'What a great place,' she said, looking round appreciatively.

They were in a fair-sized living room looking out towards the back of the sheltered housing complex, where a grassy area ended in a belt of trees. Nina could see into a little kitchen to her right, and the other door must lead to the bedroom. It all looked quite luxurious; Emily was apparently another rather affluent Moore.

'Yes, it's lovely. The staff are very kind – it's perfect for me,' said Emily, placing the miniature rose bush on the coffee table. 'Thank you, dear. I love roses. Now, tell me how you came across my name. The warden said you were researching your family tree?'

Nina made the introductions and told Emily about finding out that John Moore was dead, and then

135

discovering that he was her father. Making no mention of the paedophilia or the threats, she went on to talk about the house and the boxes of photos in the attic. Emily listened without interrupting.

When Nina had finished she spoke in a low voice. 'John Moore was my brother's boy. I last saw him at his father's funeral, years ago now, and after that he didn't get in touch again and nor did I, I'm afraid. We didn't get on – I was maybe too much of a sharp-tongued old spinster for him. So you're the Nina I used to know. I saw you quite often when you were a toddler, you were a pretty little thing. And then your mother went off with you.' She cocked her head to one side, frowning. 'But why did she tell you your father was dead?'

Nina met Sam's eyes. It was clear the older woman knew nothing about the paedophilia.

'I think she felt my father was – violent – in some way,' she said gently. 'Did you ever notice anything?'

Emily looked shocked and Nina was glad she hadn't said more.

'Oh dear – I don't think so,' said Emily. 'But that kind of thing usually goes on behind closed doors, doesn't it?'

'Yes,' said Nina. 'And as far as I knew there was no other family left to ask about things. I was so happy to find you. Could you maybe tell me a little about the Moore family?'

'Of course. And you'll take a cup of coffee, won't you?'

Emily went through to the kitchen and reappeared with a coffee tray. Sam jumped up to help her, and Emily sat back as he poured coffee from a thermos jug into blue and white mugs. Tears welled up in Nina's eyes as she looked at Emily, who was staring wistfully at the miniature rose bush. This poor old lady, a part of her own family, alone now and nearing the end of her life, remembering days gone by. All the living and loving and people now gone.

'There were three of us,' said Emily, putting her mug on the low table beside her chair. 'My brother John was the oldest, then Ruth, and then me. Our parents ran a chemist's shop. They were always very busy, stressed out you would say nowadays. John and Ruthie both married, but I never did. I was engaged as a girl but my fiancé Dan died of a ruptured appendix. No one could ever replace him, you see.'

Nina leaned across and squeezed Emily's hand. 'So you're my Great-Aunt Emily,' she said, yet more tears pricking in her eyes. 'I'm so glad I've found you. The only other blood relation I knew of is my daughter Naomi. How many children did John and Ruth have?'

Sam's phone vibrated in his pocket, and he took it outside.

Emily passed the biscuits to Nina. 'One each,' she said. 'But look. When they told me you were coming, I drew a family tree. I didn't put dates in, they're difficult to remember off-hand.'

She produced a sheet of notepaper where a family tree diagram was set out in a surprisingly clear hand. Nina bent over it.

Moore Family Tree

David John Moore m. Ruth Emily Clarke

| John Moore | Ruth Moore | Emily Moore |
| m. Sylvia Peterson | m. Peter Wright | (unmarried) |

| John Robert Moore | George Wright |
| m. Claire?? | m. Jane?? |

| Nina Moore | Paul Wright |

'Brilliant!' she said. 'This makes the different relationships quite clear. And I suppose my father was always called Robert because his father was John too. And the Wrights... so Paul Wright is the same generation as me?'

'Yes,' said Emily. 'He's about three years older than you, and you used to think he was wonderful. I didn't see him very often after you and your mother left. He was a shy, quiet boy – I think his mother had a drink problem, and that must have affected him. He had a hard time at school. His parents split up a few years after yours did, but I never knew all the ins and outs.'

Nina's mind had snapped back to the list she'd found in the house. There were two Wrights there, Paul and another – Paul's mother, or his father? For the life of her she couldn't remember if the second name was a man or a woman. George Wright was the 'Moore' in that family, anyway. She would show the list to Emily in a minute. She checked to make sure it was in her bag, realising guiltily that she hadn't been paying attention to what the old woman was saying.

'So Paul and I are what – second cousins?' she said.

'Yes,' said Emily, as Sam came back into the room. 'Your fathers were first cousins, so you and Paul are second cousins. You and George Wright are first cousins once removed. One generation apart. Though nowadays people tend to say 'cousin' for any kind of relationship.'

'I see,' said Nina, impressed. 'I've never understood all that 'once removed' stuff. Thanks, Aunt Emily. Look, Sam, isn't this helpful?'

Emily looked flushed and pleased, and Nina leaned across and squeezed the old woman's hand. Here at last was a member of the Moore family she would love. How tragic; she could have loved Emily all those years, if Claire hadn't lied... Oh God – why hadn't Claire kept in touch with Emily at least?

Sam was examining the family tree. 'Excellent!' he said. 'You can put in Naomi, too.'

Nina wrote Naomi's name under her own. 'My daughter,' she said to Emily. 'She's ten. I'll bring her to see you another time. Could you have a look at some photos and see if you recognise anyone?'

With the help of her powerful magnifying glass Emily was able to identify quite a few people on Nina's selection of photos. As well as John Moore and Claire there was George Wright and his wife Jane, as well as Paul, the little boy who was on several photos, and a few friends and neighbours from the time when Nina and Paul had been young children. Nina sat wishing she'd brought some of the older, black and white photos as well. She showed Emily the address list, but apart from telling them about a few people who were dead Emily was little help with this. Most of the people on the list must have been friends of John Moore, and Emily hadn't known them. But it was a start.

Nina gathered the photos together and slid them back into their envelope. When she looked up again Emily was sitting with her eyes closed, a thoughtful expression on her face. Nina raised her eyebrows at Sam, feeling guilty. They had tired poor Emily out.

'Aunt Emily, we'll leave you in peace, thank you so much for helping,' said Nina, reaching for her handbag. 'Would it be all right if I came back another time quite soon? There are more photos, older ones, and I'm sure the moment we're on the road home I'll remember lots of things I should have asked you.'

Emily smiled. 'I hope you will come back. And bring your girl. You two and Paul and George are all the family I have now. Maybe you can all come sometime.'

Nina kissed her great-aunt goodbye, feeling she had found something very precious. And now she had found Emily she couldn't possibly rush back to Arran at the beginning of the week as she'd planned to. No, she would try to get in touch with one or both of the Wrights, and come back and see Emily with them if possible. Maybe they could take Emily out to lunch somewhere. One or two more visits before they headed north was an absolute must now.

They picked up Naomi, who had thoroughly enjoyed her afternoon fence-painting, and drove back to Bedford, pulling up in front of John Moore's house as the church clock was striking six. Nina rummaged for her keys.

'I think I'll hire a car,' she said. 'Then we'll be better able to visit Emily and do any other business while you're away, Sam. You've been wonderful about playing chauffeur, thank you so much.'

'Good idea. There's a garage round the corner from the supermarket. I'll come by tomorrow morning with the family info that I gathered for you – there's nothing significant you don't know, but some of the dates might be useful. I'm leaving for London late morning to have lunch with an old friend, and then it's off down to Devon after that.'

'Lucky you. Devon's lovely,' said Nina, keeping her voice light.

It was hard to know how she felt about Sam leaving. He was the only person here who knew everything that was happening to her, and the thought that she would be alone with the situation wasn't appealing. And to be honest, she enjoyed his company. He'd respected her wish to be 'business-friends', and Nina wondered suddenly if she was going to regret limiting their relationship. It was too late to change that now, though. The important thing was to sort the John Moore situation and get back home.

'Can we go for pizza?' said Naomi, and Nina laughed.

'After all you ate at lunchtime? Sam, for goodness sake don't tell your mother, will you?'

He grinned. 'My lips are sealed. Ladies, I'll love you and leave you. I have a pile of paperwork to organise before my trip.'

'Does he love us?' said Naomi, as Sam drove off down the road.

Nina shooed her in the front door. 'You can't love

people you've only known for five minutes. You scoot upstairs and get washed and as you were so good today we'll go to that pizzeria by the river.'

Naomi scooted, and Nina followed on slowly. You could fall in love in five seconds, she knew that. But she hadn't, had she?

CHAPTER FIFTEEN

Sunday 23rd July

To Nina's relief Naomi was still asleep the following morning when Sam appeared with his folder of family information. She hadn't mentioned her tentative plan to stay another few days, and now she could tell him without Naomi's eagle eyes zoning in on things that weren't there... or were they? Nina didn't know herself how she felt about Sam; he was so mixed up in the sordidness surrounding John Moore.

Sam's grin stretched right across his face when she told him she wasn't ready to leave yet. 'Brilliant! We never did go for that pizza with Naomi, maybe we can when I get back.'

Nina couldn't help laughing. Naomi had eaten her own pizza last night and a slice of Nina's too.

'Well, if Naomi has anything to do with it we certainly will,' she said. 'Thanks, Sam. Have a safe trip.'

His eyes met hers, and there it was again, that spark of attraction. This time, however, he made no move towards her.

'I will. And Nina — don't worry. You're going to

get through this. You must feel as if there's bad stuff everywhere you look at the moment, but we'll get it straightened, you'll see.'

Nina didn't answer. He was right, but discovering that your father had been a paedophile and your mother had lied to you about him all your life – bad stuff didn't get much mightier than that.

Alone again, she sat down with the address list and Sam's laptop. Now to see if she could find a phone number for Paul or George Wright.

There were two Pauls and seven George Wrights in Bedfordshire, Hertfordshire, and Buckinghamshire. Okay, Paul was probably going to be easier to track down than his Dad.

Nina picked up her mobile, then stopped. Ten o'clock on Sunday morning was maybe too early to phone. Better wait an hour or so.

She used the time to call the police for an update in the investigation, only to be told that David Mallony was off that day but would be in touch with her early in the week. Depressed, Nina hung up. She didn't expect them to get excited about John Moore himself, the man was dead, but there was still the anonymous letter writer and threatening phone-caller, not to mention all the possible victims, including herself. Oh well, it was Sunday.

She went upstairs and lured her daughter out of bed with the promise of warm croissants for breakfast, then when Naomi was under the shower she tried the first Paul Wright's number. The voice in her ear sounded calm and awake, and Nina's hopes soared.

'I'm researching my family tree and I've found

relations called George and Paul Wright,' she said after giving her name. 'My father was John Moore – he and George Wright were cousins.'

There was a long pause before the voice answered. 'Well, I guess I'm your Paul Wright,' he said. 'So you're little Nina who used to play with me on Sundays? Gosh, I – I don't know what to say – I hadn't quite forgotten about you, but... what a long time ago it was. I haven't seen my father for years, we don't get on. But – Uncle John – is he - ?'

Nina explained about John Moore's death. It was impossible to tell what Paul Wright felt about her getting in touch like this. He was polite and interested in her story, but there was no 'wow, how fantastic' tone in his voice. He did ask several questions about his uncle and the house, which he was evidently familiar with. Nina hesitated for a second before suggesting a meeting, but Paul agreed immediately.

'As a matter of fact I'll be driving right past Bedford late this afternoon, on the way home from friends. Shall I stop by then?'

Nina agreed to a visit between five and six o'clock, and punched the air as she put the phone down. She had found another relation, and even if Paul didn't get on with his father, he should be able to give her a phone number for George Wright. And according to Emily, they were all the family left. So she'd done it – she had found everyone who could possibly help her reconstruct the years she and Claire spent with John Moore. The feeling of relief surprised her in its intensity, and she went to splash cold water on her face. It was going to be all right. Her programme for the week now was to talk to the Wrights, especially George, who would remember more than Paul, visit Emily a couple of times, and see Sam when he returned, after which she'd be free at last to take Naomi back to Arran. Would it be 'Goodbye Sam' forever? Nina didn't know any more.

She and Naomi spent the afternoon at a craft workshop near Biddenham where children could make their own candles from beeswax, something Naomi could do despite her sprained wrist. By quarter to five they were home again, and Naomi ran to email her friends with the candle-making news. Nina went through to the living room, rubbing her stomach, which was churning nervously. Wow, oh wow. Soon now she would meet another relative, the second in two days, and this one was her own generation. It was exciting, in spite of the bad stuff. Hope flared inside her – how amazing it would be if she liked Paul as much as she liked Emily.

She sat arranging the last of the black and white photos into 'people' and 'no people' piles while she waited. Hallelujah, that was the photos organised. Maybe Paul would be able to identify some of the family on these, and she would take a new selection to show Emily on Tuesday too.

A thought struck Nina and she frowned. With Naomi there, she wouldn't be able to go into the paedophilia problem with Emily. But then – did Emily actually need to know? It was such a terrible thing... Why spoil the last years of an elderly lady's life? Nina stared blindly at the last photo, remembering the yearning look on Emily's kind, wrinkled face when they left. An old woman, watching her new-found family leave. A lump rose in Nina's throat. She had found both a father she had no wish to have, and a great-aunt she would love. How very – surreal it felt.

The doorbell rang at ten past five, and Nina hurried along the hallway. The man on the doorstep was oddly like the little boy on the photographs. Paul Wright was slightly built and only a few centimetres taller than she was, with deep brown eyes and a shock of jet-black hair falling over his forehead. His smile was shy and appealing.

'Nina. How amazing after all these years. You used to steal my jelly babies, you know.'

Nina smiled and shook hands. 'Well, you're one up on me if you remember. I have no recollection of you at all, but I'm really glad to see you now. It's such an odd feeling, finding relatives I didn't even know existed.'

He followed her into the hallway, staring round with a wistful expression on his face.

'This place hasn't changed much,' he said. 'We used to visit at weekends, Sunday lunch and all that. I was gutted when you and your mum left. I remember crying into my pillow, and having a tantrum one Sunday because there was no Nina to play with after lunch.'

'Oh – I'm sorry.' Nina was touched.

He patted her arm. 'It was hardly your fault.'

Nina led him into the living room, and he wandered round the periphery of the room, stopping to look out of both windows before settling down on the sofa and looking at her.

'I can understand why your mum left, you know. I was scared of Uncle John. He used to shout at me when

I dropped my peas on his floor. Peas are hard to keep on your fork when you're little, and somehow it always was peas back then. My own dad was no better. He used to clout me around the ears if I made a mess at the table.'

He pulled a face at her, grinning, and Nina managed to grin back, but really, it wasn't funny, was it?

'I don't know what to say,' she said. The more she heard about John Moore the more she despised him. But thank God, she could feel a rapport with Paul. It was the same feeling she'd had with Emily, but this time she'd be able to ask what – if – he knew about John Moore's paedophilic activity.

'It was a long time ago. We can congratulate ourselves on being much nicer people than our fathers,' he said.

Nina nodded. Other than accept it, there was nothing they could do about the past. 'You're right,' she said, realising the pun too late.

He rolled his eyes and she laughed.

'Sorry. What I'm trying to do here is find out about the family I didn't know I had. There are loads of photos, can I ask you to have a look at a few? In return I'll bring you a glass of wine – or a coffee, if you'd prefer that.'

'Sounds good. I'll have a glass of wine and we can toast each other,' he said, sitting down at the table and reaching for a pile of 'people' photos.

Nina went through to the kitchen and opened a bottle of white wine. She was shaking crisps into a bowl when Naomi appeared from the study.

'Come and meet your second cousin, once removed,' said Nina, as Naomi took a coke from the fridge. 'We're going through some of the old photos and I want to ask him about some family stuff, too, but if there's anything on TV you want to watch we'll go through to the study.' She deliberately made things sound as boring as she could.

'Can I shoot bubbles?' said Naomi.

Nina agreed, glad they had Sam's laptop. Naomi would sit in front of it till she was prised away. She introduced her daughter to Paul, who didn't really know how to converse with ten-year-old girls, then helped Naomi log into her game. Oh – here were the two photos they'd found first, the woman with the small boy – Paul – and the one with the cat in front of the shabby house.

'Mum and me and – oh! That's Mitzi!' he said, smiling broadly when she showed him the second photo. 'She loved sunning herself on the wall there. Mum used to get mad because I let her sleep in my bed; it was like cuddling a real live teddy bear. Can I have this one?'

'Sure,' said Nina. 'Was that where you lived?'

'We moved there when I was about nine,' said Paul. 'It was a pretty crappy building as you see. My dad's business went bust; he used to buy and sell cars but he was a real swindler and it caught up with him eventually and he had to sell the house. He was arrested for fraud but they couldn't prove anything so there were no charges. Then he turned his talents to any kind of dodgy business he could find, and Mum and I broke right off with him. He's twisted, somehow; he manipulates people to get what he wants. But it never works out. He's never made his fortune again and he's very bitter about it. Or he was, last time I saw him. That was about two years ago. He spends quite a lot of time abroad nowadays.'

Nina pulled a face, disappointment heavy in her gut. George Wright sounded almost as forgettable as John Moore. No way did she want to contact a man like that, so maybe meeting new relatives was going to end right here with Paul. But at least he was a normal human being, and she had Emily too.

Keeping her voice low, Nina told him about the paedophilia on John Moore's computer, the threatening phone call and the letters.

Paul's face was appalled. 'Oh my God, I'm so sorry,' he whispered, leaning towards her on the sofa. 'Mum always called Uncle John a dirty old man, and I know my dad collects porn too. You must be gutted.'

Tears shot into Nina's eyes. At last, at last, here was someone who really could understand what she was going through. 'I think the worst part is feeling so alone with it all,' she said, struggling to keep her voice steady. 'I'm so glad to have found you and Emily, though I haven't told her about the pornography, or the blackmail.'

Paul was frowning. 'You know blackmail's the kind of thing my Dad would do,' he said, his face grim. 'Threatening people is right up his street; he wouldn't care that you're his own flesh and blood. And after he lost the money he really had it in for Uncle John. You should be careful, Nina. He's dangerous because he has no feeling for right and wrong.'

Nina felt her cheeks blanch. 'I should tell that to the police,' she said. How horrible, her father's own cousin could be the blackmailer.

'Don't worry, they know all about him. And you said he was on your address list too? I should think the police are already checking him out. The problem is, nothing ever happens to people like him and Uncle John, does it? They're much too good at hiding their tracks and they get way with stuff time and again.' His voice couldn't have been more bitter.

Nina sipped her wine, thinking. It was true that criminals like her father and his cousin weren't always prosecuted successfully, but there was something wrong with Paul's reasoning.

'But Paul, whoever wrote the blackmail letter talked about screaming his head off and suffering; it was from one of John Moore's victims. Your father is about the same age as mine, isn't he? So George couldn't have been a victim.'

'Oh, my Dad's clever,' said Paul dryly. 'Pretending to be some unfortunate ex-victim in order to get money out of John would be all in a day's work to him.'

Good point, thought Nina, they had no idea how accurate the letter was. Paul sat there looking as if he was going to say more, and Nina waited. In the end, though, he changed the subject.

'Let's have a look at the newest photos.'

Nina showed him the pile of colour photos, and he sat down to examine them, refusing her offer of something more substantial to eat, saying he had to get back to his girlfriend in Newport Pagnell. He was able to identify both his parents and grandparents in some of the photos before he had to leave, and promised to have a think about the past and get back in touch in a day or two.

At the door he hugged her briefly. 'Nina. It makes me sick to think you're going through all this and it might be my dad behind it. If you need anything, or if you just want to talk, give me a call. You're not alone anymore.'

Nina hugged back, closing her eyes tightly. Emily was a gem, and now she had Paul, who wasn't exactly your strongman protector type, but he was nearby and he understood, and that was enough to help her deal with the knowledge that her father and his cousin were criminals. Low-life. Not the kind of people you could be proud of.

She waved goodbye as Paul drove off, then turned back inside, a picture of the farmhouse, the B&B sign waving in the wind, sliding into her head. She could be proud of what Claire and Grandma Lily and Grandpa Bill had achieved, and she would make damn well sure that her own daughter could look back one day and be proud of her too.

Chapter Sixteen

Claire's Story – Bedford

'What the fuck are you doing here, Claire?'

The voice came from behind and Claire swung round on her bench by the river, dismay obliterating her brief moment of peace. Robert was standing there, hands stuffed in his pockets, glaring.

Claire swallowed panic. Dear Lord, coming here had been a huge mistake. She'd found herself with an unexpected day to fill, as the London friend she was visiting this week had been obliged to go into work to deal with a staffing emergency instead of hitting Oxford Street with Claire. A shopping trip alone, especially when you were only window-shopping, had limited appeal, and quite spontaneously Claire hopped on a train to Bedford. She walked through town and along by the river to see her old home. How odd it felt, wandering along the pleasant river pathway, looking at the expensive houses on the other side of the road. For a long moment she stood staring at her old home, resentment flooding through her. According to the phone book Robert still lived there, so he must be doing well for himself, even after giving her all that money. It was so bittersweet –

she would never regret her marriage, because of Nina, but the thought that he was financially so much better off than she was made her blood boil. She sat down on the bench to recover, not thinking for a minute that Robert might be at home at two o'clock on a Thursday to notice her, but here he was. And what in the world was she supposed to say now?

She stared at him, eyebrows raised and a carefully polite expression on her face. It wasn't easy, but she managed to sound calm. 'I'm not here to see you, don't worry. I'm visiting Carol this week, and I thought I'd have a look round Bedford again while I have the chance. I'll be gone before you know it.'

He snorted, then to her dismay he lowered himself into the far corner of her bench. 'Come to see the house you could have lived in, huh? Bad decision, Claire. As usual.'

He was as unbearable as ever. Thank God she hadn't tried to re-establish contact between him and Nina. Claire stood up. 'It was. And I'm not staying here for you to hurl insults at me.'

He accompanied her across the grass towards the pavement and the quickest way back to town, and Claire's stomach churned in spite of her brave words. But there were people about; she needn't feel threatened. She would walk away from him and go for a coffee before catching her train back to London.

'How's Nina?' His voice was neutral, and she replied in the same tone.

'She's fine. At Brownie camp in Dunbar this week.'

'Good.' They reached the road and Claire was turning

away when a thought struck her.

'I left a lot of stuff here, Robert. I suppose you still have it?'

He snorted. 'That junk. It's all in a couple of boxes in the attic. If you want it, come in and get it.'

Claire thought quickly, unwilling to prolong the meeting. She'd left things like shoes and clothes that didn't matter now, but there were some ornaments and trinkets as well. Would it be stupid of her to go inside with him? She glanced at the front room windows. One was wide open, and people would hear her if she screamed.

'I will, thank you,' she said, managing to sound calm. 'You can bring them down to the study, please.'

Rather to her surprise he said nothing, and she followed him inside and waited while he ran upstairs. The study hadn't changed since the day and hour she left this place; how very depressing it was. His Dad's old desk and bookshelves. And the secretaire Emily had given her when she downsized to Biddenham. Claire gazed round in distaste. This house had never felt like home and her ties with Bedford had been broken long ago. Thank God.

Robert returned with two large boxes which he dumped on the floor, forcing her to crouch down, and Claire was glad she was wearing trousers. Ignoring the way he was standing there watching her, arms folded, she rummaged through the non-clothes box and found a fair-sized collection of memorabilia of her marriage. The blue vases she'd found in Portobello Road Market, goodness, she'd forgotten about them. And she'd take the Capo di Monte rose, it matched Lily's – and Nina would love the costume jewellery. Beads and bangles were important nowadays; at ten, Nina was discovering the world of fashion.

'You can throw out the clothes, but I'll take the rest with me, except the blue vases,' she said at last. 'They're too big. I'm going on to the theatre tonight.'

Quickly, she packed her possessions into the fold-up shopping bag she kept in her handbag. 'I'll come back sometime for the vases, Robert, don't throw them away. And the secretaire's mine too, strictly speaking. I'll let you know. How is Emily – and Jane and Paul?' She stared at the secretaire. It was a pity she'd lost contact with Emily. But contact with Emily might have led to contact with Robert, and Claire hadn't wanted that back then and neither had he. Ah well. No point stirring things up now.

He followed her to the front door. 'They're all fine. Send for the rest if you want it. Don't bother coming back, Claire.'

Claire shot him one more look as he stood at the door, arms still crossed in front of him, staring after her. She strode off into the afternoon, hands shaking, forcing herself not to turn round. What a fool she'd been, coming here, but at least she'd got some things back. And she had stood up to Robert – that alone was enough to make her feel stronger. Almost. A cup of coffee settled her nerves, and she sat in the café looking through her long-lost treasures. Maybe she would go back in person for the vases someday, just to spite Robert.

Smiling at the thought, Claire checked her watch. It was time to start back to the station.

Goodbye, Bedford, she thought as her train sped south. I wonder if I'll ever see you again.

Chapter Seventeen

Monday 24th July

The second weirdo phone call came the following morning.

Nina was stepping out of the shower when the old-fashioned ring tone trilled upstairs from the study. Cursing, she pulled one of John Moore's scrubby bath towels round her and ran, almost tripping down the stairs in her rush to get to the phone. It would be a wonder if she made it and a double wonder if Naomi didn't waken with all this crashing about, but there was something very insistent about the brr-brr sounds emanating from John Moore's shiny blue eighties telephone. It was impossible to ignore.

'Hello?' She perched on the edge of the desk, thankful for the net curtains at the window. Clad in an ancient orange bath towel with her hair pinned roughly on top of her head, she wasn't quite ready to face the world.

There was an odd little snigger at the other end, and a sick, churning feeling wormed through Nina's gut. For a second she considered hanging up but remembered in time that the phone was bugged now and the police would be listening in. She wasn't alone here, she wasn't alone. All she had to do was keep him on the line.

The same sing-song, high-pitched voice muttered into her ear.

'Nina, Nina. You pay for my pain or your daughter will suffer. Get your money organised. You'll hear from me again.'

The line went dead, and Nina slammed the receiver down before crouching on the floor, panting. She had never felt so outraged, so helpless. This disgusting person had threatened Naomi. Dear God, what should she do?

Get the first plane north. Home, home. The thought ran over and over in her head as she ran to make sure the front door was locked, then rushed round checking the ground floor windows and the back door were secure too. There was nothing for her here in Bedford. The business stuff could be finished from Scotland; she could easily keep in touch with Paul by email and phone, and Emily... yes, there was Emily. But even finding an absolute jewel of an aunt had no significance in comparison to Naomi's safety. This caller – was it George Wright? – had made a definite threat now.

Loneliness crept through Nina as she realised there was no one she could call for moral support. Cruel to phone Beth, who would be in the middle of preparing heaven knows how many different breakfasts. Sam was miles away and couldn't help with this anyway. She would have to let Paul know that the blackmailer and anonymous caller, who might well be his own father, had struck again, but – dear God, would Paul really want to know? He would only be hurt and ashamed. Hot tears stung Nina's eyes and she rubbed her face impatiently. This was no time to go soft. Phone the police, woman, see what they have to say.

David Mallony was terse on the phone. 'It's as if he knew the phone was bugged. The call was from a landline but that's all we know. Nina, I think you ought to go to a hotel. You and Naomi shouldn't be alone in that house after such a direct threat.'

Miserably, Nina agreed. All she wanted was to sit on the bench outside the farmhouse and watch the waves shiver up the beach below, but she needed at least another day here. She had to talk properly to the police, and she wanted to see Paul again and ask him more about their families in the days when she and Claire lived here. He might know something that would explain why Claire had spread the myth about her husband's death. And there must be something – a huge, enormous something – that they didn't know yet, because Claire wouldn't have told that lie lightly.

Nina stood in the study, tapping her fingers on the desktop. What on earth was she supposed to do with Naomi while she was talking to David Mallony and Paul? Her daughter would be one large question mark if she realised there was more going on than she knew about.

Sam's parents slid into Nina's head as she trailed back upstairs to dress. Maybe she should take Cassie up on that offer to babysit. With Naomi at the Harrison's, she'd have time to sort things out with David, talk to Paul, and get packed. Afterwards she and Naomi could find a hotel near Emily so they could both visit before flying north again.

Naomi was awake, and Nina explained the babysitting idea. It was a good job the Harrisons had a dog, she thought, amused when this was the first thing Naomi thought of.

'You get dressed, and I'll phone and ask,' said Nina, heading for the stairs.

Heavens, all this and she hadn't even had a coffee yet. And actually she should call Paul first, while Naomi was safely under the shower.

His voice on the phone was deeper than in real life, and he sounded delighted to hear from her. 'Nina! I've been remembering some of the things we got up to as kids, and I've found a couple more old snaps, too – we must get together and – Nina?'

Impossible to keep her own voice steady while she told him about the second call. She could feel his concern through the phone.

'Oh God, you must wish you'd never come anywhere near here. I think it's a great idea to find someone to take care of Naomi. Or – tell you what, I can come and stay in the house with you tonight, save you going to a hotel. I can easily stop work early today.'

'Oh – I couldn't ask you to do that, Paul. Thanks anyway. If the Harrisons can help we'll be fine.'

'Nina, it's not a problem. Think of everything we went through as kids. Our fathers weren't into helping family and my mother wasn't much better. Now we have the chance to do better. And I'd love to have another look at those photos.'

He was right, thought Nina. If Beth or Tim had made the offer she knew she wouldn't have hesitated. And what had Emily said – little Nina used to think Paul was wonderful when they were small? It would be good to have the chance to get to know him better.

'Okay – thanks. Could you maybe come by in the afternoon? We could talk about everything then, and take it from there.'

Paul agreed to come at four, and Nina rang off, glad about her decision. It made a real difference to have someone there in the background, a family member, too, to lend a hand.

She booted up the laptop and went into the telephone directory to find the Harrisons' number. For a second she hesitated – what should she tell Cassie? Simply that she had a lot of dry and dusty business stuff going on and Naomi was bored out of her skull seemed the best way. Which, when you thought about it, was the exact truth – from Naomi's point of view at least.

'Nina, of course! It must be awkward for you. Why don't you let her stay here overnight? That would give you more time.'

Nina heaved a sigh of relief. A sleepover with a dog wouldn't be a hard sell, and then her mind would be at rest about her girl. 'Thanks, Cassie, I'll bring Naomi later this morning if that's okay. I'll have to talk to her about spending the night but I'm sure she'll agree. It's a load off my mind to have someone take care of her.'

It was shortly after eleven when Nina pulled up outside the Harrison's house. The hired car was a larger vehicle than she was used to driving, and it took her three goes to get into the tight space at the side of the road.

She made a face at Naomi. 'How to look seriously uncool in one easy lesson,' she said, and Naomi giggled.

'Chill, Mom. I think you're real cool,' she said, with a phoney American accent.

Nina looked at her girl, grinning at her from the passenger seat, her hair scraped into a high pony tail. How very much she loved Naomi. If anything happened to her little girl because of all this John Moore stuff... it would be unbearable. Impossible to live with herself if even a hair on Naomi's head was harmed. Damn the anonymous caller to hell.

Cassie and Glen came out to greet them.

'Can I really stay the night?' said Naomi, as Cassie hugged her. 'And where's Kira?'

'Of course you can. Your room's all ready, and Kira's waiting for you in the kitchen,' said Cassie. 'We'll take her for a walk later on, but first Glen could do with another pair of hands to finish the fence, couldn't you, love?'

Nina carried Naomi's bag inside, her heart warming. Cassie and Glen were obviously delighted with their young visitor, and Naomi, who knew nothing about the second threatening call, was equally enthusiastic. Nina grinned as she watched her daughter struggle into a pair of Glen-sized overalls. It was plain Naomi could hardly wait to get her hands on a paint brush.

Cassie walked back to the car with her. 'Nina, are you quite sure you don't want to stay here tonight too? There's plenty of space. I don't like to think of you rattling around in your father's house all by yourself.'

Nina was touched – there were good people in the world. She should remember that in the midst of all this. 'Don't worry, Cassie. My cousin's coming and he'll probably stay over. There's a lot I have to go through with him before Naomi and I head north. I'll phone this evening and let you know what's going on. And thank you more than I can say for taking Naomi like this. It makes all the difference.'

Cassie gave her a brief hug. 'I'll leave you to phone Sam, will I, and let him know what's happening.'

Nina smiled as she drove off. Cassie was doing a bit of match-making there – and what did she think about that?

David Mallony ushered her into his office and was approving when he heard about Naomi's new home.

'Good. We don't know what the blackmailer's planning,' he said. 'If he phones again, try to keep the line open for as long as you can. Talk to him. That'd give us more time to pinpoint the call.'

'Do you think he knows the police are involved?'

'Oh yes, but he'll think he can make you comply now without telling us. I have a feeling it'll be a letter next time, with a demand for money, and I think it'll come by post in the morning. He won't want to risk being seen near the house. So it would be better if you stay on until tomorrow at least.'

Nina sat staring at the glass paperweight on David's desk. What he said sounded logical, and it was reassuring to know the blackmailer was unlikely to appear on the doorstep. She turned back to David Mallony. Now for the difficult question.

'What have you found out about – John Moore?'

'There was a large number of pornographic images

involving children on his computer. We're investigating to see if that was as far as it went. I can't tell you any more at the moment, Nina.'

In a way Nina was relieved. Maybe it was easier if she didn't know the ins and outs of what her father had done. A thought struck her – why on earth hadn't he disposed of the laptop? He'd got rid of bags full of shredded paper. What was on the shredded paper that wasn't on the laptop?

'Contact details for other paedophiles, I imagine.' David Mallony sounded depressed when she asked him. 'Leave it to us, Nina; you don't need to know the details.'

Nina was glad to accept this. She told David Mallony about meeting Emily Moore and Paul, and he listened, an interested expression on his face.

'Good for you. But you know, it's not at all certain this blackmailer is George Wright. He does have a record, but he's been pretty quiet for the last six or seven years. We're keeping an open mind there.'

Back at the house, Nina started to organise her belongings for a possible departure the next day, then went to look at the photos on the table. Paul wanted to see them again; she would leave them here in the meantime. The 'people' snaps were laid out in groups, with the 'non-people' ones in a pile at the side.

She picked up a photo of herself as a young child with Claire and John Moore. It was so frustrating that she remembered so little. She had a hazy memory of the house, more a sense of familiarity than an actual memory. There was the horrible feeling that John Moore might have been abusive in some way. But maybe she only felt that because she know about the pornography on his computer… and because Claire must have had a powerful reason for that enormous, long-term lie. Was this what Claire had been trying to say, moments before she lost consciousness? Nina swallowed.

What had her mother known?

Nina's mobile buzzed at half past three while she was packing Naomi's remaining things. And after she'd left this house – which might even be today, if Paul couldn't stop overnight with her – she would never stay here again. And oh, the relief was incredible – she literally felt lighter.

Sam's voice was upbeat. 'Hi, Nina. I'm between meetings. How's things?'

'Okay,' said Nina cautiously. 'I was about to phone you. I guess you haven't spoken to your parents today?'

'No. Why?'

In as few words as possible, she told him what was going on. Sam was horrified.

'But Nina, of course you have to go to Mum's! You don't know this weirdo isn't going to come to the house. It's much too risky!'

'I won't stay here unless Paul can stay with me,' said Nina, trying to sound reassuring. 'And I'll make sure all the doors and windows are locked, don't worry. David Mallony doesn't think the blackmailer will come here, anyway.'

Sam, however, was not to be reassured. 'David can't possibly know that for sure. And for heaven's sake, you don't know Paul Wright, and his being related to your father and George Wright is hardly a recommendation, is it?'

Startled, Nina thought of Paul's gentle brown eyes and the way his hair fell over his forehead. Maybe she didn't know him, but he was family – he'd been part of her life all those years ago. They connected.

'Sam, I'm related to John Moore and George Wright in the same way as Paul is. Sometimes you just have to trust people. Two weeks ago I didn't know you existed either.'

It was the wrong thing to say. Sam's voice was tight when he replied.

'Well, I can say the same about you, but I think I'd trust you over a stranger with a criminal family background. I'm sorry if you don't feel the same way. I thought we were friends.'

His last sentence sounded nothing but petulant. Nina gripped her phone, biting back an angry retort. She had neither time nor energy for this right now. She forced herself to sound calm.

'Sam, I don't need any more hassle here. Paul's due any minute so I'm going to hang up. I'll let you know what happens.'

She put the phone down and stared at it. Had she been too hard on poor Sam? No, she was in charge of her own life and it was up to her what she did and where she stayed. Though in a way Sam was right too, because even if Paul was her cousin, she had no idea how trustworthy he was. Sam came with the recommendation of being a lawyer, but Paul had no such testimonial. It was always tempting to judge people by your own standards, she thought, running upstairs to check that the lock on her bedroom door worked. It did, and the door was solid oak.

Nina smiled suddenly – locking her bedroom door wouldn't be unnecessary. Paul felt like family in the same way Emily did. Maybe she could persuade him to come with her and Naomi to visit Emily tomorrow. Somehow she didn't think Paul saw much of their great-aunt, and it would be interesting to know why not. Of course, maybe he simply wasn't into visiting family, but you'd think a sense of duty would prompt the odd visit. Or was that more of a girl-thing?

Paul appeared at twenty past four, clutching a well-used sports bag and a bottle of wine.

'All ready to stay, as you see,' he said, grinning at her, and Nina relaxed.

It was all right. This was her cousin – well, second cousin or whatever, and he was going out of his way to help her.

She accepted the bottle. 'Cabernet Sauvignon. One of my favourites. How did you know?'

He looked pleased. 'It's one of mine too. Must be a family trait.'

'Is your girlfriend – Melanie, isn't it? – okay about you staying here tonight?' she asked, and he nodded.

'She's going out with friends anyway. I brought a sleeping bag so if you give me a mattress somewhere I'll be fine.'

Nina showed him into the little room beside the kitchen and he dropped his bag on the bed.

'What would you like to eat?' she asked, watching him roll out his sleeping bag. 'We don't do gourmet meals in this house but I could make spaghetti, or we can send out for pizza.'

'Let's send out,' he said. 'Pizza's easier to eat when you're looking at photos and things. Can I have a look round the house, please? I was here a lot as a kid but I haven't seen it properly for years.'

Nina gave him a guided tour. He showed her which bedroom had been hers as a child, and told her about the time the two of them unravelled all Nina's children's cassettes and tied the upstairs doors together with the mess of tape.

'It was no ice cream for us that day,' he said, grinning. 'Our mums were not amused.'

Nina laughed. This was exactly the kind of thing she wanted to hear, little stories about her life. She stood in the doorway of her old bedroom, which now contained an anonymous single bed, a chest of drawers and a wardrobe. What wouldn't she give for a clear memory of those days, but nothing was coming to mind. Disappointed, she turned back to Paul, now gazing into the room she and Naomi were occupying.

'Those blue vases were your mum's, you know. She bought blue ones for herself and green ones for my mum. It must have been just shortly before you left.'

Nina hugged her arms round her middle, staring at the vases. How amazing – the only beautiful things in John Moore's house, almost, and they were Claire's. A little part of Claire still here in Bedford. She would take them home when they left.

In the attic room, Paul walked down to the far end where the mattresses lay, then turned and stared back towards the door, the expression on his face unreadable. He was breathing heavily, Nina noticed – what was going through his mind? She was still wondering what to say when he came out of his trance and grinned at her.

'I think you should do this place up to rent out. You could easily have it turned into flats, and the way the market is at the moment that might be a better investment than selling.'

'I know,' said Nina. 'Nothing's decided yet.'

No way was she going to keep this house, she thought, following Paul downstairs. She wanted to be able to draw a very definite line under John Moore and his sleaze.

Paul settled down with the photos while Nina phoned for pizza and opened the wine. When she went back to the living room he was engrossed in the 'non-people' pile, not even reacting when she made a remark about the small size of most of these photos. Nina put his wine glass down beside him and went to phone Cassie to say she'd be quite all right tonight. It would be her last night under her father's roof. And thank God for that.

CHAPTER EIGHTEEN

The pizzas were good, a Mediterranean veggie topping on a thin, crisp base, and Nina made a green salad to go with them. Working in John Moore's kitchen was a bit like camping, she thought ruefully, having searched in vain for a salad bowl. Judging by the appliances and the meagre selection of kitchen utensils, her father's cooking had consisted of heating things in the microwave and opening tins. Of course maybe he'd eaten out most of the time – he'd certainly been able to afford it. What an odd set-up this was. John Moore was so well-off, yet he'd chosen to live in this place, which was solid and warm but – dowdy. Yes, that was a good word to describe the house. But when you thought about his collection of paedophilic pictures it all became sick and sordid, too. So maybe the dowdiness hadn't mattered to John Robert Moore.

She and Paul ate in the living room, each ensconced in a corner of the sofa as the table was covered with photos. Nina was silent, pity almost closing her throat as Paul spoke of his mother's struggle to make ends meet. It didn't make for a cheerful mealtime conversation.

His childhood had been nothing like her own. After

the split with his father, Paul's mother gave up the fight to provide for her child, and lived on social security. Alcohol had played a big part in Jane Wright's life, too. So while Nina was watching her mother and grandparents struggle to start their business on Arran, Paul was watching his mother drink herself into her grave. How dreadful for him.

'What happened to you then?' she asked gently, but he looked away, shaking his head.

'Nothing worth remembering today. I survived, thanks to social services, and here we both are, back in John Moore's house as adults. You can survive anything, you know.'

He took a large swallow of wine. Nina frowned. It was difficult to see what he meant by 'survive' and it didn't look as if he was about to enlarge on it. Poor Paul. She had always been loved and cared for, but it sounded as if no one had loved Paul after his mother died.

He wiped his fingers on the paper napkin provided by the pizza company. 'Almost forgot,' he said, going over to the table. 'I found your father's parents here. Look.'

He lifted three black and white prints, and Nina took them eagerly. John Moore senior, her grandfather, and his young wife Sylvia. They must have been in their twenties here, standing side by side beside a bandstand, presumably in some park or other, uncertain smiles for the camera and uncomfortable, formal-looking clothes. Perhaps they'd been out for a Sunday walk – people had worn 'Sunday best' in those days. Nina stared, trying in vain to read their expressions and feeling the enormous distance separating them from her life today. What had

John and Sylvia Moore done to turn their son into such a monster? Or maybe it wasn't their fault, maybe young John had gone off the rails by himself. You couldn't blame parents for everything. Paul handed her another photo showing a trio of people in various shades of grey.

'My parents with Aunt Emily,' he said.

Nina took the photos. Black and white pictures of days gone by. She searched round for a pen and paper. 'Let's number them, and write down who's on which photo.'

They sat at the table, Paul numbering the photos and providing the names and Nina writing the list. Halfway down her page she squinted at him uneasily. He wasn't happy doing this, so much was clear. His earlier good humour was gone and his answers to her questions were getting shorter all the time. At last they came to the end of the first pile; Paul numbered the final black and white 'people' photo and Nina wrote down the names, Emily and her sister Ruth, Paul's grandmother. Family photos, and dear God, what had gone on behind the scenes in the Moore family?

'Thank you,' she said, putting her hand on his arm. 'I can see it isn't easy for you, revisiting the past like this. I'll take the ones you don't know to Emily tomorrow and see if she can add anything. Or – would you be able to come too? I'd be going in the morning, before we fly home.'

He shook his head. 'I'm due another visit. But tomorrow's impossible, I'm afraid. Give her my love.'

Nina hesitated, uneasiness creeping over her. She couldn't put a finger on it but her previous rapport with Paul had vanished, and something about what he'd just said didn't ring true. According to Emily, Paul hadn't visited her for years. Maybe he was too ashamed to admit it, but why would he cut all ties with his great-aunt? Confusion spread through Nina. There was something he wasn't telling her here and it was important, she could see that. Looking at those photos had stirred something up in his head... oh dear God... was this something to do with John Moore and the nasty photos... oh fuck... had *Paul* been on any of those photos? Could that be? The crying in the attic memory crashed back into Nina's brain. Screaming, she remembered the sound now, even – but had she screamed – or Paul? What had happened back then? But before she could say anything Paul flung his pen down on the table.

'God! Emily was the only one of them who was nice to me,' he burst out. 'My grandparents were all 'children should be seen and not heard'. But Emily was cool.'

'What about your parents, and mine? Were they strict too?' said Nina carefully.

He was in a strange mood now, looking at her with over-bright eyes and pouring them both a generous second glass of wine. Nina sipped, then put her glass on the table. She didn't want to get plastered and she'd already had a big glass. Hopefully the pizza would mop it up.

Paul flung himself down on the sofa and buried his head in his hands. Nina's heart began to race. What was he going to tell her?

'Your mother had the right idea,' he said at last, lifting his head and staring at her.

The brightness in his eyes was unshed tears, and she passed him a tissue without speaking.

He blew his nose and went on. 'Your mam got you out. Mine disappeared into a bottle.'

'What are you saying?' whispered Nina. Her stomach started to heave. 'Paul? What happened?'

He reached for another tissue and started ripping it into shreds. 'They hired – us – out,' he said, spitting the words at her. 'What do you think?'

'Hired – how?' Nina's voice came out in a croak and her hands holding the tissue packet began to shake. For a few seconds the world around her hummed and it was as if the colours in the drab living room were turning silver. Quickly, she put her head between her knees. When the faintness passed she leaned back again. Paul was staring at nothing and twirling his empty wine glass. He wouldn't meet her eye.

'Our fathers?' said Nina.

He nodded, still not looking at her. Nina raised her hands to her face. Dear God, what the shit had she been through in this house?

'Are you saying we were abused here in this house and our fathers collected money for it?'

Paul gave a loud moan and jumped to his feet, pacing up and down in front of the disused fireplace. 'Oh yes. Money, that's all we were worth. They took photos, too. My dad was great with a camera, you know.' His voice broke on the last word.

Nina clapped her hands to her mouth, feeling her eyes widen in horror. Dear Christ in heaven, this was worse than anything she'd ever imagined. His eyes held hers, and she could see the horror and the loathing he had felt back then; she could see how it was affecting his life today, how he could never get away from it.

'You mean we were – raped?' It was difficult to get the words out.

Paul laughed mirthlessly. 'I was. I don't know if you were. Maybe not. You were so young, and there was the necessity to give you back to your mother more or less in one piece, you see. Mine was usually too smashed to notice. It was all so fucking sordid and it hurt, Nina, it hurt like hell.'

Nina leapt up and ran to the narrow downstairs toilet, her hands over her mouth. Her gut cramped tightly as she vomited pizza and red wine into the bowl. Dear God. Why, why, didn't she remember any of this? How old had she been? Two, three?

And shit, shit – but Claire couldn't have known about that. Quite definitely not.

Could she?

The spasm over, she rinsed her face and drank from her cupped hands. Paul was waiting in the passageway, his eyes dull. He hugged her, saying nothing, and Nina held on tightly, breathing deeply and feeling the tension in her gut slacken. She knew the worst now, and she would have to learn to cope with it. She would get over this, because if she didn't, John Moore would have won. That wasn't going to happen.

Back in the living room, she took a cautious sip of wine.

'My mother can't have known,' she said, leaning back in the sofa.

Paul glared at the floor. 'Mine did. I told her after you left. I don't know if she did anything, but nothing changed over the next couple of years. Except it happened to me more often because you weren't there anymore. And then there was all the stuff with the business going down the pan. Mam and me moved away and the abuse stopped. I've never told anyone else.'

Nina felt physically drained, as if she'd run a marathon. Her muscles hurt. The thought of what had happened to her made her feel soiled, wasted, but she knew this was the feeling she would have to change. She had been an innocent child, she had *not* been made dirty by these people. Tomorrow she would tell all this to the police and then she would start the rest of her life.

Paul leaned towards her, and she saw how his hands were shaking.

'I wanted to kill him for a long time,' he said, his voice trembling. 'Both of them, Dad and Uncle John. When I was older I even bought a gun, but they were enemies by that time and I never got the two of them in the same place at the same time and that was what I wanted. I wanted to pull the trigger on your father and watch the fear in Dad's eyes while I did it. And then I wanted to kill him too. But it didn't work out.'

Nina grasped his hand and squeezed it. The anger was understandable; she felt it too. Maybe she always would.

'You should get counselling, Paul,' she said, feeling his hand shake in hers. 'That's what I'll do, I think. We need help to get over this. Dear God. My own father.' She had seen him in his coffin and she had never known. Shit, she had looked at him and felt pity.

There was nothing left to say that evening. Nina went to bed and dozed fitfully for a while, waking every time the house creaked or a car drove by outside. At three in the morning she found herself wide awake, and shivered. This was no good, she'd be dead on her feet in the morning if she didn't get some proper sleep. She would make hot chocolate and take a headache pill, heaven knows her head felt the size of an over-ripe water-melon. She'd had too much wine and she'd lost the pizza.

There was silence in the little room beside the kitchen. Nina put a mug of milk into the microwave and when the drink was made she wandered through the dark hallway to the study and sat down at the desk.

More than anything else she wanted to have a heart-to-heart with Bethany, but she couldn't possibly ring up at this time of night about something that happened when she was two years old. She would phone tomorrow. And she would phone Sam and – yes, she would go and stay with Cassie. There would be more interviews with the police now; she and Naomi wouldn't get back to Scotland tomorrow. Nina sobbed silently for a few minutes, bent over shiny mahogany. Why, why had she come here? The legacy had brought her nothing but grief.

The headache slackened its hold, and Nina rose to her feet, only then noticing the blue plastic folder Sam had brought before he left. Heavens, she'd forgotten all about this. There might be something important in here.

She sat down again and switched on the desk light. There was a small family tree, rather like the one Emily had drawn, except this one had dates and full names. Paul's mother had been seven years older than his father, she saw, unusual in those days. And beside George Wright's name Sam had scribbled 'last known residence

2011 in Thailand'.

Well. Abusing more children, perhaps. Disgusting old man. Nina paused. Paul had mentioned that his father spent time abroad, but of course it was possible that George Moore was back in the UK now. Was he on the sex offenders register? More questions for David Mallony.

Nina yawned as the warm milk and paracetamol took hold. Good, maybe she would get some sleep after all. Upstairs again, she curled up in the warmth of her bed, feeling her muscles relax. There wasn't long to wait now. Another few hours and she'd be out of this house forever.

CHAPTER NINETEEN

Claire's story – The Isle of Arran

Claire pulled two lettuces from the farmhouse vegetable garden, but her thoughts were far away from the guests' evening meal. It was time to write another letter to Robert, and this time she would send it. Lily's death, six years after Bill's, had forced her hand. If Claire was knocked over by a bus tomorrow, Robert was the one the authorities would get in touch with. The thought made her feel ill.

Claire pressed her lips together hard. Poor old Mum. Lily had never come to terms with being widowed; the loss of her husband somehow brought about the loss of her – gumption. Ever-worsening arthritis left her almost a prisoner in the house until eventually a stroke took her in her sleep. And how very alone and vulnerable Claire felt now. She knew how irrational it was, but the fear of death accompanied her through each and every day – the thought of Nina having to leave their island home to live with a bad-tempered father in England was horrifying. Nina loved Arran, and so did Claire. The farmhouse B&B was thriving, they had decorated and added new B&B

rooms, and now that Nina was old enough to be a real help the place almost ran itself.

Tears stung in Claire's eyes, and she brushed them away impatiently. She was being stupid – there was no reason to think she would die any time soon. But Nina was only thirteen, and the letter should be sent.

She checked directory enquiries to make sure Robert was still at the Bedford house. It wasn't a hard letter to write because all she did was describe the situation. She was careful to say that money wasn't a problem and she didn't want anything else from him. But he should know. And oh, God, she really should tell Nina that Robert was alive. The poor girl ought to have the chance to forge some kind of bond with her father. But would Nina ever forgive her?

She would wait and see what Robert's answer was before she did anything.

It wasn't a long wait. Less than a week later a typewritten envelope with a Bedford postmark plopped through the front door. The letter inside was typewritten too, and very short. As far as Robert was concerned, the situation hadn't changed. He had no interest in meeting Nina; he would, however, undertake to get in touch with her on Claire's death, and she should take steps to make sure he would be contacted when this happened. The letter was signed R. Moore.

Claire stared at it blankly. She didn't know what she'd expected, but it hadn't been this. So that was that. Robert was refusing to meet his daughter until she, Claire, was dead, so there was absolutely no point in endangering her own relationship with Nina by telling her about

Robert. It was as well, maybe – she knew she couldn't trust Robert with her child. On the other hand, there was the rest of the family – Nina had aunts, an uncle, a cousin – and Emily and Paul at least were nice people.

'Mum – there's a disco down the Bay on Friday, can I go?' Nina and Bethany stormed into the kitchen, and Claire managed a smile.

'Dad's collecting me, he'll bring Nina home too,' said Beth, her arm linked through Nina's.

Claire nodded, struggling to get the words out. Imagine if Nina had to leave Beth on the island. Chalk and cheese, they were, and closer than most sisters. Dear God – another five years – if she lived that long Nina would be grown up in both Scottish and English law. Robert would be powerless then. You're worrying about nothing, Claire, said the sensible part of her head. But her heart didn't believe it.

'Oh, on you go then. I suppose this is the start of the sleepless nights while you're out gadding,' she said to Nina, who rushed to hug her.

Claire hugged back hard. Forget the family in Bedford. Nina's home was here, on the island, and she had a mum with enough love in her heart to last her daughter a lifetime. Of course she did.

CHAPTER TWENTY

Tuesday 25th July

It was well after eight the next time Nina awoke. For a split second everything seemed normal, but then she saw Naomi's empty bed, and the memory of what Paul had told her the night before catapulted into her mind. She curled up into a tight ball, the pain taking her breath away.

She had been abused. Worse still, her father had organised it. It was the ultimate betrayal, and the only thing in the world to be glad about was she hadn't known him. She'd never loved him. If Claire had known about this, she'd definitely have gone to the police. Or – Nina rolled ever closer into her ball as the pain became torture, searing through her mind – maybe that wasn't as definite as she needed to think. John Moore might have been violent towards Claire too; that sounded quite possible now. If little Nina wasn't physically injured, her mother might have thought that 'least said, soonest mended, cut the ties' was the best approach to take once they were back in Edinburgh with Grandma Lily.

Nina sobbed aloud. There was a dreadful logic about

it all, but the odds were she would never know the answers. If Claire hadn't known about the paedophilia, there would be no reason for her not to demand the financial help that John Moore, who had all that money, by rights owed them. But she hadn't asked him. And didn't that mean that she must have known, and was protecting them both by keeping well away?

A wave of longing swept through Nina. How she wished she could turn back the clock, back to those days of carefree childhood, running wild on Arran, knowing she was loved, knowing she was safe. All she felt now was hurt.

Balling one hand to a fist, she thumped the duvet. She was Nina Moore and she was strong. This was not the time to throw a wobbly, she could do that later when everything was settled here. She would get up and phone Beth – moral support from her oldest friend would be the best possible start to this first day of the rest of her life. She swung her legs over the edge of the bed, and then in spite of her good resolutions she slumped, her head on her knees. In a macabre way this felt like the day Claire died. Nina had spent terrible moments sitting exactly like this in the hospital waiting room, cold coffee in front of her, while Claire's poor ravaged body was cooling in the hospital mortuary. The world had changed that day too. And today it was different again.

Forcing her mind back to the present, Nina pushed herself to her feet. She'd wallowed in self-pity long enough. It was Superwoman time and the first three things on the agenda were a shower, breakfast, and a phone call to Beth.

Paul was up already; she could hear the radio blaring out an old Beatles song downstairs. The routine of having a shower brought some normality back to the day, and so did the smell of coffee that greeted her when she went into the kitchen. She would get through this. Paul's face was pale and apprehensive. He didn't look as if he'd slept much last night either.

'Morning. Are you okay? I saw you were up in the night.' He waved towards her chocolate mug in the sink.

Nina took a yoghurt from the fridge and sat down opposite him. 'Took me ages to get to sleep, but I'm fine now.' A lie if ever she'd told one, but this wasn't the time to start another soul-searching session.

He rose to pour coffee for them both, then leaned against the sink. 'I'm sorry about what I told you last night,' he said, fiddling with a teaspoon and not looking at her. 'I should have left it. You didn't remember, you didn't need to know.'

Nina waved her spoon at him. 'Truth's always better. But I can't stay here any longer, Paul. I'll go to Cassie's tonight, and head back up north as soon as I can, after this. Thanks so much for all your help with the photos, and for staying here last night.'

He smiled, but his eyes didn't quite meet her own. It was clear he was unhappy. 'Right. Well, I'd better be off. Work waits for no man. I'll give you a ring later and see how you're doing.'

He was halfway out the kitchen door before he'd finished speaking. Nina listened as he packed his bag and rolled up his sleeping bag, clearly in a hurry to leave. Was it work pressure – what did he do, actually? – or guilt at what he'd told her? He hadn't asked what she was going to do with the information that their fathers had allowed others to abuse them, but he must realise she would go to the police. He could have done that himself, years ago. After all, he could remember what happened. Maybe he hadn't wanted to acknowledge it. Yet there was the story about the gun... but that could just have been bravado. He would hardly shoot his own father.

Thinking about George Wright reminded Nina of Sam's file.

'Paul!' she called. 'I found something yesterday that said your father spent some time in Thailand a couple of years ago, do you know about that?'

He stood in the hallway, bag in hand, unhappiness all over his face. 'He used to go regularly, but he never stayed longer than a few months. I don't know if he still goes. I imagine it was for the sex tourism. They're a lot stricter about it now, thank God. I'll talk to you later, Nina.'

Nina watched from the study as he flung his bag into his car and roared off towards the town centre. Poor Paul. She poured another coffee and took it through to the living room, comforted by its warmth in her left hand as she accessed Beth's number on her mobile. This wouldn't be an easy call.

Bethany was silent as Nina told her what had happened over the past few days. Nina could hear the wind in the trees; Beth must have taken her phone outside. She would be sitting in the farmhouse sun-trap, the old wooden bench with the view over the water to the mainland. Tears spilled from Nina's eyes and she brushed them away impatiently. How soppy, getting teary over a flaky old garden bench. But like nothing else it brought home the contrast between this dingy, depressing house with its sad tales of abuse, and the island, where there was greenness and fresh sea breezes and people who loved her.

'Dear God, Nina,' said Beth in a low voice when Nina had finished her account. 'Come home today, honey, there's nothing to keep you there. I'll come to Glasgow and meet you off the plane.'

Nina bit her lip. She wanted nothing more than to be back on the island – but if she went home today she would be running away from the new situation, instead of fighting it.

'I'll need to see the police again first,' she said. 'I'll go and stay with Sam's parents tonight, though. And there's the great-aunt I've found – Emily Moore. She's a real duck and I have to visit her again before we come home. But when I do get back I think I'll never leave the island again.'

'I wish I could help more.' Nina could hear the misery in her friend's voice. 'Do you want me to come down, Nina? Tim would manage on his own for a day or two.'

Nina swithered. Beth's presence would make things more bearable, but more complicated too. They couldn't all stay with Cassie. And the B&B was more than one person's job in the summer – Tim wouldn't really manage on his own.

'Don't worry, Bethie. Cassie Harrison will take care of me as much as I let her.'

'Nina – will I ask Mum if she knows anything?' said Bethany. 'Claire might have told her something about it, way back then.'

Nina considered. The two mothers had been good friends from the time of the family's move to the island right up to Claire's death. It was quite possible she'd confided in Morag James at some point. It would even be interesting to know if Claire *hadn't* said anything to Morag.

'Yes – but don't say that I was abused,' she said at last. 'I'm not ready to tell people yet.'

Beth agreed, and Nina broke the connection feeling both comforted and bereft. But there was no time for tears; she had to phone Naomi now and sound like nothing was wrong, which was going to need all her acting skills. Naomi mustn't know what was happening, not yet. For a moment Nina sat glaring at her phone. How the shit she was supposed to break all this to a ten-year-old she had no idea, but there must be people available who could advise her on that so she should see them first. Psychologists or something.

Ten minutes later she was congratulating herself on sounding upbeat and positive to both Naomi and Cassie, promising to join them late afternoon. That would give her time to close the house and talk to David Mallony about what – if anything – they could do about the abuse. 'Alleged' abuse, they would call it. Or even 'historic alleged abuse'. It was depressing, this would come down to Paul's word against his father's, and most likely George Wright would deny everything. Paul would need a lot of inner strength to deal with it, and the fact that he hadn't reported it himself was telling.

An odd thought spiralled into Nina's head. Was it true?

She thought of the anguish in Paul's face last night, and the expression in his eyes when he'd talked about what had happened. Yes, she believed him. One hundred per cent, and the story was backed up by the paedophilia in John Moore's computer too. With evidence like that the police would have to do something about George Wright. She would go now and talk to David Mallony face to face.

In the hallway she bent to lift the little pile of post lying behind the door. Most of it was advertisements, trite and happy little flyers contrasting starkly to her brave new world. There was a new Indian takeaway on the High Street, and the River Fitness Centre was having a half-price weekend at the end of the month, and – oh shit.

Hell. Her heart hammering behind her ribs, Nina stared at the envelope in her hand. Another anonymous letter. The same kind of envelope as the first one, the only difference being it was her name above John Moore's address on the sticky label. And contrary to what David Mallony had supposed, this *had* been delivered by hand; it was under the pile of post – the letter-writer must have watched for the postman approaching then slipped his letter through the door first. Christ, what a ghastly thought. The scumbag had been right outside this door.

Nina dropped the letter onto the desk and used the paper knife and a pen to manoeuvre the single sheet of paper from the envelope and spread it out.

Her breath caught in her throat as she read.

'Bring £20,000 in a sports bag to the crazy golf hut in Wicks Park at 1 a.m. on Wednesday 26th July. Leave it in the doorway. No police if you know what's good for your daughter. We know where she is. And we're watching you both.'

'Oh God,' she whispered. Naomi — but Naomi was fine, they'd just discussed the Harrison's garden fence on the phone. But the letter said 'we'. Who was 'we'? Hands shaking, Nina reached for her phone.

David Mallony was calm. 'You've done the right thing in telling us. I'll consult the Superintendent now and get back to you. Don't leave the house.'

Nina buried her face in her hands. She should never have stayed on here. It was a ridiculous way to spend the summer even if she was about to inherit a fortune. And how unbearable it was to think that Naomi was being threatened too. Money was nothing compared to what she and Naomi had together; Nina knew she would give up the house and all the money in a heartbeat if it meant that her daughter would be safe.

Her mobile rang and she grabbed it. That had been a quick consultation with the Superintendent.

But it was Bethany. 'Nina, I spoke to Mum. She said Claire told her your father was a 'big bully' — those were her words — and that he'd been hitting you both around. I didn't ask more till I'd checked with you but I'm sure there was no thought of sexual abuse in Mum's head.'

'And she didn't say anything about Paul, my father's cousin?' Nina forced her mind away from the anonymous letter and back to the other end of the problem.

'No. I could mention you meeting up with him and see what she says.'

Nina thought swiftly. There was no point in hiding things, least of all from Morag, who'd known her since she was five. The police were involved and unless she was very lucky it would soon be all over the tabloid press.

'Tell her Paul remembers being abused and ask if Mum ever said anything. Thanks, Beth. I have to ring off, I'm expecting a call from the police – there's been another anonymous letter.'

'Oh shit. Nina, take care, honey. Speak to you soon.'

When her phone rang ten minutes later it was David Mallony.

'Plan of action. It isn't likely that this is more than one person, but it's quite possible he's watching you, so he mustn't see that you've involved us. I want you to leave the house in fifteen minutes and walk to the supermarket on the corner. If the blackmailer's watching he'll follow you, but don't worry, one of our men will be trailing you too. Try to act naturally, do some shopping. Leave the back door unlocked and we'll go in via the street behind and wait for you. Okay?'

Nina gripped the phone. 'Okay. Oh, and Paul Wright remembers us both being sexually abused as children. Apparently our fathers hired us out.'

There was a split second's silence before he spoke again.

'I'll get someone onto it now.'

It was horrible, walking up the road knowing that the letter-writer could be observing her every move. Having police protection wasn't much consolation; it was difficult not to look over her shoulder all the time. Nina arrived at the supermarket and wandered round, blindly filling a basket with a variety of miscellaneous items. Sensible shopping was the last thing on her mind. Walking back was even worse; her steps quickened as she approached the house, and shit, her heart was thudding away in her chest – supposing she passed out on the pavement? No, no, look, she was nearly home – oh God, it had never been home – but the police would be inside by this time and she would be safe, and oh, how she needed to feel safe.

Four men stood silent and motionless in the kitchen when she returned, various pieces of electronic equipment in their arms. David Mallony switched the radio on, and loud pop music blared out.

'We'll check the place hasn't been bugged,' he murmured, bending close to her ear.

Nina started to put her shopping away, banging cupboard doors. Surely the place wasn't bugged? A few minutes later one of the men gave David Mallony a thumbs up sign.

'All clear, boss.'

'Did you really think I'd been bugged?' said Nina, turning to David Mallony.

'Almost certainly not, but with the technology available today it's better to be safe than sorry. Okay. There didn't seem to be anyone following you. Nina -'
His face became tight. 'Tell me what your cousin said about the abuse he remembers you both being subjected to.'

Nina sank into a chair, leaning over the kitchen table while she related everything Paul had told her. Telling David Mallony was easier than telling Beth. He noted down the details.

'I'll pass this on,' he said. 'Okay, we have new information about George Wright. It now seems more possible that this blackmailing business could be down to him. He was involved in a very similar scam several years ago, pretending to be a victim.'

Nina remembered Paul's face when he'd talked about his father. Her poor cousin. 'That's what Paul said. I should tell him about this. And Sam.'

'Yes. Unfortunately we don't know where George Wright is. He's spent a lot of time abroad in the past ten years, but he's also been back in the UK for spells in between.'

He was silent for a moment, his face neutral, then he leaned towards her. 'Here's the plan. It's too dangerous for you to walk to the crazy golf hut with the cash, so we're going to turn Sabine Jameson into your double and she'll do it. She'll be wearing a wire so we'll hear everything that's going on. Then we'll be able to detain whoever picks up the bag.'

'Right,' said Nina. Thank God they didn't want her to stroll through the park personally, a bagful of money in one hand. In the dark. Alone. Knowing there was a weirdo lying in wait for her. Hell, no.

'What if the blackmailer notices it isn't me?' she said.

'I don't think he will. You and Sabine are the same build, and you both have blonde hair. Plus it'll be dark, and we can arrange to have some of the lights in the park switched off. She'll be wearing jeans and your sweatshirt or jacket. I'll get onto her now to see when she'll be here.'

He strode into the hallway to make his call. Nina sat with her elbows on the table, her chin in her hands. Not two weeks ago she had been grieving about the senselessness of Claire's death. Now she was a victim of blackmail and threats – not to mention childhood abuse. Talk about changed days.

David Mallony came back while she was trying to work up the energy to phone Paul and Sam.

'Sabine's on her way and she'll stay with you for the rest of the day. She'll appear at the front door in about half an hour and you'll greet each other like long-lost friends. And if anyone at all asks, Nina – friends, family, anyone – you say that she's a friend from university.'

'Okay,' said Nina. 'I did secretarial studies in Glasgow.'

'Fine,' said David. 'Now, when she arrives the two of you should hang about in front of the house for a minute to give the rest of us time to go out the back. Be noisy, move about so that anyone watching will keep right on watching. Sabine will stay with you till she leaves to go to the park.'

'What about the money?' asked Nina.

'The two of you will take a bag to the bank this afternoon. You have to do that in case he's watching you. You'll be shown into a small room and the bag will be filled with money. Then you bring it back here.'

'Real money?'

'Fake money.'

Nina almost gasped. It sounded too incredible to be true. 'I don't think I'm cut out to be James Bond,' she said, and David laughed.

'You won't need to leap across the rooftops. We'll get him, don't worry.'

He nodded reassuringly and left her still clutching her phone. Nina glanced at the time. Twelve fifteen. The number she had for Paul was a landline, but there was maybe a slight chance he went home for lunch.

Luck was on her side, for Paul's phone was lifted on the fourth ring. Nina explained what was going on, omitting the detail that it would be Sabine who went to the park. Unsurprisingly, Paul sounded weary and upset.

'Oh God, Nina, I don't think it was a good idea, telling the police. They'll never prove anything and it's my word against my father's now. It all sounds very dangerous to me.'

Nina swallowed hard. She was lying by omission here and it was so not what she wanted. She'd only just found Paul and here she was endangering their relationship by telling him fibs. But what else could she do? David's instructions had been clear.

'The police'll be watching all the time. I don't like it either, but we need to catch him.'

'Right. I'll come by again after work if that's all right,' said Paul, breaking the connection without saying goodbye.

Nina pursed her lips. It was clear he wasn't happy, and who could blame him? And now she would have to explain what she was doing to Cassie.

Rather to her surprise Cassie took the news in her stride. 'Make sure you do exactly what the police tell you, Nina. I'll tell Naomi you can't come till tomorrow because of business, will I? Oh, and is it all right if we take her to the pool this afternoon? We would both be in the water with her.'

'She'll love that,' said Nina. 'Thanks a million, Cassie. Tell Naomi I'll call her later, and I'll phone you tomorrow morning.'

Was she being too casual with her daughter, leaving her with Sam's folks for such a long time? But it would be impossible to have Naomi here in the middle of all this, and the Harrisons were lovely people. As was their son, who was next on her list to call, and something was telling her Sam might not be quite as cool about what was going on as his mother was. And rats, his phone was taking messages.

'Sam, it's me. I'll catch you later,' she said. It was horrible having all this going on and Sam unaware of it. They'd parted on bad terms after yesterday's call, and she didn't want to be on bad terms with Sam. Either as a friend or her lawyer.

When the doorbell rang David Mallony gave her a little push.

'On you go. It's going to be fine. Remember this is your old friend, now – shrieks of joy, big hugs,' he said.

Nina had never felt less like shrieking joyfully, but Sabine had obviously missed her vocation in the police force. She threw herself into her role with such enthusiasm that Nina responded almost as if she *was* meeting an old friend for the first time in years. They hugged fondly on the doorstep, then Sabine stepped back and pointed up to the top of the house, walking up and down the gravel, asking about the rooms. They remained outside, pointing and talking, for several minutes.

'Okay. Shall we go in?' said Sabine at last, grinning at Nina.

Inside, Nina watched as the young woman pulled a package from her bag and placed it on the living room table beside the photographs.

'My wire,' she said. 'You're doing really well here, you know. Let's make coffee and then we'll get off to the bank. The boss'll have the fake money there by that time.'

Nina breathed out shakily. How normal it all sounded. Coffee and then the bank. There must be hundreds of people doing something very similar right this minute.

If only she was one of them.

Chapter Twenty-One

Nina's feeling of unreality persisted throughout the afternoon. It was difficult to drive the short distance into town and park behind the library, impossible to walk into the bank as if this was any old shopping trip, her and her old friend and everything hunky dory. She felt conspicuous with the empty sports bag – not something she usually carried for an afternoon in town – but at least they wouldn't meet anyone she knew; she didn't have to pretend this was normal. At the bank she and Sabine were shown into a small room with 'Manager' on a blue sign on the door. Nina's sports bag was taken away and returned considerably heavier.

'What's to stop the blackmailer accosting us and stealing it?' said Nina, hugging the bag to her chest as they left the bank. She should try to act normally here – but how impossible was that when her gut was performing somersaults like something from the Moscow State Circus.

'He won't,' said Sabine cheerfully. 'He's made his arrangements for his own good reasons, and he'll stick to them.'

Her heart in her mouth, Nina cradled the bag in both

arms till they were back in the safety of the hired car. Stupid, she thought. It wasn't as if it was real money, and even if it had been, money didn't matter. Naomi was the only important thing and it was unbearable that circumstances had split them up like this. The lump in her throat, never far away since she'd left Naomi with the Harrisons, swelled painfully.

Back at the house, Nina shut herself into the study to try Sam's number again. This probably wasn't the best time to phone him, bang in the middle of the afternoon, but she could try. She listened as the tone pinged out then broke off immediately as he took the call.

'Nina? How weird, I had the phone in my hand to call you!'

'Sam, hi. I'm not disturbing you, then?'

'Nope. We're having a short break before the final settlement. Nina, I'm sorry about yesterday. Is everything all right?'

'I'm afraid not.' It was a struggle not to break down and howl as she told him about Paul's visit and what she now knew about her father's treatment of her, and about the latest blackmail letter and the police in the house. Like Bethany, he was silent while she spoke.

'That's all,' she said at last.

'All! Dear God, Nina – are you coping with this – should I get Dad to come and be with you – I'll come straight back now, I – shit, this is awful.'

Nina closed her eyes. His concern was like Beth's – warming. 'Sam, it's okay. The police are being great; Sabine Jameson's here with me all the time,' she said, realising as she spoke how very alone she felt in spite of

Sabine's presence. This assignment was simply another job to the young detective, who was whistling cheerfully as she washed coffee mugs in the kitchen. Sabine would do her work here and at the end of her shift she would go home and take up her own life.

Sam's voice sounded miserable too. 'It's not okay. I'm sure they'll do their best to keep you safe and catch this person, but shit, Nina, I wish I was there to help.'

Nina forced herself to sound upbeat. 'You'll be home soon. I'm absolutely fine.'

'You are not. And I know you don't want to be involved with me but as your *friend*, Nina, I want to be involved with you. If that's okay.'

It was a struggle to keep her voice steady. He was her friend, in spite of her telling him to get lost, basically. This horrible situation would be so much more bearable if Sam was there with her.

'You know that's okay. And you're right, I'm not fine, but I'm holding it together.'

'My business here needs another hour, tops. I'll go and chivvy them all into this last meeting, and as soon as it's over I'll start back. I'll be in Bedford about nine.'

At five o'clock the doorbell shrilled into silence in the house, and Nina, huddled in a corner of the sofa texting Beth, jumped in fright. Hell, her nerves were all over the place. And she'd forgotten all about Paul's promise to come by that afternoon.

'It'll be Paul Wright, my cousin,' she said to Sabine, who was in the armchair leafing through a magazine.

'Don't forget I'm your old college friend,' she said, and misery flooded through Nina. It felt all wrong that she couldn't tell Paul what was going on. He was much more of a victim than she was.

She introduced her cousin to Sabine, feeling more and more awkward as they all sat down and looked at each other. She was going to have to lie to Paul almost every time she opened her mouth now, and how horrible was that?

'Is your plan still on for tonight?' said Paul. His eyes were dark-rimmed and his face even paler than that morning. Nina tried to sound reassuring.

'Yes. It's scary, but if the police catch this guy it'll get things over with. I'm glad Sabine's here to keep me company. Paul, are you okay?'

His hands were picking restlessly at the hem of his pullover as he sat slumped in the armchair. Nina found it impossible to imagine what he might be thinking. After all, the blackmailer could well turn out to be Paul's father.

His expression was bleak. 'I'll be fine. I'd like to stay for a bit though, if I may. I don't want to be alone today. And maybe you could do with family around.'

'Good idea,' said Nina, exchanging glances with Sabine. The younger woman's face was pleasantly neutral and Nina could take no comfort from it. It was kind of Paul to come; it showed he cared, and she wanted to help him too if he needed support, but... it did make things awkward.

He was visibly nervous, giving very short answers to everything that was said to him, and Nina began to wonder if involving the police had been the right thing to do. Maybe if she'd ignored the anonymous letter thing from the start it would all have died down and disappeared by itself. Paul had spent all his life avoiding what happened to him as a child, and then she arrived and within five minutes she had raked everything up and was rubbing his nose in it. What kind of a cousin did that make her? But there was no way she could start a heart to heart with him when Sabine was here. Nina searched around for something to say.

'Do you know where the secretaire in the study came from? It's so different to all the other furniture here.'

He gave a half-smile. 'I think it belonged to Emily originally, but I'm not sure.'

'I'm going to take it home to Arran,' said Nina. Typical. Another lovely thing that hadn't been John Moore's. She would turn Claire's room in the farmhouse into a study, she thought suddenly. The secretaire could go there, and it would be good to have something of Emily's as well. A real family room.

Sabine started a conversation about supposed old friends, and Nina joined in reluctantly. It was hellish, sitting there trying to chat about things the two of them might remember, and a huge relief when the other woman suggested catching the news on TV. As soon as the weather forecast was finished Nina went through to the kitchen and made a pot of spaghetti, opening a jar of pesto to go with it.

Paul picked at his food but made no move to leave when the meal was over. Nina sat at the kitchen table massaging her temples and watching Sabine wash the spaghetti pan. Dear God, she was exhausted. And she was going to be up for hours yet; no way would she be able to sleep until she knew what happened during Sabine's late-night trip through the park. Plus, and the thought hadn't struck her until now – would she be all alone here when Sabine left? At least Sam would be back by that time... But the odds were that David wouldn't allow Sam anywhere near this place, because if the blackmailer was watching, the arrival of a fit young lawyer would make things even more complicated. Maybe they'd send someone to guard the house when Sabine was gone; after all, there was no guarantee the letter-writer wouldn't break in and torch the place before he went to the park. Bloody hell.

'Nina, we'll talk about holidays,' said Sabine in a low voice, when Paul went into the downstairs toilet. 'If he's still here at eight suggest he goes home and comes back tomorrow.'

When they'd exhausted the subject of holidays Sabine started asking about the photos, encouraging Paul to tell them about his childhood. Nina found it hard to listen as he revealed further details about his mother's increasing dependence on alcohol, and how she'd left Paul to organise his own meals and often wash his own clothes too. She died when Paul was thirteen.

'So you were in care?' said Sabine, and to Nina's dismay Paul glowered at her.

'I don't talk about that time,' he said shortly. 'It's best forgotten.'

Tears were bright in his eyes, and Nina ached for him. Puberty was a difficult time for any child, and Paul must have had it worse than most. She would sit him down for a long talk before she went home, see if she could change his mind about going to some kind of therapy.

She squinted at the clock on the back wall, trying to do it unobtrusively. She was unsuccessful. Paul jumped up from his chair at the photos table and flung himself down on the sofa.

'Oh, don't worry,' he said, his voice shaking. 'I'll be gone soon. I have to pick my girlfriend up after her French class.'

'Paul, don't. We're all edgy and scared. It's all right.' Nina sat on the arm of the sofa beside him.

'I know. Sorry.'

He gave her a brief smile then went to the window, where he stood jiggling from one foot to the other, staring outside. Dark clouds was gathering overhead; by the looks of things it was going to rain soon.

'I'll make more coffee before you go,' said Sabine, retreating to the kitchen. Nina heaved a sigh. It was easier when Sabine wasn't in the room; all the pretending was more than draining. She joined Paul at the window and patted his shoulder, feeling almost maternal, then remembered she had promised to call Naomi. Shit. Right this minute she simply didn't trust herself to talk to her daughter as if everything was normal. Maybe a text message would be better. She pulled out her phone and flopped down on the sofa to text in comfort.

She was in the middle of her message when the phone rang in the study, and her heart leapt into her mouth.

'Oh God, Paul – suppose that's the blackmailer?'

Sabine was in the doorway. 'I'll get it. If it's him he might stay on the line longer if he thinks I'm going to fetch you.'

She left her coffee tray on the table and strode through to the study. Paul wandered out to the hallway, and Nina finished adding smilies to her text and sent the message, hoping Naomi wouldn't call right back. Not that this was likely. Naomi had only had her own phone since her father's departure to South Africa, and sending text messages was still a novelty. Sure enough, just moments later the answering text came in.

'luv u 2. cu 2morrow. xoxo'

Nina grinned. Nothing to worry about there.

She was standing up to see what was happening with the phone when a door slammed shut in the passage and Paul careered into the living room, his face deathly pale and a sheen of sweat on his brow. Nina jumped back.

'Paul! What's happ- ?'

He grabbed her arm. 'Quick! We have to go, now, bring the bag! That was the police on the phone – there's a bomb hidden here!'

Nina's legs began to shake. 'Shit – no – what – '

'Come on, Nina!'

He was pulling her towards the door, and Nina grabbed the sports bag and her handbag and ran with him out to his car.

'Sabine!' she yelled over her shoulder.

'She's still on the phone. It was her police-boss who called. I knew she wasn't really your friend, by the way. I wish you'd trusted me with the truth.'

Nina's stomach lurched as she saw the hurt expression on his face. He propelled her into his car and she flung both bags on the back seat.

'Paul, I'm sorry. They said not to tell anyone, not even

family. Shouldn't we wait for Sabine?'

He shook his head, pulling away from the kerb and gunning the car towards the main road. 'She has to join her boss.'

Nina scrabbled for the seat belt. Would this affect the plan for tonight? And what would the police do about the bomb? 'Where are we going?'

Paul's voice was shaking. 'He said to get well away for a while. They'll be in touch. We'll go to mine.'

They stopped at the traffic lights and Nina sat consciously relaxing her clenched fists. Thank God they'd got away safely. Paul turned into the High Street, and Nina looked out at people wandering along the pavement, on the way to the pub, maybe, or the cinema. Lucky ordinary people. She couldn't hear anything, but the police must be blue-lighting to the house right this minute. Was there a bomb disposal unit on standby in a small place like Bedford? And actually, going to Paul's might not be the best idea.

'Paul, let's go to Cassie Harrison's,' she suggested. It would be so great to be with Naomi again at last.

Paul pushed the car into gear as the lights changed and swung round the corner away from the High Street.

'You don't want to lead anyone who might be following us straight to Naomi, do you?'

His voice was grim, and Nina winced. He was right, they didn't know what kind of people they were dealing with here. David Mallony thought only one person was involved – possibly George Wright – but of course there was no certainty about that.

Nina shivered. George Wright and bombs didn't seem

to go together, in fact it was difficult to understand why anyone would want to bomb John Moore's house. Or – was she the target, not the house? Her and the money? Bloody hell, how improbable that sounded... and the blackmailer wouldn't risk blowing up the money... Of course he might have counted on her leaving and taking it with her – and that was exactly what she'd done. Shit, maybe he was trailing the car. She turned in her seat to see out the back window, but everything looked quite normal.

A road sign indicating Cambridge loomed up and Nina gaped at it. A sense of direction wasn't her strong point, but she did know that Cambridge was in the opposite direction to Newport Pagnell.

'I thought we were going to your place?'

'We are. This is a short cut to the best road there,' said Paul, his eyes fixed on the traffic, and Nina gave up. He must be as stressed by the developments as she was. She turned back to the window. They were still in Bedford, driving past old houses now, each much closer to its neighbour than was usual nowadays.

Neighbours... The police must have warned everyone in the street, but she hadn't seen any neighbours when she and Paul sped away from the house. But if people were told 'there's a bomb in the house next door', they wouldn't spend too much time gathering stuff together before leaving the building, would they? And – there were still no sirens to be heard, no police cars rushing to the scene, no fire engines... And had the police warned everyone by phone? Was that standard procedure?

She glanced at Paul. His face was pale, but there was a

determined set to his chin that hadn't been there before. He caught her eye and his jaw tightened. Nina felt her gut spasm. Something wasn't right. Shit. What was Paul doing? She turned again to see out the back window – still no sign of police activity. Her stomach cramped as a new, horrifying thought entered her head.

David Mallony wouldn't have called on the house phone. The police had radios to contact each other, and even if these hadn't been working for some reason, Sabine had a mobile. Paul had lied about that phone call. Sweat broke out on Nina's forehead – what the hell was going on here?

The car slowed down to swing round a corner, then headed east of town. They weren't going to Newport Pagnell, so much was clear.

'Paul, what's going on?' she managed, her voice shaking.

This man was her relation, she had trusted him, more than that; she'd been glad to find him in the horrible mess of her father's paedophilia and her mother's lie. She'd thought of Paul as a victim, like she was. Now she didn't know what to think.

He blinked across at her, and she saw both pity and determination on his face.

'I'm sorry, Nina. This wasn't what I wanted, but you left me no choice.'

'What do you mean? Paul, talk to me!'

He didn't answer. Nina balled her hands. This was her cousin and she'd trusted him... and now he was taking her somewhere and she didn't want to go.

'I want to get out, Paul. Stop the car, please.'

He gave her a little smile. 'Nina, Nina, it's all right. Don't worry. We'll get things sorted.'

Nina felt panic rising within her. She grabbed Paul's arm. 'Stop! Let me out!'

He shoved her away and the car swerved across the road, narrowly missing a lamp post as it mounted the central island and then thumped back down on the road. A van going in the opposite direction blasted its horn. Nina shrank back in her seat, shivering so hard her teeth were chattering. Hell, she couldn't make him stop the car, and starting a physical fight over the handbrake would be suicide.

They were driving round a run-down district now, and terraced houses lined identical streets. Few people were about. Nina swallowed. She was tensing herself to jump out and run for it at the next corner when Paul pulled up behind a solitary car parked at the roadside, and grabbed her forearm.

Nina could see determination and fear in the brown eyes fixed on her own . 'We're going to get out of this car and into the one in front. We'll do it quickly and very calmly, Nina. I've got a gun.'

Nina gaped at him, her gut cramping. Sam had been right – she didn't know Paul. The sweet, shy man she'd been so taken with was... it was odd, he wasn't quite gone because she could still see him in there, but he was somehow stuck behind another Paul, and this one was a stranger.

Fear made her voice shake. 'Paul – what are you doing? Let me get back to Naomi, please!'

He scrabbled in the glove compartment with his free

hand and she recoiled in fright, dizzy with relief when he produced another car key. Dear God, had she really expected him to bring out a gun? Did he have one?

'Do as you're told, Nina. We'll talk later, I promise.'

He grabbed the bag of fake money from the back seat and strode round to her side of the vehicle, gripping her arm again as soon as the door was open. Nina's legs were shaking so hard she could barely remain upright as he hurried her towards the other car. She moaned inwardly. Her handbag – with her mobile – was on the back seat of the first car. Without that she was ten times more helpless. Shit, she was being abducted and there wasn't a thing she could do about it. Half a minute later they were driving away from the terraced houses.

'Where are we going?' Nina knew it was important to keep talking to Paul. She had read that you shouldn't show fear when you were being bullied, and this was much more than bullying. What was he going to do to her, this man she'd thought she could trust? Bile rose in her throat.

'Paul - ' She started to speak, but he cut her off.

'Keep the shit quiet, can't you,' he said, his voice tight. The engine screamed as he accelerated up the road.

Horrified beyond words, Nina closed her eyes. A picture came into her mind. Arran. Home. The Firth of Clyde sparkling in the sunlight, the Holy Isle dark against the blueness of the sky. Tears burned behind Nina's eyelids. What wouldn't she give to be back there today, as penniless as she'd been at the start of the summer. But that wasn't going to happen.

CHAPTER TWENTY-TWO

Claire's story – The Isle of Arran

Claire jogged along the uneven track, then slowed to a walk as she came to the pathway that sloped steeply across the field back up to the farmhouse. Morag, Beth's mother, had laughed when she'd taken up jogging at her age after avoiding gyms like the plague all her life. Claire laughed back but kept right on jogging. She had to make sure she was as fit as possible. Fit people lived longer.

She knew it was irrational, this fear that she too would die and leave Nina helpless at the hands of the authorities. But having seen both parents die at a relatively young age, Claire's confidence that life automatically went on until you were eighty-something was more than shaken. In spite of her best efforts to be positive, the carefree days of trust in the future had been gone for a very long time.

But – she had almost made it; Nina was eighteen next week. Her daughter was a student in far-away Glasgow now, doing secretarial studies. She was living in a hostel connected to the college, sharing a unit with three other girls, and she was having a ball. It was a heady time, first freedom… but Nina had a sensible head on her shoulders, and it was right she should enjoy herself while she was young.

Claire smiled, thinking about her girl, then frowned. As of next week Nina was an adult and wouldn't have to go and live with Robert if Claire 'popped her clogs', as Lily had called it, but there was no guarantee that Robert would help Nina financially when – if – he did get in touch. Claire's death would be followed by hurt and disappointed for Nina when she discovered that her father was alive and Claire had lied about it. Would Nina hate her for the lie? Oh God, she loved her girl so much, and no matter what she did, one day Nina would resent it. Claire couldn't even revoke the clause about him being contacted in the event of her death because Rob had signed it too. It was a lose-lose situation and there was no way on earth that she could put it right. The only good ending would be if Robert died first – but if he did, they might never hear of it.

Claire panted into the farmhouse kitchen, where Jan, the live-in helper, was making lentil soup. As well as breakfasts, they now gave guests the option of a simple meal at night too. Business was booming.

Claire poured a glass of orange juice and took it upstairs with her. Maybe the best thing would be to write Nina a letter, one of the 'to be opened after my death' kind. She could explain everything and apologise for leaving her daughter in ignorance. That way at least Nina would know the truth, because Robert couldn't be trusted to be honest. Yes, a letter was a very good idea. And it wouldn't hurt to check if Robert was still at the same address – in fact she would call him right now while she was feeling brave. Claire searched through her handbag for her address book; she no longer knew the number by heart and the code had changed since she'd lived there anyway.

Slowly, she punched out the number and listened as the ring tone pringed in her ear. Seven, eight, nine times. Twenty times. There was nobody there. Tired tears of frustration filled her eyes and she slammed down the receiver, then on the spur of the moment she ripped the page with Robert's number from her address book and tore it into tiny pieces. He was gone from her life. Forget him, Claire.

Easier said than done.

Chapter Twenty-Three

Helplessness. The sensation fluttered round Nina's head while nausea dragged at her gut. She was stuck in a car with her newly-found cousin, who was in the middle of a major breakdown – what the shit was she going to do? Her stomach cramping, she tried to steady herself, clutching the door and the side of her seat and hardly daring to breathe as Paul drove on, swerving round corners and flooring the accelerator on the straight. The engine howled and Nina was thrown from left to right, the seatbelt tearing repeatedly into the tender skin of her neck. They were in another housing estate now, quite a long way from the first one, and she hadn't recognised any of the places they'd passed through. The streets became progressively dingier and more litter-strewn, and Nina breathed out as Paul was forced to slow down. At last he pulled up in front of a neglected semi, beer cans scattered across the pavement in front of the house. A fresh wave of dread broke over Nina as he switched the engine off and turned to her.

'This isn't a nice place, Nina, and I'm sorry. But no one's going to think of looking for us here so it's the best place to be.'

His voice was pitched higher than normal and it cracked on the last word. Nina's throat closed in terror. She'd heard that voice before... The blackmailer on the phone was Paul. Shit, hell... Paul had taunted her and threatened Naomi... What on earth was he trying to do? She clenched her fists to stop her hands shaking.

With growing horror she realised there had never been a bomb, or a phone call from the police. It had been Paul, getting her – and the supposed money – out of the house and away with him. He must have made the call to John Moore's phone from his mobile, right in front of her stupid nose while she was sitting on the sofa texting bloody smilies to Naomi. And then he'd gone out when Sabine answered the call... Nina bit back a moan. He must have hurt Sabine, knocked her out, or worse. And oh God – no one knew where they were... What a gullible cow she was, she'd believed every word he told her. But why was he doing this?

Paul undid both their seatbelts. 'We're going inside – and you'd better be quiet about it. Remember my gun.'

Nina said nothing, concentrating for the moment on not having hysterics. She had to get a grip; be in control – but how impossible that seemed now. Paul was waiting by the passenger seat door, and Nina was unable to prevent the shudder when he grasped her elbow and steered her towards the house. She stared round wildly, but no help was at hand. Apart from a little gang of hooded teenagers lingering raucously at the corner about thirty yards away, the street was empty of people.

'Paul, please. Let's talk. I'm sure can work something out.' She tried her best to sound understanding and firm but it was impossible, her voice was shaking. He must know how afraid she was – hell, look at the expression on his face. What a bastard; he was enjoying her fear. That was what those madmen who abducted people got off on, wasn't it? – the feeling of power over their victim.

He didn't answer, and all she could do was stand and watch as he opened the shabby front door, revealing a narrow hallway. A stained and smelly carpet covered the floor and the walls were painted what had probably started out magnolia, but time and touch and cigarette smoke had transformed them into patchy grey and beige. Stairs, the carpeting worn bare in the centre of each tread, rose into darkness on the left, and the stench of poverty and squalor was rife.

Horrified, Nina stumbled as he pushed her inside. 'Shit, what kind of place is this? Do you live here?'

His eyes were shining brightly, and yes, those were tears she saw there... maybe she could still get out of this. Hope swelled painfully in her head.

'Of course not.' The indignation in his voice would have been funny in other circumstances. He hustled her down the unlit passageway. 'This is all your fault. You've ruined everything. I have spent months, Nina, years, doing research, looking for those scumbag paedos, and it was going so well until you arrived and got the police involved. I've met a lot of – undesirable people, shall we say, and this place belongs to one of them. Oh, don't worry. He's in prison. So we'll be safe enough in the meantime and more importantly, no one will find us.'

Paul pushed her into the kitchen at the back of the house and Nina felt a hysterical urge to laugh. She hadn't been impressed by John Moore's kitchen, but this one was ten million times worse. It was indescribably filthy and apart from an ancient-looking gas cooker there were no appliances at all. A thick, pungent smell hung about the place and made her eyes water. It obviously hadn't been lived in properly for a very long time. Paul pointed to a greasy wooden chair and Nina sat, shuddering. Her legs had lost their strength again.

Paul laughed mirthlessly. 'Not quite up to your standards, is it?' he said, the sneer in his voice increasing Nina's fear.

She looked at him bleakly, unsure how to reply. This kitchen wasn't up to anyone's standards. Normal people didn't live like this.

'Paul – please tell me why you're doing this. What do you mean, you were looking for paedos?'

Keep him talking, try to get him back on your side, Nina. It was as if her own voice was inside her head now, Christ, was she going mad too? But if he didn't tell her there was no way she could help either of them. Hell, she didn't even know if she wanted to help him after this, but she had to help herself because she had a daughter out there waiting for her. Naomi, Naomi baby, it's going to be all right, please, it must be all right...

He slumped into a second chair and sat staring at her. 'You really don't know what you've done, do you?' he said, his voice a strange mixture of regret and contempt.

Suddenly Nina was angry. 'No, I don't. From where I'm sitting I've done everything right. I was trying to cooperate with the police when I came up against what seemed to be criminal activity. So tell me what I did wrong.'

He was sitting with his hands in the pockets of his jerkin, but now he leaned towards her, his expression malevolent. Nina shrank back into her chair. She would have to be more careful what she said, it would be a mistake to anger him more than she had already. She listened, horror growing inside her as he spoke.

'I've found them, Nina. Most of them. Those dirty old men who paid our dads for – us. I was made redundant last year and I went to your dad for money – I reckoned he owed it to me – and after a little persuasion he gave me what I needed. But it started me thinking, remembering what happened in that house. Those filthy pigs... so I started to look for them. Your dad - '

Nina recoiled at his last words, he said them with such venom, and he was doing it to hurt her. She could tell by the way he watched her response and smiled briefly. There was no way she could keep the anguish from her face.

'- your dad gave me some names, after a little more persuasion, and I looked them up. And you know what? All they wanted was to save their own disgusting skins. Every single one of them. It was child's play to get money from them, but that wasn't the best bit, oh no – I got to see them squirm. They were terrified their dirty little secret was going to come out, and they were all prepared to give me more names as well as hard cash. But I haven't finished, Nina, there are two more I definitely remember doing vile things to me, and I haven't found them yet. And you, stupid interfering madam that you are, have upset the whole bloody thing.'

Nina closed her eyes momentarily, overwhelmed by

the mental picture of what had happened in the attic at the hands of these men.

'And is money and seeing them squirm enough for you?' she whispered.

He laughed again, he actually laughed at that, and Nina began to sob, she couldn't help it. His laughter stopped as suddenly as it had begun.

'Enough? Oh no – but you see I'm going to give their names to the papers. And my dad's name too, and your dad's, even though he's out of it now. That way, the ones I haven't found'll still be terrified, like I – like we were, Nina. And it's not just those creeps from your dad's attic room I found. There are others, too, and some of them did a lot worse things to other kids, pretty little girls and nice little boys like you and I were. I confronted them too and got to see them squirm as well. I'm going to take all their money and then one day, when I've found a nice round number, maybe a hundred, maybe two, I'll give every single name to the papers. Oh yes, that'll be enough. One day. But for now you've buggered it all up.'

Nina stared bleakly. She was a victim of these crimes too. Was she to have no say in what they did with their abusers? Apparently not. But in an odd way she could even sympathise with Paul here.

'If you give the police the names you have up to now they'll be able to find the others.'

'You might be right about that, little cousin. But that's not what I want. I want to stand in front of these kiddy-fuckers first and watch the terror in their eyes. And I should be out looking for them before it's too bloody late, not sitting in a disgusting kitchen talking to you.'

He stood up and rummaged in a cupboard under the sink, pulling out an old piece of rope. Panicking, Nina leapt to her feet and tried to run but he grabbed her arm and forced her to sit again. With all her strength she pushed against him, but he slapped her face with the rope and began to wind it round her middle, tying her to the chair.

'Sit – still,' he said, his voice hissing in her ear.

Nina flinched. She should do as she was told for the moment. She had to stay unharmed; if he injured her she might never be able to get out of here. Trembling, she sat enduring his touch as he went on to tie both her wrists to the struts where the back of the chair met the seat, and her ankles to the chair legs. Whistling between his teeth, he produced a rag, an old tea towel by the looks of it, and used it to gag her. By the smell it had been in contact with motor oil at some point and Nina spat and jerked her head away, but he was stronger. Saliva filled her mouth and the fumes from the rag made her eyes water; dear God, nothing in her life had ever been as disgusting as this.

When she was immobilised to his satisfaction he blinked down at her, and for a second she saw regret in his eyes.

'What I have to do is keep the police occupied with you,' he said. 'If they're looking for you they won't be worrying about what my dad supposedly did, or even about sending bags of cash to the park tonight. Meantime, I'll get on with looking for my last important two. I have to get them, Nina.'

Whistling again, he began to search through the

cupboards. Nina was finding it impossible to breath calmly. The gag tasted gross, and it was cutting into the flesh at the corners of her lips. God knows what bacteria were swimming round in her mouth. Paul must be mad. Psychotic, whatever. His search for paedophiles had a terrible kind of logic, but why was he doing this to her? Why send the blackmail letters, why the phone calls? Maybe he'd thought she'd go running away home, leaving him to continue his 'work' in peace. But now? Holding her in a squalid kitchen was doing nothing to further his cause.

Nina writhed against her bonds; they were much too tight. She could feel blood pulsating in her wrists; it was agony... Hell, how long was he planning to keep her here? She stared at the floor, willing herself to stay calm. Naomi, baby, don't worry, it's going to be okay. But was it?

Paul was watching her, his expression mocking. 'You had it all, you know. Your mam got you out, you had a good life. A proper home – a *baby*. And I know you might need a little persuasion to stay here and help me with this, so I'm going to fetch your baby,' he said, his new high-pitched voice echoing round the bare kitchen. 'Little Naomi, she's always been able to wrap you round her little finger, hasn't she? First I'll go to the police and tell them we were both abducted but I managed to escape. You, unfortunately, weren't so clever, and how would I know where they've taken you?'

Nina struggled to keep panic at bay. He mustn't, he must not bring Naomi here. She moaned into the gag. What could she do now, what could she do to stop him?

Paul smiled, and Nina had to look away because oh, it was like something in a horror movie. His eyes were shining and his face didn't belong to the man she had met just a few days ago.

'First the police and then the hospital. The abductor had a knife, you see. A little realism'll make sure they believe me. I need hospital treatment and that's when I'll go off by myself leaving them all looking for you on the Luton bypass, because that's where we were heading when I managed to escape, isn't it? And then I'll go and comfort my poor little cousin Naomi, she must be so frightened without Mummy. You can stay here together. Searching for you will keep all those policemen so busy they won't worry about what I'm doing, looking up those last two scumbags.'

He took a kitchen knife from a drawer and held it up to the light, watching it glint before stabbing it twice, viciously, into his lower arm. Nina gasped, the shock and the gag combined almost preventing her from breathing. Paul was mad. He would do anything. And shit, fuck...

Blackness swirled in front of Nina's eyes. He was going to bring Naomi back here and she couldn't stop him. So no way could she leave this house even if she did manage to get free. She'd have to wait in this awful place for Naomi... Dear God, what would this do to her little girl?

Paul wound a towel round his bloody arm. 'You know, after what happened to me when I was a kid, nothing much hurts anymore.' He bent over her and jerked the bonds on her wrists tighter still. White hot pain seared up Nina's arms, and tears ran down both cheeks and soaked into the gag.

The front door slammed behind Paul, and she heard a key in the lock.

CHAPTER TWENTY-FOUR

The car engine spluttered into life, then roared as Paul drove off. Nina slumped in her chair, but straightened immediately as the movement caused the rope to dig even more cruelly into her ribcage. Silence fell heavily in the dimness of the kitchen, and Nina closed her eyes, fighting dizziness.

Sweat broke out on her brow as she thought about Naomi. Her little girl was in danger. It was imperative to think carefully, plan what to do. But what could she do, tied to a kitchen chair in a house 'somewhere near Bedford'? The horror of the situation threatened to overcome her, and she forced herself to breathe normally. Passing out here would help no one.

Come on, Nina. For a second she heard Claire's voice in her ear, and it calmed her. And she needed to be calm, because nobody was going to come to this house to look for her. She would have to get free herself and phone David. Her mobile was still in her bag in Paul's car, the first car, but even a house as squalid as this one might have a landline.

But supposing it didn't?

Panic gained upper hand again, and for a few

minutes Nina fought against the rope binding her to the chair, swearing frantically in her head as her efforts caused nothing but pain. The binds were unmoving and eventually she gave up and sat panting into the foul-tasting gag. Dear God – she could choke and die on her own saliva here. Why, why had she followed Paul so blindly when he'd yelled that a bomb was hidden in the house – idiot that she was, she had put her life and Naomi's into the hands of a madman.

Right. It had happened and she had to do something; she couldn't sit here till Paul came back with Naomi. She had to get out, get help, get away. If she didn't she could lose everything, including Naomi, for God knows what Paul was capable of. Think, Nina.

The police would believe Paul when he went to them with his story. To them, he was a victim, not a violent psychopath. Unless – of course! The sudden hope was almost painful in its intensity, and Nina gasped aloud. John Moore's landline was bugged. Paul's call to lure Sabine to the phone would be traceable, so the police would know that he was mixed up in this even if Sabine was unable to tell them.

The moment of relief was short-lived as she realised that someone who was capable of successfully finding and blackmailing paedophiles would have thought of this and used an anonymous, prepaid phone. Nina gave way to the storm of sobs that shook her bruised body against the binds and the hard kitchen chair. Please God Cassie wouldn't leave Naomi alone with Paul. Please God he wouldn't hurt her girl.

The storm abated, and Nina gathered her strength for

a new bid for freedom. She could *not* stay here on this chair in near darkness. Grubby windows only made the dimness more apparent, and Paul had switched the light off when he left. The yellow glow from a streetlight in the lane behind the house was only illuminating the area of kitchen nearest to the window.

If she could find the knife that Paul stabbed himself with and somehow jam it in somewhere, she could maybe rub the bonds on her arms against the blade. It was worth a try, anyway.

By jerking one side of her body she was able to move the chair a few millimetres. The friction of the rope on her wrists was agonizing after a mere handful of jerks, but there was no other way.

Frustration filled Nina's mind as the chair turned oh, so slowly until she was facing the sink and the drawer where Paul had found the knife. She would have to cross three metres of disgusting floor to reach it. Time after time she jerked her body forward, and gradually the chair moved. The tiles were old, old lino, and some were loose, which didn't make her journey any easier. After every five jerks she awarded herself two quiet, steady breaths. The little routine helped her carry on. It was five lashes of the whip, followed by two recovery strokes, again, and again, and again.

Tears of desperation and pain were trickling down Nina's face long before she got to her destination. Blood from her wrists ran down her hands, warm and sticky, and the mixture of tears and saliva soaking into the foul-tasting gag made it more obnoxious by the second.

One last jerk brought her to the drawer. She could see

the glint of metal; there would be a knife in there.

There was. Several painful moments of pushing and shoving with her right arm opened the drawer enough to reveal an unsavoury collection of cutlery, including a couple of sharp knives. The problem was she couldn't get at them. There was no way she could lift anything out with her elbow, and she wasn't able to bend her head far enough to get into the drawer with her nose and chin. For long, demoralising minutes she tried, thinking, shit, this has to work, I've come all the way from the table and it was so bloody painful, I *deserve* it to work. But it was hopeless. In a fit of rage, she pushed against the sink unit with all the strength in her right arm.

The chair creaked and moved, then the backrest parted company with the seat and Nina fell. Her head hit something cold and hard, and briefly she saw stars.

Winded, she lay still, then hope surged through her... if she wriggled a bit she could free her right wrist... yes... one good pull – yes! Her right hand was free.

Barely taking time to catch her breath, Nina pushed up into a half-sitting position, yanked her left hand free and tugged the gag from her mouth before sliding over to the drawer for a knife to cut the rope from her feet.

She was free. Thank Christ. Nina leaned on the sticky sink unit taking deep breaths of revolting air. Both wrists were bleeding, but the wounds were superficial. Her ankles were okay, her jeans and socks had saved them from the worst of the chaffing. She couldn't move, though – her feet had gone to sleep and were tingling back to life. It hurt almost as much as the bonds had.

Come *on*, Nina, she thought savagely. You can be a

wimp later. You have to call the police.

A quick check through the downstairs rooms revealed no phone and Nina moaned aloud. The only other option was to go to a neighbour for help, but would they help her if she did? What kind of people lived round here?

Loneliness swept through her as she realised that she couldn't risk it. But Paul had driven past a row of shops on the way here. She would find them, get someone there to call the police for her, and then come back in case he returned with Naomi.

Nina ran to the front door and jerked it open, stopping dead on the threshold as the sound of rough voices yelling obscenities came from her left. Shit, kids were fighting round the corner. She could hear thuds and screams and the sound of glass breaking. She would go right, then, as fast as she could. No sooner had she made this decision than a crowd of youths appeared from the right too, and Nina slid back into the house and closed the door. It sounded like hell out there. Maybe, if she was lucky, the police would come to break up the fight.

More youths were careering down the street now, and Nina went to look out the back, but yobs were racing along the lane there too. She stood at the front room window – the fight itself was out of sight, but there was a lot of running about and shouting, and the occasional tinkle of glass breaking. Surely someone must have phoned the police, even here. The arrival of a police car would be the answer to her prayers.

The fight continued, more and more kids joining in. And still no police – wait – there was a car coming... Nina's hopes rose, then plummeted.

Hot frustration filled her as she watched Paul park in front of the house and stride up the path, a plastic bag in one hand. He was accosted by a tall youth, who ran up screaming something, and to Nina's horror her cousin pulled out a gun. The youth backed away, hands raised in the best Wild West fashion, and ran off down the road.

Nina leaned against the living room doorway as Paul entered the house. She would show him she wasn't afraid. But she was afraid, she was terrified she wouldn't get out of here alive. But at least Paul was alone; he hadn't got Naomi yet.

'Aren't you the clever one, all untied and making yourself at home.' He waved the gun at her. 'Good job I have this, that's a nice little war going on out there.'

He had a large bandage on his left arm, clearly a professional job. Nina felt sick with dread. Had he managed to get hold of Naomi after all – was her daughter locked up somewhere else? Horror chilled its way into her very soul. There was no point in asking; he could tell her anything and she wouldn't know if it was the truth or not. But she had to show she wasn't beaten.

'Paul – we need to get out of this situation. Let's work out what I can do to help you.'

His eyes were bright. 'I've been thinking about that. You and Naomi – especially Naomi – will be the perfect bait for my poor innocent victims.'

Nina's mouth went dry. He gestured with the gun in the direction of the kitchen.

'What do you mean?'

He gave her a little push towards the kitchen and she walked in front of him, only just managing to breathe normally. But panic would help no one. He grabbed her shoulder from behind and forced her down on the one remaining chair.

'We could get them easily, Nina. Nice pic of Naomi on the right websites and they'll be queuing up to get her.'

'I hope you're joking,' said Nina, determinedly calm. He laughed, and she slumped in the chair. It was no use; he was playing with her. All that effort had been for nothing – she had failed. Dear God, would she ever see her little girl again? She offered no resistance as he lifted the rope from the floor and bound her hands in front of her. When he was satisfied she wouldn't be able to use them he grunted, and Nina smelled both beer and curry on his breath. She let her own breath out slowly. No way could she be sick here.

'Well, the police are busy searching for you a long, long way away,' he said, taking a can of beer from his bag. 'And your boyfriend's with them. Seems a pity really, all that effort for nothing. But they're all very concerned about you. I've told them everything I know and I've been sent home to rest; they won't be looking for me till nine tomorrow when I have to go and make a statement. But I'll pop round and get Naomi first. That old couple won't be able to stop me. Nice little dog they have, but it isn't what you'd call a Rottweiler, is it?'

Nina's mouth went dry. He'd found out where the Harrisons lived and gone to have a look at the place. She spat the words at him before she could think. 'Leave Naomi alone. You don't need to involve her in this.'

He ignored this. 'As soon as she's safely here I'll get her pic on the web, along with one of me when I was a nice little kid too, and go on with my search. Shit, Nina, I wish you'd stayed away from Bedford and left me in peace to do this.'

How she wished that too, but Nina said nothing more. He didn't have Naomi yet. There was still time to escape.

'Right. Upstairs,' he said roughly, pulling her to her feet.

Nina's gut went into a painful spasm. Was this when he raped her?

He manhandled her up the stairs and into the largest room. A stained and smelly double mattress was the only piece of furniture, and Nina was hard put not to moan. Paul kicked his shoes off. He made no attempt to touch her inappropriately, though he stood outside the disgusting toilet while she used it, then made her lie beside him on the mattress and bound her left foot to his right. Nina couldn't stop the shudders as she lay there, Paul's leg warm against her own.

'Sweet dreams!' he said mockingly, and placed the gun inside his trousers.

CHAPTER TWENTY-FIVE

Claire's story – Glasgow

Claire stood in the doorway, her eyes roving the six-bedded bay. The smell and the atmosphere here were almost identical to those in another hospital almost twenty years ago, and for a second the past shimmered in front of her. It was noisier here, with visitors round nearly every bed and children running up and down the corridor. The event she'd been anticipating for months had happened.

Nina was lying on top of a bed by the window, eyes closed. Beside the bed was one of those see-through hospital baby cribs, and in it lay Claire's brand-new granddaughter.

For a moment Claire stood motionless, emotion making it difficult to breath. This was the next generation of her family. In spite of her fears time was passing and life was going on, and in a sudden flash of understanding she realised she had no control, she had never had control, that things happened and would continue to happen in their own momentum. Worrying made no difference.

Her eyes fixed on the baby, she crept over to the crib.

Nina didn't waken, but the baby's eyes were open. She looked exactly as Nina had the day after she was born. Claire pulled up a blue hospital chair, and for a long moment she and the baby held each other's gaze. Claire could feel the smile on her face spread to become joy in her heart.

But how angry she'd been when Nina told her she was pregnant. Still a teenager, not even finished her course yet, unmarried, though that didn't count for anything these days. Claire couldn't understand how the girl had been so foolhardy. It wasn't as if they'd never discussed birth-control.

Nina brought up her pregnancy quite casually over coffee one Friday when she was back on Arran to celebrate Bethany's birthday. Claire was completely gobsmacked – this kind of thing happened to other people's kids, not her sensible, hard-working daughter.

'What are you going to do?' she demanded, and Nina raised her eyebrows.

'I'm going to have a baby, what do you think I'm going to do?' she replied defiantly. 'Okay, it wasn't planned but we'll manage, Mum. When my course is finished I'll get a job and find day care. Alan'll help, too. We're looking for a flat.'

Claire liked Alan, but he wasn't much older than Nina and was in the middle of a degree in business studies. It was a chaotic situation if ever she'd seen one. She watched helplessly as her daughter moved into student digs with Alan, only to move out again four months later and heavily pregnant. So there wasn't going to be a happy end with wedding cake and confetti.

Nina stirred on the bed and opened her eyes. Another lump came into Claire's throat. All the joy in the world was right there on Nina's face, and Claire knew she should show her own delight. For shame, she chided herself. Misery-guts. Try to be happy for once in your life.

'Hello love,' she said, leaning forward to grasp Nina's hand. 'And congratulations, she's just gorgeous.' Her voice trembled, and she could see happy tears in Nina's eyes too.

'Thanks, Mum. Do you want to hold her?'

A few moments later Claire was sitting with her granddaughter in her arms. How well she remembered the time when Nina was tiny; Lily had come to London and they'd had a positive orgy of baby-worship. Those were the days of effortless happiness, and how very much she wanted to feel like that again, for this new little girl.

Claire came to a decision. She would let the past go, because she had to. The past was unchangeable, and the future was uncontrollable. She would live today and be happy. Misery-guts adieu, Claire.

Decision made, Claire smiled across at Nina. The family had grown, there were three generations again. Claire kissed the baby's head. Whichever way you looked at it, she was rich as a king today.

Chapter Twenty-Six

Wednesday 26th July

Nina jerked awake. What the hell – she was – oh God, she was still stuck in this awful house and Paul was snoring beside her. How unbelievable, she had actually slept here. Her gut cramped and she lay still, panting in shallow breaths until the spasm passed. Thank Christ she hadn't woken him. Moving as slowly as she could, she turned her head to look round the room. A heavy blue curtain was pulled across the window, but she could see it was pretty light outside.

Fear was sharpening her brain; she was wide awake now. She had to get out of here, and without disturbing Paul. Ignore the rumblings and twitches in her gut, she inched gingerly away from the malodorous body beside her, taking great care not to move her left foot. Paul's breathing didn't change, and Nina lay motionless, planning furiously. She had to free her foot. Slowly, slowly, she pulled herself into a sitting position, listening all the time to Paul's breathing. It didn't change.

The rope was greasy and difficult to loosen with tied hands but at last she felt it slacken. Squinting at Paul and holding her breath, she pulled her foot from the noose. Hah! She was free.

The snoring continued, and Nina rolled over until she was crouching beside the mattress. If the floor creaked now she'd be done for. Slow-motion, nice and easy, Nina, whatever you do, don't wake him.

Testing the floor at every step, she crept to the door and inched it open. Out on the landing she paused. Should she make a run for it – or creep downstairs one step at a time? Fear was screaming at her to run, quick, as fast as she could, but her head insisted on caution. She inched down the stairs, stepping on the edge of every second tread only, gripping the greasy bannister and going as fast as she dared.

The bottom tread creaked and Nina froze, but no howl of rage came from the bedroom. She scurried through to the kitchen and seized a knife from the drawer, still half-open after her efforts last night. Jamming it between her knees, she rubbed her bound wrists along the blade. A few good sawing movements and she was free. Right. Quick, quick. Hush to the door, and run, Nina, run, as far away from here as you can get.

Fingers trembling, she eased the front door open and squeezed out, the rope burns on her wrists stinging in the coolness of the summer morning. The contrast between the stench in the house and the early-morning air hit her like something solid, but there was no time to stand around taking deep breaths. Away, away; she had to get back to Naomi. Please God her baby was safe in bed at Cassie's and not tied up in some other hell-hole of Paul's.

Stumbling down the path, she came to the next hurdle.

The creaky gate had fallen shut. With the bedroom window tilted and facing this way, she couldn't possibly risk opening it. Jagged branches tore at her clothes and scratched her hands as she forced her way through the hedge – which way now, which way? Nina trembled in silent frustration. She had no idea, but Paul's car was facing right so she turned left and started to jog along the uneven pavement.

The street was deserted; why was no one up yet? Didn't they have jobs to go to? The combatants of the previous evening were gone, but shards of glass on the pavement marked where the fight had been. And dear God, look at the blood in the gutter. Where the hell was she, anyway? Dilapidated houses and litter-strewn side streets loomed up as she continued down the road. In a different area she could have knocked at someone's door and asked for help, but not here.

Her heart gave a great leap at the next corner. Yes! Oh, thank God. They had driven down here yesterday. About two hundred metres up this road was a roundabout, and if she turned right there she'd soon be in a more civilised area; she was so nearly safe. Run, Nina, run...

A loose paving stone wobbled under her foot and she stumbled, her stomach cramping yet again. The thought of Naomi spurred her on, her breath ragged in her ears. The next street she crossed was wider. Hallelujah, there were the shops she'd remembered seeing yesterday. Maybe –

Hope plummeted. None were open yet – but she was nearly at the roundabout now. She would flag down a car. That would be safer than knocking at one of these shabby, anonymous doors. Please God she would find someone respectable, some woman driver who would call the police for her. She had so nearly made it, help was within grasping distance.

The sound of her own heavy breathing meant she didn't hear the car behind her till it drew level. Nina jerked to a halt, dizzy with horror, gaping helplessly as Paul wound down the window; he was laughing, oh God how horrible. This was a hideous caricature of the gentle, shy man who had greeted her the first time on the doorstep of John Moore's house. He leaned out the window and Nina moaned.

'Race you to Naomi!' he yelled gleefully, and gunned the car towards the roundabout.

Chapter Twenty-Seven

Wednesday 26th July

Horror chilling through her, Nina stood motionless as Paul's car circumnavigated three-quarters of the roundabout and disappeared. Her feet felt as if they were stuck to the ground. It took a huge effort to wrench them free and run on. Naomi must still be at Cassie and Glen's; I'm coming, baby, stay safe, Mummy's on her way.

Pain stabbing through her cramped leg muscles, Nina staggered towards the roundabout. No one at all was about, and shit, she needed help. Right now. But the buildings to her right looked like warehouses, and the one across the road was a derelict factory. For a second her feet faltered – should she go back and risk knocking on someone's door? No – onwards was best; a car must come soon, she would flag it down. The thought of Paul speeding towards Naomi spurred her exhausted legs on.

The first car to approach blared its horn and swerved round her when she jumped into the road and tried to wave it down. Bastards. They must have seen that she was in trouble. But of course in an area like this it was equally likely she was out to rob them. Another car was approaching and she waved even more frantically.

The car stopped, and a dark male face glared out, a painful reminder that Sam must be worried sick.

'Please. I need help. Can you phone the police for me?' Her voice sounded ragged.

The man in the car laughed scornfully. 'Yeah, right,' he said, and skidded off like Paul had.

Nina swore. Time, time, she didn't have it. Paul would soon be at Cassie's, and God knows what he'd do when he got there. She had never felt so impotent. It was like one of those nightmares where you keep running and running and it's so important that you arrive somewhere on time, but you can't find the way...

The third car stopped too, and Nina gasped in relief when she saw two women in the front. Panting, she repeated her plea. The woman in the passenger seat raised her eyebrows.

'Police? Why?' Her face was reluctant but not hostile, and Nina bent till she was level with the women.

'My cousin's driven off to get my little girl and I'm afraid he'll hurt her.' It was difficult not to scream at the women, but that would certainly frighten them off. 'Please. Do you have children?' she added, and the women glanced at each other.

'Your cousin from round here?' asked the driver, and Nina felt like shaking them both.

'No, but he kept me in an empty house here overnight. I've just got out. Please, phone the police for me. My name's Nina Moore. Please.'

Again the women exchanged looks, and the driver gave a slight nod. Her companion reached into a bag at her feet and produced a mobile. Nina stood panting. Thank God. Help would soon be on its way. The woman pursed her lips at Nina before punching out 999.

'I guess I need police. Crazy woman here called Nina Moore wants help. At the Leeway roundabout.' She disconnected and dropped the phone back into her bag. 'They're comin',' she said, winding the window up again. 'And we're goin'.'

The car jerked as the driver slammed the gearstick in and drove off. Nina sank to her knees on the dirty pavement. Oh God. She had no way to tell if the woman really had called the police. And even if she had, they still didn't know to protect Naomi. Should she stop another car?

But the next two cars didn't stop and after that there was a lull. Nina trudged towards the roundabout. She had failed. Paul would have reached Cassie's by this time. All she could hope was that Naomi would be asleep in bed. And she might be, she wasn't an early riser. But then again, if Paul rang the bell and introduced himself, there was no reason for Cassie and Glen not to believe whatever he told them, even if they did know by this time that Nina was missing. After all, Naomi knew Paul. Worst case, Sam's parents might even waken Naomi and bundle her into Paul's car.

Nina stood at the roundabout, dry sobs mixed with shivers shaking her body. She had never felt so out of control and so – beaten. Nobody stopped to help her; there were no good Samaritans at the Leeway roundabout this morning and dear God, she was so dead. What would Paul do with Naomi? He would be furious that Nina had escaped, Christ, it would be all too easy for a grown man who was mad and hurt and unhappy to take out his frustration on a small girl... Please God he won't hurt Naomi... Nina buried her face in her hands. If the woman had called the police they should be here any second, surely. But it was another five minutes before she saw a blue light flashing in the distance, swooping up to stop beside her.

'Christ, Nina.' David Mallony was out of the passenger seat and helping her into the back before Nina could draw breath.

'Paul. He's gone to Cassie Harrison's to get Naomi,' she whispered, and David pulled out his radio.

The car sped off, Nina slumped in the back seat. She had done all she could, but – would it be enough? Naomi was still in grave danger... David was here; she wasn't alone any more – more than that, she was safe – but how unimportant that was beside what could be happening to her child. Nina sat shaking, taking noisy, painful breaths, unable to stop her teeth chattering.

David clicked his radio off and turned to her. 'They're onto it. Are you hurt? Do you need a doctor?'

Nina shook her head. 'Sabine?' she whispered again. It was easier than talking.

'Alive but unconscious. She has a serious head injury, but she's stable,' said David. 'Nina, tell me everything.'

In a few short sentences Nina covered the horror of the past several hours. Unfortunately she hadn't noticed what make either of Paul's cars were, all she could say was that the first was silver and possibly an Opel, and the second light green metallic. She described the house she'd been held in, then listened while David passed on the information over his radio. And all the time she was trembling so hard it was painful, and her breath was burning in her throat.

Bedford town centre didn't look as if anything untoward had ever happened there, and Nina gazed out at now-familiar streets, willing the car to drive faster. She felt as if an elastic band at breaking point was holding her gut together. Soon, soon she would know if Naomi was safe; this not knowing was the worst, the most terrible thing. She had tried so hard, but it might all have been too late.

The minute the car stopped at the police station Nina scrambled out to see if there was any news. Sam was waiting outside the door, and he seized her and hugged her hard and God, how awful she looked and she stank too, she knew she did, of that terrible house and all the stress and sweat, but Sam was holding her as if he'd never let her go.

'Naomi?' she said into his chest. She felt his body tense up and pulled away to see his face.

'Nina, we'll find her,' he said, but his voice was dull.

Oh God. Darkness swirled. But she'd known really... Naomi... her baby. The elastic band broke and Nina retched painfully then swallowed burning saliva.

David Mallony finished talking to another police officer, then strode across and gave her arm a little shake.

'Nina, you have to hold it together. Wright's got Naomi. She went out to the garden with the dog a short time ago, and when she didn't come back Cassie Harrison went out to look, and found the dog but no Naomi. We have to assume that he has taken her. I need you to tell us every detail you remember about where you went, and what Wright said.'

Nina stepped away from Sam and felt the world sway. Shit, she had to get a grip here. 'Try her mobile. It's 078432084.' David nodded at another officer.

Nina sat in a grey interview room, Sam beside her holding her hand while she dredged up every detail of the past twelve hours. Someone brought her tea and toast, and she picked at it. She had to keep her strength up but Christ, how impossible it was to eat toast when her daughter had been taken by a madman. Naomi must be terrified. She would realise very quickly that Paul wasn't normal and dear God in heaven why had nobody picked up on this long ago?

A young officer appeared with the news that Naomi's mobile was beside her bed at the Harrison's, and the brief hope that she'd be easily traced was gone. Nina closed her eyes. Could nothing go right for them? Here she was, Naomi's mother, and all she was doing to help was tell a couple of police officers about the state of the bloody lino in the kitchen she'd been held in. Fear for her child was eating its way through Nina's gut, and she clutched her middle. Oh God. She was going to be sick soon.

A police doctor, a woman, arrived halfway through her statement and insisted on dressing Nina's wrists. Nina sat still, not heeding the sting of antiseptic and refusing to halt the question and answer session with the police officers. Any one of these questions could be the one that helped find Naomi. Before she was finished news came in that the police had found the house she'd been held in, but there was no sign of life there. Paul's own flat in Newport Pagnell was deserted too. Nina shuddered. Paul, by his own admission, had spent the past year tracking down paedophiles. Not only that, he now wanted Naomi to 'help' him – he was going to put her photo on some ghastly website... Suppose he had taken Naomi to another place he thought wouldn't be found? This place could easily be connected to one of the 'kiddy-fuckers' he'd been meting out his self-justice to.

Saliva rushed back into Nina's mouth and she swallowed it down to churn around in the tea and toast mess in her stomach. Never in all her life had she been so afraid; even breathing was painful. Suddenly she remembered something.

'Paul spoke of a girlfriend. Melanie.'

David nodded. 'We'll check that too. We'll be searching his home.'

Nina sat back. There was nothing left to tell them; nothing more that could help find Naomi. This was worse than any nightmare, a hundred times worse than the fear for her own safety was the previous day. Waves of numbness were alternating with waves of panic. This very minute her child could be tied to a kitchen chair somewhere, helpless and terrified. The mass in her stomach shifted and Nina ran for the toilets.

Sam was waiting in the corridor to hug her after she'd been sick and dear God she needed someone to hold on to. Sobbing, Nina clung to his jacket.

'I should never have left you,' he said into her hair.

'Nina, I wish I'd been there for you.'

'It wouldn't have stopped him,' said Nina, hearing the dreariness in her own voice. 'Paul wants revenge and he wants money, and me coming here and involving the police stopped him getting both and it's made him mad, Sam. Why the hell didn't I notice sooner? I was so caught up in this bloody finding-family thing that I wasn't thinking straight, it was all cousins together, and I wanted a cousin, I wanted a family, and shit, why didn't I notice?'

Sam led her back to the interview room. 'He was clever. He said all the right things.'

Nina sat down again. The police officers had gone, and there was another cup of tea waiting for her. She pushed it away. 'Do you think he'll let me buy her back?'

She rocked back and forward on the police station chair, and Sam rubbed her back without speaking. Nina was grateful for his silence. There was no reassurance anyone could give her right this minute.

David Mallony came back in and leaned on the table. 'We're going to drive around with you, see if we can find where you changed cars,' he said. 'Paul may have a base of some kind nearby.'

Nina, David, Sam and a policewoman drove around for over an hour before Nina admitted defeat. They found the district where she and Paul left the first car, but she couldn't remember enough to pinpoint the correct street. They were all so alike, with their identical council terraces and scrappy front gardens. She'd been absorbed in Paul at that point; she hadn't been watching where they were going. There was no sign of the car, either; Paul must have moved it.

'Okay – at least we've got the area,' said David eventually. 'We'll get a house-to-house inquiry going. Someone may have seen Paul. You should rest, Nina. You're exhausted.'

David drove them back to John Moore's house, where the first thing Nina did was have a boiling hot shower. Not that she cared how she looked or smelled, but all that was keeping her going now was the thought that any minute, Naomi might be found. Which meant she had to be ready to go at a moment's notice to help her child. She emerged from the bathroom to find Sam packing her things into her case and two plastic bags.

'You're not staying here another minute,' he said.

All she wanted was to leave this house forever, but – 'What if he comes back here? What if he phones?' she whispered.

'He won't, he knows the landline's bugged. And it's up to the police to watch the place. They're going to seal it, anyway. Come back to my flat, Nina. Or Mum and Dad's.'

The memory of Naomi happily preparing to paint Glen Harrison's fence flashed into Nina's mind and her legs turned to jelly. She fell to her knees, head bent to the floor, sobs shaking her body. Sam knelt by her side, patting her back but not attempting to stop the tears.

'Nina, there are dozens of police officers out searching,' he said. 'Don't give up, they must find her.'

Sniffing, Nina allowed him to help her to her feet. How very much she wanted to believe what he had said. But how often did you read about little girls being taken and then found later in ditches, raped, bleeding, dead. And Paul would be angry about what had happened, he'd be looking for revenge not only on his own abusers now, but also on her. On the other hand, he knew from his own experience what sexual abuse did to a child. So he wouldn't allow the same thing to happen to Naomi, would he? He was a victim – but then weren't paedophiles often victims first, and then lost themselves in a never-ending vicious circle, repeating the abuse they'd been subjected to?

The numbness was returning, replacing pain with blessed nothingness, though Nina knew if suffering would bring her girl back, she would take it all. She grasped the handle of her suitcase. 'Let's go to yours. And I should phone Beth. And Naomi's Dad. But first I want to call David; there might be more news.'

Unlikely, in the forty-five minutes since she'd seen him last, or he'd have phoned and told them. But David was all the contact she had to Naomi at the moment, and oh, what a frail thread of contact it was.

Sam handed over his mobile, and she called David on the way to Sam's flat.

'Nothing yet. We've got dogs out in the areas you were taken to,' he told her. 'Mrs Harrison gave us Naomi's nightgown for the scent. Rest up for the moment, Nina. I'll call you back in an hour or so.'

Sam's flat was comfortable and modern, an enormous blue L-shaped sofa dominating the living room, and crammed bookshelves round two walls. Nina sank into the sofa, dread weighing her into the cushions. Thoughts of Naomi were circling round her head in a quite unbearable spiral; but she had to bear it because, oh fuck – she had caused it. She had caused whatever was happening to her child today.

Why the hell had none of Paul's teachers or social workers seen that he wasn't normal? The abuse he'd suffered as a child must have unhinged him, but no one had helped him, and heaven knows how long he'd been like this. Nina shivered. She must have been affected too, how afraid she would have been, a poor little wide-eyed three-year-old who didn't understand what was happening to her. Incredible to think she'd managed to block out something as momentous as sexual abuse. She had no memories of it – how had she been abused, and how often, and by how many people?

A lump rose in Nina's throat. Claire had told Morag that John Moore had been 'hitting them both around'. Had Claire known about the sexual abuse and simply not told Morag? It didn't sound like Claire, and she and Morag were such good friends. So either Claire knew nothing or... the thought was like a sudden breeze of fresh air...

...or little Nina hadn't been abused. Was that possible?

Fighting the weakness that was still threatening to overcome her, Nina thought about her three-year-old self. According to what she knew, she'd been a talkative, confiding child. Wouldn't she have spoken about it to Claire, or Lily, if anything bad had happened to her? And as paedophiles normally abused either boys or girls, but not both, it was actually unlikely that both she and Paul were victims of any one group of abusers.

The one thing Nina was sure of was that Paul had been

abused. He couldn't have lied about that so convincingly. She'd seen all the way into his soul, that night he told her about it. So if Paul had lied about her being abused, he'd done it to scare her away and leave him in peace to continue his revenge scheme. The blackmail letters and the calls hadn't worked, so he'd notched up the horror-programme for her.

Nina sobbed aloud. There was no way to know, but surely, surely, Claire would have intervened if she'd known that Paul was being abused?

Sam appeared from the kitchen with a glass of orange juice and a sliced banana on a plate.

'Eat,' he said briefly. 'I'll phone Mum and tell her you're here.'

He left her alone, and Nina managed two pieces of banana and a sip of juice before pushing the plate away. Was Sam on his landline? She wanted to phone Bethany.

He came back and gave her the handset almost as if he had heard her thought.

'Mum's coming up later,' he said. 'She's in a bit of a state; she feels it's her fault.'

'It's not,' said Nina, her voice thick. 'He would have got Naomi even if she hadn't been outside. I'm sure he had plenty of tricks ready. Look how he got me into his car – false bombs and everything. He was so convincing, Sam – it's my fault, not Cassie's.'

And if anything happened to Naomi today Nina knew she would blame herself for the rest of her life.

Sam patted her shoulder. 'I'll leave you to call Beth. Eat that banana, Nina, it'll give you energy.'

As soon as she heard Beth's voice Nina dissolved into

tears, and it was a few minutes before she was able to talk coherently. Beth was horrified, and for more long minutes all they could do was cry together.

When she ended the call Sam came back and sat beside her on the sofa. Nina sipped her juice, her teeth chattering against the rim of the glass.

'This is like waiting for Mum to die,' she said. 'She was in a coma for days. I was pumped full of adrenalin all the time, ready to cope with her death. I hardly slept. And now – it's the same kind of feeling again. Sheer horror and nothing to do but wait.'

Sam put an arm round her and Nina closed her eyes. When would she be able to hold Naomi in her arms? Dear God, she'd known about the paedophilia but she still allowed her only child to come and be a part of it all. She'd been the worst possible kind of mother to her little girl. If only... if only she'd never heard of John Moore, never come to Bedford, and never inherited all that blood money.

In and out, in and out, there was nothing to do except breathe and wait for news to come.

Chapter Twenty-Eight

Thursday 27th July

Nina slept fitfully on Sam's spare bed that night, fully clothed in case the police called and she could rush to Naomi. Going to bed when there was still no news of her child was horrendous, but she was so tired... She'd phoned Alan, who was distraught but decided to wait in South Africa in the meantime. Nina could almost understand this, after all, she and Alan would draw little comfort from each other's presence and the journey from Cape Town was over twelve hours even after the plane took off, and dear God surely Naomi would be found by that time. But it was another rather chilling reminder that she was the only 'close' family her child had.

David Mallony called shortly before midnight to report they would continue door to door inquiries the next day, but in his opinion Paul had taken Naomi somewhere else.

'This wasn't how he'd planned things; he'll need time to re-think,' he said. 'We'll put out an appeal tomorrow, Nina. Can you get us a recent photo of Naomi? You won't have to speak; we know who has Naomi so all we need is a police appeal to the public to keep their eyes open. And of course all the airports and ports are already alerted. He won't get her out of the country but I don't for a minute imagine he's trying to. He'll be holed up somewhere making new plans.'

Nina's sleep was broken, full of dark, frightening dreams. Every so often she jerked awake, heart racing, only to fall back into uneasy sleep. Dismal visions of Glen and Cassie and Emily, all shouting 'help, help', chased no less fearsome dreams of Claire and her bruised and broken face. Nina awoke at six with tears on her cheeks and knew she wouldn't sleep again.

There was silence from Sam's room as she crept past to the phone and punched out the number of the police station, only to be told there was no news but the search parties were already out again in the estates. Nina stood by the kitchen window, forcing back panic. It was a beautiful morning; brilliant sunshine mocked her as it sparkled on the chrome sink. Inside she felt as dark and oppressive as it was possible to feel, and that wasn't going to change until she had her girl back. Today, please, that must happen today.

She showered mechanically, breathing deeply as the piping hot water flowed over her weary muscles and feeling about a hundred and fifty. Were old people like Emily tired and sore like this all the time? It was a horrible, draining feeling.

Emily... Emily had said quite a lot about Paul. But... Nina stood still, remembering. She'd missed part of it. For a few moments in the middle of the conversation she'd been thinking about something else, hadn't she, yes – the names on the list. She'd missed some detail about

Paul. Emily had a phone in her bungalow, but quarter past six was much too early to call. Nina pulled on jeans and a sweatshirt. She would wait till seven and phone the home, ask someone to check if Emily was up. And later she and Sam could go to The Elms. Her great-aunt might know something about Paul that would help find Naomi. Nina shivered. Talking to Emily was the only bloody thing she could do. The police weren't going to let her and Sam go out and search housing estates, but no way could she sit around all day and wait. She had to do something to help find her child.

Sam still hadn't surfaced, so Nina booted up his computer. Beth had e-mailed two photos for the police appeal. Taken a couple of weeks ago, one showed Naomi laughing as she played with Fifi the farmhouse cat, and the other a more earnest Naomi doing a jigsaw on a rainy afternoon. Nina sent them on to the police station, then sat sobbing over the keyboard. Naomi had been missing for twenty-four hours; the 'golden hours' were long gone.

'Hey, come on. Come here.' Sam was beside her, gathering her into his arms.

Thank Christ Sam was here. She wouldn't have managed any of this without him. Nina told him about her feeling that Emily might have mentioned something about Paul.

'Good thinking,' he said. 'And that goes with something that occurred to me in the night. You should take every one of those photos to show Emily, because one of them might remind her of something that could help.'

'Hell, Sam, there's hundreds of them. Do you think she'll be able to get through them all?'

'I'm sure she'll give it her best. It means telling her what's happened, but you have to do that now anyway.'

Nina pictured Emily's kind old face and the lump in her throat grew again.

'I need a mobile,' she said dully. 'I need to have a number for the police and Beth and Alan and – in case anyone has to contact me.'

Another thought struck her and she winced. 'Oh God, I don't know anyone's number any more...'

'You can borrow my old mobile,' said Sam. 'If you send everyone on your email address list a mail with the new number they can get back to you with theirs.'

He produced the phone, and Nina wrote her email and sat clicking through her address book. She arrived at Claire's address and burst into sudden, shocking sobs. She would never send Claire another email.

'Dear God, Sam – why, why, why didn't Mum tell me about John Moore? None of this would have happened if I'd known.'

'She couldn't have known what he was,' said Sam.

Nina closed her eyes. She would never understand it. How on earth had Claire managed not to know what her husband was? It didn't seem possible.

Sam was watching her face. 'Do you believe she was doing what she thought was best?'

'Yes.' It was a gut reaction. There was no way she could doubt Claire's intentions.

David Mallony was out at one of the estates, but his sergeant broke the seal on John Moore's door for Nina and Sam. He told them Sabine was still critical in the intensive care unit, and Nina felt her face blanch. Paul had injured Sabine to this extent before he'd lost it so completely. Now he'd be capable of even more craziness and violence...

The sergeant also showed them the text of the appeal due to go out on TV and online that morning. It was short, simply asking for information about Naomi, who was 'with a distant relative in need of medical attention'. Nina read it, her lips pressed together hard. How many times had she seen a similar appeal and thought vaguely that at least the child concerned was with a relative? She'd had no idea. She swept the photos into a plastic bag and almost ran from the house.

At nine-thirty they were parking under the big tree at The Elms. Emily was waiting, the coffee table cleared in anticipation of the photos. She put her arms round Nina, patting her back in a frail, old ladyish way, and Nina only just managed not to cry again.

'Oh Emily. We need to know everything you can tell us about Paul, please. We don't know enough to find him and Naomi. And I think you said something last time but I can't remember what it was.'

Emily sat back. 'He was a strange child,' she said frankly. 'A sweet little boy, but as he grew older he became wild and distant. His mother was a nice girl when she was sober but she was an alcoholic, poor thing. I didn't see much of Paul after you and your mother left. That broke up the family; there weren't many Sunday lunch parties after that and I was too busy with my own life to worry about Paul. Then later his parents split up. He was sent to boarding school, I'm not sure when. After Jane's death, I think.'

'I see,' said Nina. 'We didn't know that; he skated over it when he was talking to me and later he clammed up when Sabine asked him. Do you know why he was sent there? Was it because there was no one to take care of him or - '

She broke off. Emily was frowning and shaking her head.

'Well, there was that too, but I rather think there was something more. I remember shortly before Jane died – Paul must have been eleven or twelve – she had him at some kind of nerve doctor, a psychiatrist, I suppose. I think he was having problems at school, and I always assumed it was because of Jane's alcoholism.'

'A psychiatrist,' said Sam, sitting straighter. 'Jeez, Nina, that explains a lot. Childhood trauma can cause... um...'

Nina gave him a warning look. Emily still knew nothing about the paedophilia or the abuse, they should break the news gently. She soon saw that she had underestimated her great-aunt.

'Young man, you're talking in riddles,' said Emily, frowning at him. 'What trauma do you think caused Paul's problems?'

Nina glanced at Sam and took Emily's hand. It was time to tell the truth.

'It seems his father and others abused him sexually when he was a young boy,' she said, hearing the tremble in her voice. 'At least Paul says they did, and at the moment it appears to be true. I'm sorry, Emily. There were paedophilic images on John Moore's computer, too.'

Emily sat still, then gave a sigh. 'There is such

wickedness in the world. All you can do is hope you never come across it,' she said softly. 'And now we have. My own sister's boy. And your father.' She reached towards a box of tissues on the coffee table, her hand shaking visibly. Nina was unable to keep her own tears back, and for a moment they both sat wiping their eyes.

Emily tucked her tissue into her sleeve. 'The important thing is to get your Naomi back. We can deal with Paul later. He needs help.'

Sam unpacked the photos, and Emily fetched her powerful magnifying glass. Nina sat beside her making a list, as she had done with Paul. Come to think of it, Paul hadn't been happy doing this, so maybe there was something on one of the photos. He'd been very interested in the non-people ones too, so it was important to look at them all.

Nina had filled three pages of her notebook when Emily wilted. Alarmed at her aunt's pale face, Nina rang the buzzer for the warden.

'Yes, that's quite enough for the moment,' said the woman, helping Emily to her feet. 'Come on, Emily love, you can lie on your bed and rest for an hour or two.'

'I want to go on. We might find something important,' protested Emily, and Nina squeezed her hand.

'I'll leave the photos and the pad,' she said. 'If you're up to it later you can carry on yourself, and we'll phone this afternoon anyway to see how you are. But don't make yourself ill, Emily. You've been a great help, thank you so much.'

The mobile Sam had lent Nina trilled out its sea shanty ring tone when they were on the way back to Bedford, and she scrabbled in her pocket for it, her heart pounding. Was this - ?

David Mallony's voice was grim in her ear. 'No news yet, though we've ruled out a few places,' he said tersely. 'But there's information coming in about the Wright family. I won't tell you on the phone but - '

'We'll be with you in – ten minutes,' said Nina, glancing out. And how horrible it was that she'd driven up and down this road so many times now that she knew within a couple of minutes when they would arrive anywhere. Her summer should have been on Arran, with Naomi pony-trekking and running wild along the beach. Not this.

Nina's breath was catching in her throat as they hurried into the police station. Information that couldn't be passed on over the phone wasn't going to be good news. And it wasn't.

'Paul's girlfriend doesn't seem to exist,' said David Mallony. 'That was presumably a ploy to make you feel safe in his company. Okay, George Wright is currently in Thailand. Colleagues there are out looking for him but as he's apparently been there for weeks there's little doubt he's unconnected with what's been happening here. When they find him we'll have him questioned about the abuse Paul's accusing him and John Moore of. But we can be fairly sure that Paul himself is our blackmailer this time round. And I'm afraid that's the good news.'

'Shit,' said Nina. What was coming now? Not the worst news, because Naomi was still missing – could there be any other bad news?

'There are paedophilic images on Paul Wright's computer too,' said David, his eyes holding hers. 'Seven in all. Three of them are the worst grade. Now it could be that Paul was doing what he said, researching the abuse dished out to him. Many victims do that, so at the moment we have to keep an open mind about what it means.'

Nina gripped the arms of the chair she was sitting in. Was Paul a paedophile too? And – worst grade? What did that mean? She tried to speak but failed, dear God, all she wanted to do was curl into a ball and howl. No. That was wrong. All she wanted was five minutes with her so-called cousin. What wouldn't she be capable of doing to the man who had taken and quite possibly harmed her daughter. The thought of what might have happened to Naomi – of what might be happening right this minute – crashed into Nina's brain and she choked, fighting for control.

David fetched her a glass of water. 'Try to stay calm. He told you he was 'researching'. At the moment there's no reason to think he'd be abusive in that way himself. His former employers have given him a good character, too. He lost his job through no fault of his own. Don't imagine the worst before we know more.'

Nina sat back, feeling the numbness take over again. She passed on what Emily told them about Paul, then buried her face in her hands. If Paul intended to use Naomi as bait for the men he was still looking for, God knows what he would do. Maybe that had been his intention all along, ever since he'd seen what a beautiful daughter she had. Naomi could be anywhere if that was the case.

'And you're quite sure she's in this country?' Sam asked the question for her.

To Nina's relief David Mallony was positive about this. 'Yes, the ports and airports were alerted as soon as we knew Wright had her. She's in the country, and the odds are he hasn't taken her too far away. The appeal's being broadcast regularly, Nina, and people are keen to help in a situation like this. It's quite probable we'll get reported sightings of Naomi all over the place. We'll check them all out, but the likelihood that they *are* Naomi is small. So don't get your hopes up with every sighting, that would drain you.'

Nina swallowed. How was she supposed to not get her hopes up? The hope was almost killing her every single second, because it was all she had left to hold on to.

'Where do we go from here? Should we print posters and things?' Her voice sounded almost normal – how the shit was she managing to sound normal?

'We'll hold off with that for the moment. We're still investigating Paul's flat and his computer, and we're finding all kinds of places to check. I'm hopeful we'll find Naomi in one of them. That's all I can tell you at the moment. And Nina – I don't know if this helps, but – '

Nina gazed at him.

'Very few paedophiles are attracted to both girls and boys. So Paul's abusers probably had no interest in abusing you, back then.'

Nina nodded silently. So she'd been right about that. Did it make Naomi any safer today? Unfortunately not. Paul was on a mission now to get revenge not only on his own abusers, but on paedophiles in general. Many might say it was a worthy mission. But it had put Naomi in terrible danger.

'What do you want to do now?' said Sam, back in the car.

Nina rummaged for a tissue. 'This is doing my head in, Sam. I feel numb one minute and terrified the next. Let's go back to the estate where Paul and I changed cars. Maybe if I walk about a bit this time I'll find where he parked.'

Sam drove to the top of the High Street and turned left over the bridge. Nina pulled out the mobile he'd lent her. Several people had sent messages of support, but of course the one name she wanted to see on the screen wasn't there. Oh God, if only she could press a couple of buttons and have Naomi's voice in her ear. She wrenched her gaze from the mobile out to the street they were driving along. Sam stopped at a zebra crossing and a little family of four passed in front of the car, and Nina stared bleakly. This could be her and Sam, in another time and place. A white, blonde mother and a dark-skinned, handsome father, swinging a cute and laughing little boy between them, an older girl skipping along at their side. She squinted up at Sam. His mouth was tight, and she could feel the band of tension round her own head. If anything happened to Naomi she would go away from this place and she'd never see Sam or Emily again and she'd never want to, either.

They came to the estate where the car-change had taken place and Sam pulled up in front of a solitary shop, a newsagent's, where a wire guard criss-crossed in front of the window. Nina hunched into her jacket, cold in spite of the warmth of the day.

'Let's walk about a bit,' she said, and Sam nodded. They headed downhill, and Nina stared round in resignation. There were so many streets, most of them mirror images of the last one; they couldn't possibly walk through them all. This was hopeless. It was the only thing she could do to help Naomi and it was hopeless.

'I didn't see any shops, and the street wasn't as wide as this one,' she said, stopping at a crossroads and looking right and left. They continued down to the next junction, where the intersecting street was narrower. Nina peered to the left and shrugged. This wasn't anything like as poor a district as the one where she'd been held captive, but there was no great affluence here, either. She turned a full circle, looking as hard as she could for something, anything that could give her that one vital clue to lead them to Naomi. There was nothing.

'Hell, Sam, this is no use. I wasn't looking at the scenery; I was concentrating on Paul and how scary it all was.'

He frowned. 'Did you notice any people about?'

Nina pictured the scene, her eyes closed. 'I heard kids shouting in the distance when we were walking to the other car. Smaller kids than Naomi. But that's all. There was no one nearby who'd have seen us.'

'Little kids. I wonder if there's a swing park or something nearby,' said Sam, and called out to a passing teenager.

'Hey, man! Any swings around here?'

The youth shook a finger at him. 'You're way too old for swings, Grandpa!' he said, his face one big grin. 'You try 'em out right along there and see!' He pointed down the side road.

'Thanks man!' Sam gave him a thumbs-up.

Nina started along the road, not allowing herself to hope. Crossing the first junction they came to she slowed down, gazing up the narrower street.

'Wait! It was along there,' she said, excitement stirring inside her. She strode along, Sam following. 'Look, we drove down here and – yes, I remember now, I saw that house with the green curtains, we parked - ' She ran further up the road, ' – right here! Quick, quick, I have to phone David, they should come straightaway – she might be close by!'

Nina's teeth were chattering as she pulled out her mobile. She could be within a few yards of Naomi right now.

David's voice was calm, but she could hear the urgency behind his words.

'Nina, get right away from there. Immediately, and quietly. If Paul is nearby with Naomi and sees you and Sam searching around, the first thing he's going to do is leave again. Go back to your car and wait. I'll be in touch.'

Sam was listening in and he pulled her back along the road. 'He's right. Come on, Nina!'

She allowed herself to be propelled back along the road, but it didn't stop her looking round frantically as they went. Naomi, baby, are you here? If she shouted with all that was in her, would Naomi hear?

An elderly woman was trudging along the road with

a carrier bag. 'Looking for something, dearie?' Her voice was rough but kindly.

'My cousin brought my daughter to stay somewhere on this road but I don't know the number,' said Nina, wondering if there was actually any point in lying about it. 'Have you seen her? Ten, shoulder-length blonde hair, looks like me only – better.'

The woman gave a snort of amusement. 'Wait till you hit my age, dearie. I did see a young chap with a girl this morning, I noticed because I've lived here all me life and I reckoned I knew everyone, but these two were new to me. We don't get many casual visitors hereabouts. Why don't you ring someone's bell and ask, if you're sure this is the right street?'

She waddled on up the road. Nina gave up. The police could search more effectively than they could, and the last thing she wanted was to frighten Paul – and Naomi – away from the area. If they were here in the first place. She passed on what the woman said to David and followed Sam back to the car, where they sat staring at each other. New hope was painful in Nina's chest, and she had to make an effort to breathe normally. The police were coming. She could be within minutes of holding her daughter.

Or maybe not. She could be within minutes of sitting in an ambulance as it blue-lighted towards hospital, Naomi with God knows what injuries pale on the stretcher beside her. Or – the worst thought in the world – she could be within minutes of watching police cars scream up and park diagonally across the street, officers running to stretch tape across the entrance to one of these houses – the start of a murder investigation. When her mobile rang she could hardly control her fingers enough to answer it.

'Naomi isn't here,' said David. 'Go at once to the police station and I'll meet you there, Nina. There's more news.'

CHAPTER TWENTY-NINE

Claire's story – Edinburgh

'Waah, Gran – did you really walk up these steps all the time when you were little?'

Claire laughed, feeling her breath catch in her throat as she and Naomi arrived at the top of Waverley Steps, coming up from the train station. The escalators were off, and a tired stream of early Christmas shoppers were pounding their way up and down the stairs, helped or hindered by the wind that was a permanent feature there.

'I certainly did. You get used to it, you know. Let's go and have some orange punch before we visit Santa.' Claire breathed in, smelling the roast-chestnuts-mulled-wine-too-much-traffic smell that was so peculiarly Edinburgh at Christmas. She and Naomi were spending the weekend here, a belated treat for the little girl's sixth birthday.

They wandered along bustling Princes Street, Claire's hand gripping Naomi's. She could hear children singing carols further along the street. *Good King Wenceslas* was followed by *Jingle Bells*. Sweet, high-pitched, slightly out-of-tune little voices, accompanied by a whiff of mince pies from the stand by the roadside – how lovely it was to be back. The ghost of Christmases past. And how odd to think that Nina was younger than Naomi was now when the two of them returned home to Mum and Dad in Edinburgh.

Claire pulled out her purse when they reached the stand, and bought a paper cup of mulled wine for herself and one of orange punch for Naomi. This was perfect, a visit to her home town with her granddaughter – how blessed she was. The tension that had ruled her life for so many years was all but gone – she had made it. Nina was grown up and the two of them and Beth were successfully running the B&B; whether or not Robert was alive and well she had no idea, and while she couldn't quite say she didn't care, it wasn't such a huge obstacle to her peace of mind. Being a Grandma had helped her get things into proportion. She had a wonderful family, a beautiful home... she even went on the odd date now. Life was good. Who cared what Robert may or may not do? In any case she had every intention of living to be a hundred and fifty, so Robert would never have the chance to contact Nina. Miserable git that he was.

Most importantly, she had come to realise that the very fact that in all these years Robert had never taken the trouble to contact his daughter would prevent Nina forging any real relationship with her father. Robert had rejected Nina. And maybe someday the opportunity would arise for her to sit down with her girl and have a frank talk. Explain things. And if it didn't – no matter.

'Can we visit Santa now?' Naomi was jumping up and

down, blonde hair escaping from the Swedish woolly hat one of their foreign visitors had sent her. Happiness surged through Claire. It was almost Christmas and Santa was real; the magic was still intact.

Count your blessings, Claire, she thought. You're the luckier grandparent. You have a daughter who loves you and a granddaughter who thinks you're wonderful. Nothing's worth more than that.

"Course we can,' she said.

CHAPTER THIRTY

As soon as he walked into the room she saw it, and it was all she could do not to scream.

'Don't touch,' said David Mallony. He placed the evidence bag on the interview room table.

Nina stared through clear plastic. Naomi's blue and white striped sweatshirt lay there, unfolded, looking for all the world as if the girl had pulled it off and flung it down on the table.

'Where did you find it?' Did this calm voice really belong to her?

'It was on a sofa in number ten, near to where you remembered leaving Wright's car,' said David steadily. 'This proves Naomi was in that house at some point. There's no sign of either of them now, though, so it may simply have been a stopping-off place. According to the neighbours, the people who rent it are on holiday. And we've found the car registered to Paul Wright, so he must be using the other one, the one you transferred to beside this house. It possibly belongs to the people who live in that house so we're investigating that too.'

Nina sat still, her eyes devouring the sweatshirt. All she wanted to do was rip the bag open and bury her face in soft cotton, blue and white to match the blue sweat pants Naomi wore to play badminton back on Arran. She'd folded it and put it into Naomi's bag on – yes, on Monday. She hadn't seen her daughter for four days.

'It feels as if we're running along three steps behind him all the time,' she said, the pain back in her chest. Oh God – perhaps her heart was broken. 'This doesn't bring us any further forward at all.'

'It still might. We know Wright has access to that house and we'll keep it under observation in case he comes back,' said David, lifting the bag again. 'Nina - '

'I know,' she said dully. 'Go home and rest.' And how impossible was that?

Back in Sam's car, Nina called The Elms, only to be told that Emily was asleep and the warden didn't want her disturbed. Nina sagged in her seat. They had run out of things to do.

'Let's go home, like he said,' said Sam. 'Have something to eat, and you can phone Bethany and Alan. And you know, maybe they'll find something quite quickly now they have his car and that flat to investigate too.'

Back home, he made them BLTs, and insisted Nina finished hers and drank a full glass of orange juice. She didn't have the energy to argue with him. She felt dead inside; the pain in her chest was gone and the agony she'd felt on looking at Naomi's photos that morning seemed very far away. Would there never be any positive news? And talking of news, she should watch the appeal on television. It would be on after the bulletin at the top of the hour. Apprehensively, she stared as TV adverts for this and that danced across the screen. Perfect families, those soap powder people. All clean and smiling and Mum and Dad and the kids. Shit. They said you couldn't miss what you'd never had, but you could, you could. How very much she missed being part of a family like that.

The sight of Naomi's face filling the screen jolted Nina more than she could ever have imagined. First the smiling photo was shown, while a male voice read the text. Towards the end the jigsaw photo was substituted in, and Nina sobbed aloud. How sweet and serious Naomi was with her jigsaw, and right this minute no one could tell them if she was alive or not. No one except Paul. Impossible to imagine what she would do if she lost her child. The thought, the dreadful hope that Naomi might soon be found was all that was keeping her upright today.

Sam hugged her as the appeal gave way to the weather forecast. 'Come on,' he said briskly. 'Millions of people are on the look-out for Naomi now.'

Nina swallowed. 'I want to go back to the police station. If anything comes in I want to be there.'

'Well – let's call by, anyway. You can't sit there all day. And don't forget Emily – we should check on her too and that might be more useful than hanging around at the police station.'

Nina heard his mobile ring while she was in the bathroom, and came out to hear him say goodbye to David.

'The police have your handbag, it was still in Paul's car,' he said, thrusting his phone into his pocket. 'Nina, David says there are reporters camped out in front of the police station, so we shouldn't go there. Thank God they don't know you're here.'

'Hell,' said Nina. 'I suppose should be glad they're publicising it but being hassled by the press is the last thing I need. I'll phone The Elms again.'

She called the warden, and was told that Emily was up again sorting photos and they were welcome to join her. Nina smiled sadly. What a treasure Emily was, and what a great pity it was that they hadn't known each other all this time. A desolate by-product of Claire's lie.

Emily's cheeks were pink and there were two rows of snaps on the coffee table in front of her. To Nina's surprise most of them were from the 'no-people' selection; only a few had recognisable figures in them, and none were anyone she knew. Unless Paul was one of those indistinct children...

'You've found something,' she said, sitting beside Emily on the sofa without taking her jacket off.

'I rather think I have,' said Emily, gripping her magnifying glass and staring at one of the photos. 'I haven't thought about it for years. Your father and George Wright used to go fishing. It was always a 'man-thing', the women-folk stayed at home but sometimes the men took Paul. They went to an old farmhouse belonging to a friend of George's – there was a stream with bass nearby. There are quite a few photos of the house, and some more with different youngsters and fishermen outside – look. You can see that's the same building in the background here... and here. George was a keen photographer and the scenery was lovely, but there are... a lot of photos of the place. I'm not sure what to think.'

Nina bent over the coffee table. A couple of images

were from the black and white selection, but the rest were colour. Five showed rural scenes, both with and without an old stone farmhouse in the background, and another handful showed various figures sitting around the garden in front of the house. Young Paul was there, and another boy. Had George taken these? Maybe the farmhouse was – what a truly horrible thought – a place where her father and Paul's had taken children to be abused. Nina began to feel sick.

'Emily, where is this farmhouse?' she said, taking her great-aunt's hand. And how difficult it was not to scream out loud, for this was certainly another place David Mallony would need to check out.

Emily rubbed her eyes, a distraught expression on her face. 'That's the stupid thing, I'm not very sure. I was only there once; we had a family picnic one Sunday. It was a long time ago, you were barely toddling around. It's not far from Bedford, I know, less than half an hour in the car.'

'I'll call David. I'm sure they'll have ways of identifying the landscape,' said Sam, pulling out his mobile.

Nina listened to his side of the conversation, staring at the photos spread out on the table. How innocent it all looked, English countryside and people from decades ago. But the innocence might have been flawed.

Sam finished his call and gathered the photos together. 'I've to scan them through from the office here,' he said, leaving Nina and Emily looking at each other.

'Scan?' said Emily, and Nina thought how the world had changed since Emily was her age.

'The computer system here can make copies and send

them to the police computer,' she explained.

Sam returned, having forwarded the images, and Nina hugged her great-aunt.

'I'll phone this evening and let you know the latest,' she said. 'Emily, thank you so much. I'll probably see you tomorrow.'

For where else would she go if Naomi was still missing – and if Naomi was found, then Emily would be their first port of call, always provided that Nina didn't have to keep vigil at her daughter's hospital bedside.

It was two hours later when the phone call came. Nina spent the time on Sam's sofa staring into the glass of juice he brought her, knowing how fragile her composure was. The thought of losing control was terrifying, and Naomi might need her soon. Please God Naomi would need her, please God Naomi was alive.

Sam grabbed his phone and held it between them, and Nina could see how his hands were shaking too.

'We've found the farmhouse. It's near Millburn, to the north of Bedford,' said David Mallony.

Nina's heart began to race, thudding behind her ribs. She pressed both hands against her chest.

David continued. 'It's called Cummings Farm. The land was sold off years ago, and an elderly couple called Wilson have lived in the house for years. It's fairly outlying, a long way to the nearest neighbours. Anyway, the people at the bottom of the lane noticed a pale green car going up and down to the farm yesterday, but it's not there now. The Wilsons aren't answering their phone, so we're going in to check.'

'I want to come too,' said Nina immediately. This was

important, the best lead they'd had, was she wrong to feel convinced this was where Naomi was? Or had been...

'Nina, there are literally thousands of pale green cars in the area. At the moment this is no more weighty than any of the other leads from Wright's computer,' said David. 'You can't rush around checking everything yourself, you'd be exhausted in no time.'

'I want to come,' said Nina. 'Please.' She heard David Mallony sigh.

'Okay. We'll pick you up in five minutes. But you must do exactly as you're told.'

She could hear he was already in the car.

'I will. Can Sam come too?'

'The more the merrier,' said David Mallony dryly, and Nina clicked off her mobile.

The car, an unmarked police vehicle, picked them up and Nina squeezed her hands between her knees as they sped north along the A6. David was right, she'd make herself ill if she went on like this. But surely this must be it – a remote farmhouse known to Paul, an elderly couple not answering their phone – and the pale green car noticed by people in the same lane. Maybe she was driving towards Naomi at last, and there was still no way of knowing what her child had suffered all this time. Nausea, never far away now, welled up again and she leaned back, taking shallow breaths through her mouth.

Millburn was a village, larger than Biddenham, and a mile off the A6. The driver stopped in front of a red sandstone church on the High Street, and Nina saw that two more police cars and a paramedic on a motorbike were waiting. So maybe the police were taking this more seriously than the other leads from Paul's computer; they didn't take paramedics to every single check, did they? The churning in her gut increased. David Mallony went to consult his colleagues, telling Nina and Sam to stay put.

Nina sat watching the policemen gesticulate as they conferred. Anger was beginning to replace the nausea. 'Shit, Sam, how dare Paul do this?'

'I know. Just – hope as hard as you can,' he said.

Nina rubbed her face. It wasn't hope she was feeling now, it was dread, but he was right. She should hope. She tried to concentrate on being positive.

David Mallony returned and bent to the back seat window.

'The farmhouse is further along the lane beyond the church. There's a belt of trees between it and the village, so we can't see anything from here. We don't want to warn Wright if he's there, so Kev and Phil are going to scout through the trees and see what's going on. Then if necessary the rest of us can drive on up to the house.'

He got back into the car and sat with them, and Nina appreciated the gesture although she knew that nothing today could be of any comfort. The other officers stood around outside.

After about ten minutes David Mallony's radio crackled, and he spoke with presumably either Kev or Phil, but the voice was so distorted that Nina couldn't understand more than the odd word. David's contributions were merely short affirmatives. He lowered the radio and turned to Nina and Sam.

'They've been round the outside of the building and there's no sign of life and no car. The others are going up there now. We'll move up the lane a little too,' he said, edging the car along behind the other vehicles, stopping after a few hundred metres.

From their new standing place it still wasn't possible to see the farmhouse, and Nina shivered. This waiting was horrendous. As bad as the day they'd done the last brain function test on Claire, with Nina in the waiting room, knowing what was coming. Today, she didn't know what the outcome would be, and the dread was mixed with heart-piercing hope. Another ten minutes passed before the next report, and again David Mallony had to translate.

'No answer at the door and no one in the outhouses. We're going right up there now but you stay in the car, okay, Nina?'

In a few moments the farmhouse came into view, an old, somewhat ramshackle building with homey tubs of petunias by the front door and cheerful blue and white checked curtains at the downstairs windows. Nina's brittle hopes plummeted. This place looked a lot more like an elderly couple's home than a paedophiles' retreat. The car drove round the house and pulled up by the back door, and Nina saw a policeman jiggle with a window that had been left tilted. In seconds it was wide open and the officer was climbing in.

'That's why you should never go out without closing your windows,' said David, and Nina nodded, her eyes never leaving the window. She jumped in fright when the back door of the house opened and the police officer jogged towards the car, his gloved hand clutching something pink in a plastic evidence bag.

'It was on the kitchen floor,' he said, holding up the bag to show a pink and white rubber band bracelet. 'Is it - '

Nina's head was buzzing and she couldn't see properly. Waves of dizziness were threatening to overcome her. She opened her mouth, but her voice had gone.

'It's Naomi's,' said Sam. 'I've seen her with it. Nina, put your head down.'

He pushed her head between her knees and the giddiness receded. She scrabbled for the door handle.

'Nina, stay in the car!' said David, getting out himself. 'Wright has a gun, remember? When – if – we want you to come, I'll get you.'

He disappeared into the farmhouse. Now all the policemen were inside except one who was standing at the corner of the building, and Nina saw with a shock that he was armed. There was the sound of an engine, and the paramedic appeared up the lane and parked on the far side of the car. Nina moaned.

'Dear God, Sam, is she - ?'

David's voice. 'Nina! Come quickly!' The shout came from within the house, and Nina was out of the car and running, the paramedic close behind her.

Naomi baby, I'm coming, Mummy's coming, I'm right here...

She crashed through the back door and pulled up short in a large farmhouse kitchen. Which way, which way? The house was silent; it was cold, and seemed deserted – and –

Naomi?

Chapter Thirty-One

Claire's Story – Glasgow

Something was hissing behind her, but her eyelids were too heavy to open. Panic surged through Claire as she realised she couldn't move. And her face... something was wrong, her face was broken, tight, something hard was covering her nose – oh God, what was happening? Where was she?

'Talk to her,' said a voice. 'She isn't deeply unconscious now.'

'Mum?'

The surge of panic came again as Claire heard the fear in Nina's voice. It took a monumental effort, but she managed to crack her eyes open. Brightness stabbed into her head but not before she saw the orange curtains hanging round the bed – oh dear Lord, she was in hospital. The thing on her face was an oxygen mask. In a way it was reassuring. They would look after her here, wouldn't they? Her thoughts drifted into nothing; it was easier.

A bang nearby focussed her mind again. Nina was still there, and she was talking.

'...and Morag's looking after Naomi. It'll be okay, Mum. They're experts here, it's a specialist unit so you're in the best possible place.'

Again and again Claire tried to open her eyes, but they wouldn't obey her. It was so horrible. She couldn't see Nina, but that would be Nina's hand holding hers, wouldn't it? She tried to squeeze the cold fingers, but her own remained lifeless. She must be really bad; a specialist unit wasn't going to be on the island. Had they taken her to Glasgow? Oh dear Lord.

Nina was silent again, but Claire could hear her daughter's uneven breathing; she could sense Nina's fear. What was going on? Heavier darkness swung into her head, and a shiver ran through her body. She was hurt; she was badly hurt, maybe she was going to die here... No, no, she couldn't leave her girls. Oh God, she didn't want to die, please God... But the darkness was all around now.

A new thought struck and Claire's mind was suddenly clear. Robert. If she died now Robert would get in touch with Nina. What a shock that would be for her girl, to have a long-dead father appear and say – what? What would Robert tell Nina? And what would Nina say, what would she think of Claire for lying to her all these long years? How stupid she'd been; she should have written that letter to Nina, the one to be opened after her death. Nina would never know why her mother had lied about her father's death. But maybe she could still put that right.

For a long moment she gathered her strength, then at last she managed to open her eyes. Nina was sitting by the bed, eyes closed and her face pale as... as death. Claire feasted her eyes on her girl. All she needed to do was tell Nina that Robert was alive. Nina must have felt her gaze, for she opened her eyes and leaned forward, clutching Claire's hand.

'Mum? Is there something you want?'

Thank God, Nina had realised she wanted to speak. Claire opened her mouth but no sound came out. She tried a whisper.

'I'm sorry. I should have told you.'

'Don't worry, Mum, it's all right. You can tell me later.'

'Robert.'

But her voice was gone again, swallowed by the hissing of the mask on her face, and Nina didn't understand. Claire tried again, with the same result.

Nina patted her shoulder.

'Relax, Mum. Have a rest for now. I'll go and phone home, tell them you're awake. Morag'll be so...'

Claire's eyes closed again and she felt herself drifting as Nina continued to speak. Dear God, if she went to sleep now she'd never be able to tell Nina about Robert. All at once she knew that was exactly what was going to happen. The darkness was different now... This wasn't just floating towards sleep, this was... distancing... leaving... listening to the person she loved most in the world, and knowing she would never see Nina again, or Naomi... She should have told Nina right at the start... or at least, when she had grown up... but Nina would forgive her, Nina loved her...

The world was closing in... her world – Edinburgh, and Bedford... and Arran; she was standing at the top of the hill now, the Firth blue and sparkling down below. Nina was running towards her... how terrible to leave with no goodbye...

CHAPTER THIRTY-TWO

'Nina!'

David's voice came from upstairs, and Nina stumbled through the cluttered kitchen. Her breath hoarse in her ears, she thundered past the ancient coffee machine on the counter, the old-man slippers by the Aga, and upstairs past the trio of framed embroideries on the stair wall. Two policemen at the top motioned her into a room facing the front of the house. Three more strides and Nina gathered Naomi into her arms, feeling the terrible tension in the girl's body. Naomi was sitting on the double bed, shivering, her eyes wild, but she was alive, thank Christ, she was alive. Sheer, blessed relief flooded through Nina as she rejoiced in every heave of Naomi's chest as they sat there clutching each other, both trembling. Her baby was here; she was holding her little girl.

David touched her shoulder and spoke quietly. 'She was locked in, Nina, but the key was in the door. We need to find out if she knows where Wright has gone – she didn't answer when I asked.'

Nina stroked the hair from Naomi's face. 'Do you know, sweetie?'

Naomi shook her head then burst out crying, and Nina

couldn't prevent her own tears.

For a few moments she and Naomi hugged and sobbed together, then Nina wiped her eyes. Time for supermum.

'Sweetheart, you're safe now. We've got you. Naomi – are you hurt? What did he do to you?'

The million dollar question, and Nina leaned back to look into Naomi's face. Her daughter was pale and wide-eyed with fear, her face tear-streaked and filthy, and she was clutching Nina with shaking hands. Hell, no child's hands should ever have to shake like this.

'He kept grabbing me and pushing me around,' she whispered. 'And he wouldn't tell me where we were or nothing, he was horrible, Mummy, why did he do that?'

Nina stroked the tangled honey-coloured hair back from the pale face, feeling the tightness inside her gut begin to ease. It didn't sound as if Paul had abused Naomi, but the girl's use of the word 'Mummy' showed how insecure and frightened she was. Nina swallowed. What, oh what was she supposed to say to make the situation less frightening for her child?

'I think he's a – he's not normal, lovey, he's not well. Darling, did he touch you under your clothes? Did he make you touch him? Did he – ' Hell, Naomi wasn't a baby, she would know the word – 'Did he assault you?'

Naomi burst into noisy tears and Nina could barely make out what she was saying. 'No. But he kept pushing me around everywhere and shouting and then laughing. And at the first house he took photos of me and he said they were the before photos, and he was going to use them to catch some bad men who wanted me to look different afterwards – after what, Mummy, what did he mean?'

Nina closed her eyes, hugging Naomi tightly. Christ, Paul could have returned here at any time, and who knows what would have happened to her lovely daughter if they hadn't arrived here before him. Thank God for Emily and her efforts with the photos.

David Mallony was standing in front of the window. 'That's what we're going to find out, Naomi. The main thing is you're safe. We'll get you three out of here now, Nina. The police doctor will check Naomi soon.'

Nina felt Naomi's body relax a little. David sounded so authoritative and in control, just what they both needed right now. Sam was standing in the doorway, and he moved back as she led Naomi from the room.

'Sam, thank you,' she whispered, and he touched her cheek as she passed.

Back at the police station, Naomi told what little she knew and then they were allowed to go back to Sam's flat, well away from all frightening associations for Naomi. It was a good couple of hours before the wildness in the little girl's eyes began to diminish. Sam phoned round their families and friends while the same police doctor who'd seen Nina the day before questioned Naomi closely and conducted a brief examination which involved some very personal questions but fell short of removing any of Naomi's clothing. Afterwards Nina took the doctor into the kitchen to talk. The woman's first words were what she wanted to hear.

'She hasn't been sexually assaulted,' said the doctor.

'She spoke quite openly about her experience and what Wright had said and done. She wouldn't have been able to do that if anything had happened. It's been a terrible shock for her, though. Naturally. Talk to her about it, but don't force any confidences, take things at her pace. And it might be an idea to tell her a little about your own encounter with Wright; she doesn't know anything about that yet and it would give her the feeling that the ordeal wasn't hers alone. No gory details, though, play it down. I'll leave some tranquillizers. You can each have one at bedtime and they'll give you a good night's sleep.'

Nina went back to the living room, where Sam was with Naomi on the sofa, carefully sitting well round the corner. Naomi had a fat cushion clutched across her chest, but Nina noticed that the trembling had stopped.

'Come on, you,' she said, putting a hand on Naomi's head. 'Bath time. Sam doesn't have any smellies that you'd like, but we'll put a good squirt of my shower gel into the water and you can lie in the bubbles and I'll tell you about Paul Wright locking me up in a horrible house all night.'

The doctor was right. Hearing about Nina's imprisonment jolted Naomi out of her own situation. They discussed mental illness and child abuse quite openly, and Nina's last lingering fear vanished. Naomi's behaviour in the bath was the same as always, and her body was unmarked. Nina left the girl drying herself with one of Sam's massive bath towels.

Sam was in the living room with a bottle. 'Wine,' he said, pouring her a large glass of red. 'If anyone deserves it it's you. Are you okay?'

Nina sipped, then put the glass down and looked at him. He stepped across the room and took her in his arms, holding her tightly, and she could hear his heartbeat and the sound of his breathing. She fitted her forehead against his neck, feeling how their breathing coordinated. In, out. Slowly, she began to relax. Now if she could stay right here for about four months she would be okay again.

'I feel like I've had the biggest fright of my life,' she said.

'Well, you're not alone,' said Sam. 'And if I - '

'Stop snogging.' Naomi marched into the room, her face still pale. 'I'm hungry, I haven't had anything to eat all day.'

Nina went to hug Naomi. A hug could work wonders; she and Sam had just proved it.

'Right,' said Sam, rubbing his hands. 'What would you like? I could make spaghetti, that's quick, or pizza, that takes a bit longer, or we could send out for a curry or go for a hamburger – you choose.'

'Chicken Tikka,' said Naomi, her head on one side as she considered. 'And chapatis and normal rice.'

They ate at Sam's breakfast bar, and Nina was glad to see the colour return to Naomi's face. The safe routine of having something to eat was helping them both. Although it wasn't really routine, thought Nina; they had never eaten with Sam, unless you counted the picnic by the river where Naomi had gone off in a strop. The bad mood was a thing of the past today; the little girl was listening to Sam's account of the beaches he'd been to in Devon with an almost-smile on her face.

'I want to go to the beach too. When can we go home, Mum?' she said, mopping up the last of her sauce with a chapati. 'Home to Arran, I mean.'

'As soon as they let us,' said Nina. 'I'll talk to David Mallony tonight. We'll go on Sunday at the latest.'

And how good it would be to be back on the island, back to fresh air and healthy living. Of course they would have to visit Emily first. And Cassie and Glen.

'Good,' said Naomi. 'Will you be coming to see us sometime?'

She was looking at Sam, and for the life of her Nina couldn't read her daughter's expression.

'Maybe I will,' he said, glancing at Nina. 'I've never been to the islands. We'll see what we can fix up, will we?'

He gave Nina the ghost of a smile. 'I'll bring you the last lot of documents to sign.'

Nina grinned back, feeling that it was forever and a day since she'd been able to grin at him and mean it. 'You'll be very welcome, Sam.'

Was it her imagination or did his face fall slightly when she said that? It was clear that he was still hankering after a relationship, but she would need several gallons of fresh island air in her lungs before she'd be able to think thoughts like that. On the other hand, she could search for years and never find a man as supportive – and, yes, as fanciable – as Sam... A couple of deep breaths on Sunday should do the trick. She smiled again and his face brightened.

Nina gave Naomi one of the doctor's pills and sat by Sam's spare room bed until the little girl fell asleep. Naomi's face was flushed, and lying there in her Snoopy nightgown she was the very same child who slept in her little room under the farmhouse roof on Arran, lulled by the sounds of the sea. Nina heaved a sigh. They had survived. Everything was going to be all right.

Sam was on the landline when she went back to the living room. He was talking to David Mallony, but the conversation was coming to a close.

'They haven't found Paul yet,' said Sam, replacing the handset on its base. 'David thinks he's holed up somewhere on one of the estates. Apparently there's a fair-sized paedophile network around here and Paul has contacts to them.'

Nina shuddered. It was more than time to leave Bedford, leave David and his team to close the case.

'We'll go on Saturday. All I want to do now is get Naomi well away from here,' she said. 'The bad stuff won't seem so immediate when we're back home. Island life is so different.'

'Nina – I meant what I said about visiting you on Arran,' he said. 'I know you don't want to think about what we could have together, but one day you might and till then I'll be making a nuisance of myself. Be warned.'

Nina laughed, and held out her glass. 'I'm warned.'

Sipping, she wandered through to check that Naomi was okay. Because... and the thought made her shiver all over again – Paul was still out there somewhere. They weren't safe yet.

CHAPTER THIRTY-THREE

Friday 28th July

To Nina's relief Naomi slept right round the clock. She was sombre when she awoke on Friday morning, however, and Nina decided the best thing to do was to keep busy as well as give Naomi plenty of cuddles and opportunities to talk about what had happened if she wanted to.

The other important thing was to get back to Arran asap. Nina wasn't sure if Naomi had realised Paul was still at large, but hell, this wasn't something she wanted to talk about till there were a few hundred miles separating them from Bedford. She sent Naomi to help Sam make breakfast while she booked flights for the next day before e-mailing their arrival time to Beth, grinning when a reply appeared within minutes. Beth must be doing the mails too, sitting at the kitchen table as she always did. And wow – just one more sleep here in sunny Bedford and then they'd be travelling north, her and her girl. Nina hugged herself.

'Beth's meeting us at Glasgow tomorrow,' she said, sliding onto a high stool at Sam's breakfast bar and reaching out to rub Naomi's shoulder. 'She's taking the car, if she can get it booked on the ferry, to get us home as quick as she can.'

Naomi's face lit up. 'Great. And then can I go riding on Monday? My wrist's better now.'

Nina's heart contracted with love. 'You certainly can. We'll get the next trekking course organised for you too.' She smiled at the girl, glorifying in the answering smile from Naomi. How great it was not to have to count the pennies any more. Naomi could even have her own pony... It was going to take a bit of getting used to, this having money.

'So what are we doing today?' asked Naomi, and Nina turned to Sam.

'Should we pack up the last few things at the house first, then go and see Cassie and Glen?' she suggested. 'We'll go to Emily on the way to the airport tomorrow.'

'Okay. I'll tell Mum to expect us for coffee this afternoon.'

Nina phoned David Mallony for permission to break the seal on John Moore's front door, and was told there was still no sign of Paul, but the police had traced the owners of the farmhouse on holiday in the Lake District.

'We haven't found anything to link them to the Moores or Wrights,' he said. 'I think the connection there must go back to the previous occupants, the people who had the place when Paul was a lad, and they've been dead for years. I'll send an officer to meet you at John Moore's house; he'll watch the place while you're inside. Until Wright's found we have to be very careful.'

'Thanks, David,' said Nina. Thank God there would be a policeman with them at the house. The thought of going back was daunting.

She rang off and gave the phone to Naomi to call her father, careful to keep her voice neutral. Alan's reaction to Naomi's abduction became more infuriating every time she thought about it. It wasn't so much that he hadn't come back to the UK, after all, South Africa was a long way away – but now that she'd been found, a few concerned phone calls from her father would have helped distract Naomi and reassure her that she was loved. But Alan seemed to have relegated both Naomi's abduction and her own to a 'getting lost in the supermarket' level of importance. Sam was doing a much better job at providing her child with concerned fatherly support. And Nina wasn't quite sure what to make of that.

John Moore's house looked exactly the same as the very first time she'd laid eyes on it, and Nina glared at the ivy-clad walls with distaste. Definitely, this would be the last time she'd come here. After all that had come to light these past couple of weeks she had no wish to go inside even now, but there were still some things here she wanted. The blue vases from the bedroom, for instance. They'd been Claire's, and spending the past twenty-five years with John Moore hadn't made them less beautiful.

The police officer broke the seal and stationed himself at the front door while they trooped inside. Naomi started to hunt round for her missing ipod, and Nina went into the living room. The air smelled musty; it was as though the house had been shut up for centuries and not a few days. And there was the sofa where Paul sat and told her a pack of lies – and she'd believed him.

'Nina, stop it. Let's find the stuff you want and get out of here,' said Sam, rubbing her shoulder.

Nina heaved a shaky sigh, staring at the big table, where two stray photos lay gathering dust. The rest were still with Emily. She would collect them when they visited tomorrow.

'There's nothing in here,' she said. 'I'll have a quick look in the study and then pack the last odds and ends from the bedroom. Sam, could you maybe bring the big box of china down from the attic? There might be something nice there, like those vases.'

He gave her a salute and bounded up the stairs two at a time. A shriek of triumph told Nina that Naomi had found her precious ipod, and she went into the study to see her daughter booting up Sam's old laptop.

'It was under the microwave. I'll charge it up here now. And Mum, could we take that little desk home? It would look quite nice in my room.'

Nina glanced at the secretaire, her lips twitching. So much for her own plans for it. And if Naomi was developing a taste for antique furniture it was just as well they'd inherited John Moore's millions.

'Sure,' she said, going through to the kitchen. 'Sam can organise to have it transported up to Arran.'

Or if he kept his word and came to see them on the island, he could bring it himself, if he drove up. And talking of Sam, where was the man? He'd been up in the attic for ages, and there were no thumps and bumps telling of him shifting stuff around.

Nina ran up to the first floor. The vases were still on

the chest of drawers in the room she and Naomi had occupied, and she pulled a couple of towels from the airing cupboard to wrap them in.

'Sam?' she called. 'We're about finished here. I'm packing those vases; I'll take them on the plane. Have you found the china?'

No answer. Nina stood still. Silence from the attic; nothing was moving up there.

'Sam?'

Nina's stomach cramped uncomfortably when once again, no reply came from above, and she dropped the vases on what had been Naomi's bed. Something was wrong... Sam? She crept out to the landing. The attic door above her was cracked open, dim electric light shining round its edges like something from a horror film – but now she was being ridiculous.

And yet...

Nina stood at the bottom of the attic stairs, the hairs on the back of her neck rising and her breath catching painfully in her chest.

Paul was up there. She could smell him. She would never forget that smell.

The house remained silent. Ice-cold fear was pumping through Nina's body with every beat of her heart. Oh no no... Naomi... She had to get Naomi out of this house, immediately, right this instant. It was Naomi Paul would be after; she was the one he'd wanted to help catch his paedos. Thank Christ there was a policeman at the door. And dear God in heaven – Sam, what had happened to Sam? But Naomi came first. Her heart breaking, Nina turned away from the attic. Be normal, Nina. Paul mustn't know he'd been rumbled...

'Get a move on, Sam – I'll take this lot downstairs,' she called, aware that her voice sounded nothing like her own but unable to do anything about it.

Quick, quick, quick, downstairs and away, Nina – and thank heavens Naomi was down there on the laptop and not trailing round after her mother, looking for souvenirs. Down, down, as if everything was normal... She was in the study now, pulling Naomi from the desk, smothering the child's protest with one hand.

'Shh! Paul's upstairs. We have to get out of here, come on!'

Naomi's face turned pale and she followed Nina without a word. Nina eased the front door open, and they slid out and stood in an odd little huddle on the doorstep with the policeman on duty.

'He must have knocked Sam out,' whispered Nina, clutching Naomi to her side, sick horror making her legs shake. When was this going to end? Paul had a gun, until more police arrived they were in grave danger yet again. Why had he come back here, to the scene of his suffering as a child? He couldn't have known they were coming today, hell, he must have *chosen* to hide out here. In the attic room. How completely macabre that was. Nina stood hugging Naomi while the constable radioed for reinforcements.

'They'll be with us in minutes,' he said in a low voice. 'The boss says try not to upset him, he might take it out on Sam Harrison. You two stay put – he won't be able to shoot at you from the attic windows while you're here under the eaves. I'll go in and see what's happened to Sam.'

293

He slid inside, disappearing up the stairs, treading lightly.

Nina craned her neck to see along the road. This would definitely count as an emergency; the police would be blue-lighting through town. The best thing would be to get hold of Paul by whatever means it took, and get him help. A psychiatric –

With appalling suddenness a shot rang out upstairs, and two starlings screamed heavenwards from the garden next door. Nina and Naomi clutched each other again.

'Was that a gun?' Naomi's face was pale.

'Hell, yes.' Nina's breath caught in her throat. Who had Paul shot at? But it must be the policeman, if he'd been going to shoot Sam he'd have done it before now. Or – had they got into the kind of situation where a hostage – Sam – ends up getting killed... Dear God, what should she do... there was still no sign of the police. Nina made a spot decision.

She handed Naomi her phone. 'Call David Mallony, his number's there. Tell him what's going on. I'm going to see if Sam needs help.'

Naomi grabbed her arm. 'No! You can't – he might shoot you too.'

Nina cupped the child's face. 'Sweetie, I have to. He won't shoot me. And we can't just do nothing. So you get phoning – and stay right here, okay? Under the eaves where you're safe.'

Naomi nodded, her face rigid. 'Are you sure he won't shoot you?'

'Positive. It's you he wants, to, um, help him trap some

other people. He won't risk you running away. I won't be long.'

She turned back into the house and raced upstairs. Dear God let Sam be safe. Alive. She'd only just found him... And please let her get out of this safely too – she had a child who needed her. Maybe she should have stayed with Naomi. But imagine if Sam was hurt or even died because she hadn't gone to help him – she wouldn't be able to live with herself if that happened.

There was no sign of the policeman on the upstairs landing and no sound from Paul. Nina climbed the attic stairs, her heart thumping. Her mouth was dry but steely determination filled her head as she stood on the little landing, staring at the attic door. It was slightly open, but all she could see was the stairs.

'Paul, I know you're up there. Where's Sam? And the policeman? What happened?' Good, she sounded in control.

Footsteps approached down the stairs on the other side of the door. It swung a little further open, though there was still nothing to be seen of Sam or the young policeman.

'Nina. They're both up here, but they're not saying much. We need to talk, Nina. I need to get those last two bastards.'

Fear and adrenalin rushed through Nina and she swayed on her feet. Paul's voice was high, cracking on almost every word; this time he really did sound mad. And Sam...

A hand on the wall steadied her. 'Paul. Of course we can talk. I want to get them every bit as much as you do.'

And she did, didn't she, even though he had lied about them abusing her as well. This was so hard – she was revolted by what he was doing, yet the state he was in today was due to her coming here and stirring things up. If she hadn't done that, Paul would have finished his 'research' and handed his findings over to the police. Which would have been a much tidier end to the whole affair than the one they were seeing now. And the thought that her actions had caused her cousin to have such a king-sized breakdown was truly appalling.

Utter stillness in the attic room. Oh God. What was he doing now?

'Good, up you come. But remember I've got a gun, Nina. And nothing left to lose.'

But she had everything to lose. Paul's plan had gone horribly wrong, from his point of view, and she had no intention of confronting him. And where the shit were the police?

'Actually, I think I'll stay right here and talk. You don't have to do this, Paul, the police will find those scumbags for you. How did you get in here, anyway? The place was sealed.'

Was Sam alive? Nina's world began to spin around in front of her eyes, and she crouched down till the dizziness passed. Paul was mad – was he a psychopath? Psychopaths could kill people without a second thought, couldn't they? Look what he'd done to Sabine. But the important thing was to keep him talking until the police arrived.

A thump shook the staircase as Paul sat down on the stairs on his side of the door. Leaning sideways, Nina could see one of his feet. He began to talk, his voice cracking and strained.

'Well, Nina, the kitchen window opens if you just breathe on it from the right direction. And you must know why I have to do this. Maybe you didn't harm me personally, but your father did. And mine. And all their horrible friends. I was raped and assaulted every weekend, Nina. Years it went on. Can you imagine what it did to me?'

'I can't imagine, Paul, but there are people who could help you. Doctors, therapists. You don't need to go through this alone and you certainly don't need to hurt me and my family like this.' She wished the words back the minute they were said. The last thing she wanted was to antagonise him.

Too late.

'Me hurt you? That's a joke. You know, Nina, before your Mam took you away, you came upstairs one day and found me crying after your Dad and one of his filthy friends had been having it off with me while my Dad took the photos. You started to cry too, because I was crying, and then your Mam came home and found us and God help me, I couldn't tell her what had happened. I told her your Dad had hit us both. And paedophilia didn't even cross her mind, she was so horrified that you, her precious baby, were hurt, but you hadn't been hurt, Nina, it was me who'd been tortured and raped. And it was you who was taken away, your Mam saved you, Nina, but nobody saved me because my Mam was pissed out her mind on the sofa.'

The anger had gone and his voice was thick with tears.

Nina began to feel sick. What on earth could she say to him? Maybe he would never get over what he had gone through. What wickedness there was in the world. That's what Emily had said, and it was true.

A faint sound came from below as the front door opened and closed. The police, thank Christ. She had to keep talking now, keep Paul's attention on the conversation. He mustn't realise someone else was here.

Nina opened her mouth, but before she could speak he started to howl, a nerve-shattering high moaning sound, like an animal in pain. The sounds of him scrambling to his feet and running round the attic came down the stairs, and then she heard breaking china, the thump of something heavy and solid hitting the floor, and a series of muffled thuds. Shit, shit, he was kicking something – hell – was he kicking Sam?

Before she had time to think Nina was on her feet and running up to the attic room. If Sam was unconscious and being kicked... he could die here today, and she'd never get the chance to find out what they could have together.

'Sam!'

'Nina! Come down here!' It was David's voice, along with several pairs of heavy feet thudding up the stairs.

Nina stared across the attic. Sam was motionless on the middle of the floor, face down. The policeman was nearer, eyes closed and blood seeping into the floorboards from his left shoulder. Paul was crouched on the floor by the window, howling. Nina took a few steps into the room – and then she saw the gun in his hand. She froze.

When he spoke his voice was like an old man's, weak

and shaking. 'Nina, Nina. How stupid do you think I am? I know you've got police there. And you know what? I'm going to make sure they can never touch me.'

Fear burned sour in Nina's mouth. 'Gunman goes on killing spree in Bedford attic.' It might be tomorrow's headline. And Naomi – Oh God, Naomi. How would she ever recover if Nina died here in a hail of bullets?

'Paul, please. Let me help you.'

He was crying, pitifully, like a child in pain, and she was crying too. A dim memory slid into Nina's head and then came sharply into focus. It was the day he'd talked about, the day Claire found them crying.

She was just a little kid, in her room, scared because Paul was up here in the attic, howling like he was now. She'd gone up to see why Paul was howling... She couldn't open the door at first, but then she managed and she sneaked into this room and Paul was pulling his trousers up and running towards her, his face full of terror and disgust and loathing and pain... and she screamed and screamed and they fled from the attic and Paul slammed the door shut and he stood there and banged his head on the wooden T on the door, again and again, bang bang and she couldn't stop him... then she screamed again and they stumbled back to her room together. Dear God, how could she have forgotten that?

Shaking, Nina glanced behind her. David was there with two other officers, and they were all armed. David jerked his head towards the stairway, but Nina shook her head. She took a careful step towards Paul and he lifted his head and gazed at her. His eyes were dark, and she had seen that expression before, that day when he'd run across the attic towards her...

'All I wanted was to make them suffer too,' he whispered. 'They turned me into something I wasn't, Nina. I never had a chance, I - ' His voice broke.

Nina dropped to her knees and edged towards him. 'Paul. You have a chance now. Come downstairs with me and I'll help you. The police know you were a victim first. I won't press charges, Paul, I promise. You could come to Arran, you could...'

His face was sheet-white and his eyes were unfathomable. 'No. I couldn't. But you're right you won't press charges, Nina. You won't get a chance. I'm out of here.'

Before she could move he turned the muzzle towards his head and pulled the trigger. Nina screamed as David Mallony grabbed her and pulled her away. Paul was slumped on the floor under the window, a huge hole in his forehead. Her ears ringing, Nina pulled away from David and scrambled across the attic to Sam.

'Sam? Sam, love!' She dropped to her knees beside him and cradled his head. Thank God, he was breathing. She patted his face, and his eyelids flickered.

'Sam, baby, hang on. David! Call an ambulance!'

'Here already, they're on their way up,' said David, squatting beside the young policeman. 'Steve? Keep still, help's on its way.'

Nina knelt beside Sam, her arms round his head. Sam was hurt, Paul was dead, Naomi was God knows where, and she would never know exactly why Claire had acted as she did, all those years ago – but that was no longer important. Today was important... Sam had to be okay;

she couldn't lose him too. Paul had his peace now, but she and Sam were only at the beginning of their story. Please let them have a story.

Nina sobbed quietly as a green-clad paramedic bent over the still form under the attic window and then rose again, shaking his head.

Paul's mission was over.

Chapter Thirty-Four

Sunday 30st July

Heathrow was mobbed as usual. Feeling more depressed by the minute, Nina glared round the crowds in the departures area.

'Can I buy a magazine? Please? Except I don't have any money left.'

Naomi was hopping impatiently from one foot to the other, and Nina made a face at her before handing over a ten pound note.

'Here. But I want the change, okay?'

Naomi ran into the newsagent's and began to investigate the magazine rack. Nina followed, unable to let her daughter out of her sight. They were travelling a day later than planned, but Nina couldn't leave until she was sure Sam would be none the worse after his ordeal. They'd kept him in hospital till Saturday afternoon, and he'd had an almighty headache all day yesterday.

Nina shivered. They had still escaped lightly. Waiting at the hospital on Friday while the doctors examined Sam had been terrible. Only Glen and Cassie were allowed in with him, and Nina, unable to sit still, went up to the neurosurgery department to visit Sabine. What she saw there was horrifying; Sabine had wires and tubes connecting her to a life support system, the same kind Claire had been wired up to, and the right side of the young woman's body was twisted and lame. David Mallony told her the doctors were talking of permanent brain damage now.

It was an incredible relief to go back downstairs to A&E and find Sam sitting up on his trolley talking to Glen and Cassie.

They spent Saturday quietly, visiting Sam in the morning and Emily in the afternoon. The old woman was visibly saddened, and Nina thought guiltily that Emily might well have been happier if they'd never met. But that was impossible now, and at least she could do something for her elderly relative. Cassie and Glen were going to visit regularly, and Nina knew that she and Naomi would travel down several times a year. Emily deserved that much at least. As for Paul – if George Wright agreed, she would have Paul's ashes sent to Arran. She and Naomi would scatter them on the beach and her cousin's last resting place would be a beautiful one.

Nina sat on the plane, eyes closed as they thundered along the runway and lifted into the sky over London. She'd come here to find out about her family, but questions still remained and something was telling her they'd never know the answers. Claire had lied, and all this happened. Nina remembered her mother's blue eyes and the pride glowing on her face as she watched Naomi collect her prize at the Easter gymkhana. How Claire had loved being a Grandma... she was so much more relaxed after Naomi's birth. A smile tugged at Nina's lips – in spite of the lie, Claire had done her best for their little family. She believed that one hundred per cent.

When she opened her eyes the city was gone, and clouds and more clouds were rushing past the window. A lump rose in Nina's throat. Somewhere down there was Sam, but in a few weeks' time he'd be driving north, the secretaire in the back of his car. And right this minute Beth would be on the ferry approaching Ardrossan; she would drive up to Glasgow and the plane would land and the three of them would hug like they'd never let go.

Then later this afternoon they would all be back on the same ferry, the 'Caledonian Isles', heading for Arran.

Heading for home.

The End

If you enjoyed *The Attic Room*, you might be interested to read this extract of *The Cold Cold Sea,* Linda Huber's second novel:

THE COLD COLD SEA

Prologue

A glint in the sand caught her eye and she crouched down. It was a beautiful pink shell, exactly like the one she'd found yesterday. She eased it out from under a thick strand of brown seaweed and brushed it gently with one finger. It was covered in sand and wasn't nice to hold like the other one. She looked round for someone to help, but her dad was right along the beach with his back to her, staring at something up towards the hotel. She hesitated for a moment. The sea was just nearby. She would wash the shell herself and then she would take it home and give it to her Granny. She smiled at the idea.

The sun was hot on her shoulders as she turned towards the water. It was difficult to rush along the loose sand; coarse grains were rubbing the skin between her toes. Nearer the ocean the beach firmed up and she stopped to empty her sandals. It was the only thing she didn't enjoy about the beach, the way sand got everywhere.

What she liked best, of course, was the sea. It was like magic, the way the colour changed all the time. Today it was shining blue in the sunshine, sparkling like the jewels in her mother's ring. She giggled as her toes met the first of the baby waves fizzing up the beach.

The water was cold but it was silvery-clear, rushing up round her ankles and pulling her in to play. She bent over and swirled the shell in the sea. Immersed in her task she rubbed and rinsed and rubbed again, oblivious to the cold water creeping up her legs. The shell was cleaning up nicely. It would look so pretty on her Granny's windowsill, lined up with all the other shells they had collected last year.

Satisfied with her work, she stood up straight, jerking in surprise when she saw that the water was up over her knees now. She could feel the waves swirling round her legs, pulling her this way and that. It felt as if she was wobbling on a trampoline. It would be easier if there was someone to hold her hand. She looked back at the beach.

Both her parents were tiny figures in the distance now, much too far away to hear her if she called. The sea was right here, teasing her. She giggled again as the wash from a distant motorboat slapped and tickled against her thighs. This was better, it was fun again now.

Further out the waves were white-tipped and rolling towards her, and she remembered the picture book she and Daddy had read just before coming here. A fairy tale princess had caught a beautiful white horse on a wave, and rode away to the place where the sea joined up with the sky. If only she could do that too. She stood on tiptoe and walked a few paces to see if there were any white horses nearby.

Quite suddenly the water was deeper, and it was freezing cold too; it was splashing right up over her tummy. A larger wave almost lifted her off her feet and she cried out in panic, sobbing when she realised that she had dropped Granny's beautiful shell. Tears hot on her cheeks and teeth chattering, she struggled to regain her balance then waded a few steps in the direction of where the shell had vanished.

But the shell was nowhere to be seen. The water took hold of her again, pulling at her and pulling and all at once it was right up to her chin and there were no white horses at all, just cold cold water. It got in her eyes and nose and in her mouth, too, when she tried to shout for help.

Salty water was burning in her nose and pulling her down; the sea was filling her up and washing her away and she couldn't stop it. The whole world was getting smaller... it was so cold. She was floating in cold white water now, just floating, and then suddenly everything was gone.

Part One

The Beach

Chapter One
August 22nd

Maggie stood in the doorway and stared into Olivia's bedroom. It was tiny, like all the rooms in the cottage, but this one was still. Toys, games... everything in here had been motionless for a week now. Baby dolls vied with Barbies on the shelf, an assortment of soft toys lay strewn across the bed, and Olivia's darling Old Bear was sitting on a wooden chair by the window.

Maggie could hear the sea battering against the cliffs. High tide. The beach would be covered in water now; surging, white-tipped waves beneath a flawless blue sky. How beautiful Cornwall was, and how lucky they were to have a holiday cottage here. That's what they'd thought until last week, anyway. If this had been a normal day they'd have been picnicking on the clifftop, or shopping in Newquay. Or just relaxing around the cottage, laughing and squabbling and eating too much. All the usual holiday stuff.

But nothing was normal any more, and Maggie knew that tomorrow was going to be the worst day yet. The twenty-third of August. Olivia's birthday. Right now Maggie and her daughter should have been making the cake Olivia had planned so happily, the raspberry jam sponge with pink icing and four pink and white candles.

No need for any of that now. Maggie stepped into the room, grabbed the pillow from the bed and buried her face in it, inhaling deeply, searching for one final whiff of Olivia, one last particle of her child. But the only smells left were those of an unused room: stale air and dust.

'Livvy, come back to me, baby,' she whispered, replacing the pillow and cradling Old Bear instead, tears burning in her eyes as she remembered holding Olivia like this, when Joe had whacked her with a plastic golf club on the second day of their holiday. She'd had two children then. She hadn't known how lucky she was.

'I didn't mean it, I didn't.'

Her voice cracked, and she fell forwards, her kneecaps thudding painfully on the wooden floor. How could she live on, in a world without Olivia?

'I'm sorry, Livvy, I'm sorry!'

She had barely spoken aloud all week, and the words came out in an unrecognisable high-pitched whimper. Bent over Old Bear on the floor, Maggie began to weep. Her voice echoed round the empty cottage as she rocked back and forth, crying out her distress.

But no-one was there to hear.

Printed in Great Britain
by Amazon

55286012R00176